LANDER'S CHOICE

STONE SOVEREIGNS #2

C. S. WACHTER

Shadowfall Publishing

Lander's Choice
Book 2 of Stone Sovereigns

Copyright © 2020 by C. S. Wachter
www.cswachter.com

Published by Shadowfall Publishing

Printed in the United States of America

Wachter, C. S.
Lander's Choice / C. S. Wachter
Book 1 of: Stone Sovereigns
ISBN: 978-1-7340591-3-7 (paperback)
ISBN: 978-1-7340591-4-4 (ebook)
Cover Design by: Mountainview Books, LLC

Print formatting by: Mountainview Books, LLC

For Jesus my redeemer and Lord.
Thank you for your grace and mercy which are new every morning.

And for my grandson, Reed and my granddaughter River.
You are such a special blessing.

ACKNOWLEDGMENTS

Special thanks to Jan, Barb, and Kelly.
The best critique partners a writer could want.

CHAPTER 1

Lander clenched his teeth, the muscles in his jaw bunching. He pulled Becky closer into his side. Was facing the Vortex at this moment the destiny his mother had mentioned? The swirling whirlpool called to him with a siren song of promise. What it promised, he didn't know, but he had no choice. Hunt would force his compliance. Already had when he ordered Michael shot and then refused to allow Lander to heal him until they were in the Core.

Lifting a prayer to the God of the Bible, the God Pop-pop Ian had trusted, Lander closed his eyes, turned Becky into him and wrapped both arms around her. Pulling her head into his chest, he jumped into the black hole at the center of the Vortex, Becky's scream drowned out by his own.

A second later, his fall slowed. Castor, Desma, and the others within the protection of his shield were drawn down behind him. His translucent bubble upholding them as the twisting maelstrom of pink, blue, and green light spun like a silent tornado.

Lander looked down over Becky's shoulder and uncurled his fingers. The four Stones resting on his palms glowed with blinding brilliance in tones of blue-green and deep maroon. Lander blinked. He shifted his gaze and confirmed everyone he had committed to transport to the Core was safe within the boundaries of his shield, standing as if they were supported by a flat, solid floor not hanging within a shimmering ball.

Becky's warmth against him drew his attention. She raised her dark brown eyes to his. A hesitant, trusting smile lit her face and a shaft of guilt pierced his heart. She was so beautiful in her white skinny jeans and flowing, gray, sleeveless top. It was his fault she was here now, not home, where the most serious things she would worry about were keeping her grades up and writing essays for scholarships.

She turned her head and rested a cheek against his chest, her soft breathing ruffled the fabric of his graphic tee shirt. Resting his chin on the top of her head, Lander's gaze sifted through the shadows around him, seeking out Michael. One of Hunt's men knelt next to Michael's inert form. It took a moment for Lander to realize the man was helping Michael, talking to him while bandaging his leg. Lander puffed out a breath in relief.

The bubble shuddered, then began to drop, slowly at first, but picking up speed.

"Lander." Castor's voice carried a note of intensity from behind Lander's right shoulder. "Listen to me." Lander wanted to ignore the man, shut out everything around him except Becky resting in his arms. Overwhelmed by all that had happened in the last week, he rebelled at the idea of Castor lecturing him.

"This is going to take hours and you're going to need to stay focused the entire time, Lander. If not, the shield will collapse on itself and we will all die. Do you understand?"

Castor's words triggered an old memory.

"I'm tired, Pop-pop. Can I stop now? Please?"

"No, Lander. You must learn to focus without break or rest. Balance and stay invisible. I'll be back in an hour.

Another image ghosted into Lander's mind. Sweat had beaded his brow and dribbled down along his hairline from his temple to his chin as a hungry mosquito droned in his ear that blistering hot day two summers ago.

"Come on Pop-pop, none of the other kids have to do this."

"Stay focused Lander. I'll be back tomorrow ..."

His grandfather's gritty voice echoed inside his head. But the strict lessons he never understood before now made sense. Ian's training made Lander strong, created within him the ability to focus when his attention was split. Even now, with his concern for his friends bleeding through on a surface level, a deep part of his brain fed focus to his shield.

He glanced over his shoulder at Castor's probing eyes. Becky pushed against him, drawing his attention back to her; she stepped away. A chill replaced her comforting warmth on Lander's chest. Avoiding contact with the pulsing shield, she slipped past Lander, and moved with slow, awkward steps toward Michael.

"Lander?" Castor demanded his attention.

"I've got this, Castor."

"Are you sure? It's asking a lot. When we came up with Ian, he, Cyanne, and Jerod took turns holding the bubble secure." Castor's gaze dropped to the Stones glowing on Lander's hands and his eyes widened. "That's incredible! I've never seen Stones of Power throw off so much light."

A crooked grin lifted one side of Lander's lips. "Pop-pop Ian may not have told me about where I came from, but he made sure I worked hard every day. Even without these." He bounced the Stones lightly on his palms, then as they wobbled, he wrapped fingers around them in a tight grasp. Balancing two different Stones in each hand took effort. He grimaced and shifted his gaze back to Castor. "Anyway, I could hold a shield before I learned about the Stones. Maybe not so big, or for so long, but this isn't hard for me."

The tilt of Castor's brows broadcasted his doubt to Lander loud and clear without him needing to say anything. *Probably thinks I'm over-confident ... well ... maybe I am.*

Desma shook her head, her lips pressed into a flat line as she moved next to Castor. "Don't get cocky kid. Ian and your parents had years of experience. Wait until you've been at it for six ... or eight ... hours. Let's see how *hard* it is for you then."

"No, Desma." Castor's calm voice and soft hand on Desma's shoulder drew her eyes from Lander to Castor. "The boy's right. Ian did train him hard and look at the Stones; have you ever seen any others shine so brightly?"

Desma huffed. "Yes. I see them. But remember, Lander, when you start to lose focus or tire, Castor can help. He may not be a Stone Sovereign, but he is Gifted as a Stone Worker. Don't let foolish pride keep you from asking for it. The shield can shrink without proper attention and trust me, the effects of exposure to the Vortex without shielding are ... deadly."

"You've seen that?" Lander's knuckles whitened as his grip tightened around the Stones.

Desma's eyes lost focus for a couple seconds. Her face stiffened, she turned, and walked a few paces away.

"She doesn't like to talk of it," Castor said, "but when she was younger, Desma worked with the ... you would call them doctors. The Core can be a dangerous place. Trust Desma. You don't want this shield shrinking, especially when we pass through the light and heat of the Flux. If it does, those around the edges will be at risk for injury ... even death."

Lander swallowed hard and a shiver raced through him. "I understand. I'm sorry if I seemed to blow off your advice. I'll ask for help if I need it."

"Good boy." Castor patted Lander's shoulder then moved

to join Desma. They sat on the invisible floor, Desma's head on Castor's shoulder, her eyes closed.

Lander turned to face outward. The shifting lights beyond his barrier swirled into a mottled mix of colors, quavering, as if he viewed them through water or a pane of distorted glass. He had no idea how fast they were traveling, but his stomach left no doubt the Vortex was pulling his fragile bubble downward at an unimaginable speed.

Doubt curled invisible claws into his mind, ripping at his self-confidence. He reached out and rested the first two fingers of his right hand on the cool surface of his sphere. It vibrated and the first inklings of immense heat shot up his arm. He pulled back his fingers and looked at them expecting to see a blistering burn. They looked normal, the skin smooth and unharmed.

"Umm ... everybody. You all might want to keep away from the shield. I mean ... don't touch it."

He swallowed and focused. Setting a second shield within the outer one.

"You don't need to do that." Castor pushed to his feet. "We should be fine with the one layer. Just make certain you keep it stable. If you waste your energy on an inner shield, you might lose both by the time we get to the Core. Don't worry. You'll be fine."

Lander allowed a scowl to distort his features. *I wouldn't be worried about it if you hadn't said anything!*

"Alright. Yeah. That makes sense." Lander released the scowl and allowed the inner bubble to dissipate.

By now, Hunt and his men had settled on the flat portion at the base of the bowl opposite where Lander stood. Some slept while Hunt and Talen spoke in soft tones.

Lander closed his eyes and focused, checking that his shield held at full strength. Once he confirmed its potency, he walked to Becky and sat next to her. The guard who had wrapped Michael's wound continued to sit at his side, across from Becky and Lander. No one spoke. The only sounds were the constant hiss of the Vortex against the sides of Lander's shield and Hunt's and Talen's whispers.

A faint odor of burning laced the air and Lander wondered about oxygen levels in the closed environment.

Becky dropped her head onto Lander's lap. Hours passed. As they descended; Lander's awareness of the stresses and intense heat blistering his bubble increased. The air within had grown stale and warm. When Becky drifted off to sleep, he slipped out from under her, settling her head on his rolled-up sweatshirt.

He focused, cupping the now faintly glowing Stones of Power in his hands. Soft footsteps behind alerted him to Castor's presence.

"How are you holding up?" the big man asked.

Lander shrugged, pursing his lips. "It's harder now. How much longer?"

Castor glanced at his watch. "Maybe another hour. Maybe less."

"You said you could help. How? You're not a Stone Sovereign. What can you do?"

In response, Castor pulled his Stone of Power from his pants pocket, cupping it in his left hand. "You're right, I'm no Stone Sovereign, but I can do this." He closed his eyes and his Stone sparked a golden glow within. A moment later, Castor stepped closer and dropped his right hand on top of Lander's Stones. They flared as if given new life.

The pressure within Lander eased and for the first time in more than an hour he pulled in a deep breath. "Thanks."

Castor nodded without saying a word.

Time passed at the speed of a moving glacier. Castor stayed by Lander's side, his Stone adding strength to Lander's. When light began to show in a pinprick below, Lander thought it was his imagination. Until Desma joined them. "There it is. Not far now. The Core."

As if on cue, their globe began to slow. The pinprick grew into a dot, then the size of a basketball. People stirred, shifting positions, and rising to their feet. Everyone except Michael. Becky approached Lander. She met his eyes.

"How's Michael?" he asked.

She shook her head. "I don't know. He's been unconscious for most of the trip. Glen, the guy who was helping him said he was lucky the bullet missed major arteries and veins, but a bone may be fractured. I think Glen gave Michael something to knock him out so he wouldn't try to move."

Lander nodded, hoping he would have the energy to heal Michael after maintaining the powerful shield for so long.

The sides of the Vortex narrowed then disappeared. Lander's bubble hit the ground and bounced a few times, throwing everyone off balance. Lander met Castor's eyes and the two let go of their focus. The travelers stumbled as the supporting base of the shield vanished and they now stood with trembling legs on hard, blue-tinged rock.

Lander sucked in a gasp and his eyes grew wide. The land before them dropped in a gentle incline to a broad, shallow basin. Beyond the valley, pale blue light flowed out of two immense tunnels leading off in different directions. Between the travelers and the lighted fissures, taking up most of the valley, sat a city. Lights glimmered in buildings of all shapes and sizes. Nothing Lander had read in his mother's journal prepared him for this. He had imagined small villages, not cities the size of Camden.

"Shavah Deklakh." Desma breathed out the words as if they were a prayer.

"Yes." Hunt's voice sounded loud on the heels of Desma's whisper. "The city of your clan, Lander Devlin … or should I say Lander Deklakh. I wonder if they will welcome you."

CHAPTER 2

Lander." Becky's call pulled Lander out of his stunned daze. Turning, he sprinted the short distance, dropped to his knees, and joined her at Michael's side, still clutching the four Stones of Power. He pulled in a breath. Unfamiliar, coppery scents infused the blue-tinged air. They pricked his nose and coated his tongue. He closed his eyes, blocked out the alien landscape, and focused.

The Stones flickered with weak pulses, tickling his palms. He struggled to pull a response from all four. Nothing. Fear of failure soured his stomach. He needed to help Michael; if he couldn't heal his friend, then what purpose did his being special serve?

A vibration ran through the Stones. Striving to settle his churning gut, he pushed down the fear. He slipped his mother's Stones of Power into a pocket and cupped his father's two blue ones, rubbing their cool, smooth, flat tops, their weight familiar, his connection with them strong.

They pulsed, then sparked to life. He focused and the glow

grew brighter. Warmth filled Lander and he shifted in closer to Michael, his knees now touching his friend's side as he leaned over him.

Talen's voice droned behind him. It sounded like an insect buzzing in the distance, far from Lander's consciousness, as he plunged into Michael, seeking out his leg, locating the injury. In his mind's eye he saw the break, a hairline fracture. A simple repair. A moment later, Lander sent a final, full-body, healing impulse, then pulled out of Michael and released his focus.

Dizzy and breathing hard, Lander reached his left hand out to his side. Becky grabbed it, took his Stone, and helped him sit back on his heels. He shifted and straightened his legs, tingles skittered up and down them, evidence he had focused on Michael longer than he realized.

"We need to get moving." Talen's voice broke through Lander's haze.

He was saying something before. Doesn't matter. Lander wanted to shake his head, clear his muddled thoughts, but the idea of moving stirred the still-present nausea in his stomach. Instead he leaned back into Becky, grateful for her care and support.

Michael groaned and lifted his right hand to his forehead. "What ... what happened? Are we still on the island? Where...?"

"Hey ... Michael. Do you remember? Hunt had you shot to force Lander to bring us through the Vortex." Becky's soft voice soothed Lander's frayed nerves, until his eyes caught movement to his right. Talen and Hunt approached. Lander's muscles clenched.

"Well, young man." Hunt moved to a position in front of Lander. "I see you've succeeded in healing your friend's injury. Well done. I've kept my end of the agreement. We've reached the Core; he is healed. It's time for you to keep yours."

Hunt held out his hands, palms up and wiggled his fingers. "First off; you need to hand me those Stones. I'd rather not burden you with something that could—oh so easily—tempt you into reckless action."

Lander's hand curled into a tight fist around his father's Stones. He considered denying Hunt and using his Stones of Power to force the issue. But keeping the barrier strong for the trip through the Vortex, followed by healing Michael, left him shaky and drained. And one look at Hunt's icy, pale blue eyes killed the thought. Lander glanced at Becky. With an angry snort, she gave him the Stone she held. He handed the blue Stones to Hunt, then pulling his mother's two from his pocket, dropped them onto Hunt's waiting palms as well.

"Excellent." Hunt nodded as he passed the Stones to Talen. "Now, my boy, as Jerod's son and a Stone Sovereign, your welcome in Shava Deklakh is assured." He drew in a deep breath through his nose and narrowed his eyes. "My return, however, might not be met with ... open arms. If my welcome—or my people's welcome—is anything less than cordial, you must smooth the way for me. Otherwise, I may have to give Mr. Talen permission to use the Wasp."

His eyes shifted to Becky who had helped Michael onto his feet and stood glaring at the man. "Understood?" He raised his eyebrows in anticipation.

The Wasp. Lander swallowed bile and the muscles in his leg twitched at the thought of the searing pain of its sting. Though Talen no longer held the control device that activated Lander's anklet, the man held the trigger to the one they had fastened on Becky.

Lander swallowed the words of denial forming on his tongue and nodded. *For now. Just for now, old man. I'll play along ... for Becky.* He pushed up onto his feet, swaying from the effort. Exhaustion overwhelmed him as he glanced behind at Becky and Michael, locking his knees against the jelly-like weakness invading his legs.

Castor moved past him, taking Becky's place next to

Michael, pulling Michael's arm over his shoulder. The guard who had stayed with Michael repeated the action on Michael's other side.

"I'm good! I'm good! Geez." Michael shook both off, waving them away. "Whatever happened, I'm good now." He met Lander's eyes. "Hey, man. Thanks! Don't know what you did, but ... thanks!"

"Sure."

"Very touching," Talen said. "But you heard Mr. Hunt." He inclined his head toward the city. "Let's move."

Castor and Desma led the way. Becky and Michael took up positions on either side of Lander and followed. Hunt, Talen, and the other guards brought up the rear, holding their weapons as if they expected trouble.

Lander's gaze roamed over the extraordinary city that stretched out into the distance before them. Far overhead, a ceiling of translucent rock shone with the same blue-tinged light as the tunnels. Beneath his feet, a similar radiance glimmered. The color reminded him of pictures of deep-sea creatures he had seen in biology. He envisioned being held within a glass bowl surrounded by an immense bioluminescent creature. Only here the bowl was called the Sentinel Band—the thin layer of rock that protected the Core from the intense heat and energy of the Flux—and the creature was the Flux, molten, powerful, incomprehensible.

As his eyes adjusted to the curious light, more details came into focus. The land dipped down before it rose again in a series of sharp elevations that led up to a bowl-like plain where a vast city sat. Curved stairs cut into the vertical rises gave access from one level to the next. The two lowest levels were nothing more than narrow ledges that looked like park areas with smatterings of blue-green bushes and trees. Fixtures resembling streetlights glowed at regular intervals with pale blue illumination. Several monuments added vertical interest to the landscape.

Above the narrow shelves, the final level broadened out

across a valley. Though there were a few immense boulders several stories tall on the near side of the ledge, small, round, blue-gray boulders, set close together, filled much of the vale. *Houses? The boulders are houses!*

Beyond the houses, the land grew rugged. Thickets of blue-green shrubs and trees grew between large swaths of bare rock, but the plants looked stunted and scruffy. Though the tunnel to the right looked impassable, the one to the left had the appearance of a major thoroughfare with lights bobbing in both directions along the way.

Becky's grip tightened on Lander's hand. "This … is … unreal. I can't believe I'm standing in a hollow core at the center of the earth. And people are living here." She gave him a sideways look that sparked with excitement. "Not that I didn't believe you … or that I didn't just make that surreal trip down the Vortex. But, Lander, this is incredible! I could never have envisioned this."

Michael stared, his mouth hanging open. "She's right. I feel like I'm caught in an episode of that old show, The Twilight Zone, you know? I keep thinking I'm going to wake up."

"Imagine how I feel?" Lander huffed out a quick breath, letting it hiss over his teeth as he reached out to place a hand on Michael's shoulder, needing the stability, as his legs once again decided to turn to Jell-O. "This is where my parents came from and I know nothing about it. Pop-pop Ian sure knew how to keep secrets."

"Don't be too hard on him," Castor said, looking back over his shoulder. "He tried his best to give you a good life on the Surface and protect you from Hunt."

"This is your family's city," Desma said. "Shava Deklakh. The city of scholars. There are parchment scrolls here dating back to the time of our descent, the time of Noah's flood. This is your heritage, Lander; allow yourself to experience it with an open mind.

"For the last sixteen years I've wanted nothing more than to return here." Hints of sorrow laced her words. "And yet ... now that I'm here ... it seems so small and dark."

"Is this all there is to the Core?" Disappointment filtered through Lander at the thought. He had hoped it would be more impressive.

Light laughter bubbled from Desma and Castor chuckled. "No." Castor shook his head and chuckled again. "This is just one of three great caverns that make up most of the Core. Shava El'Ruhan, where Desma and I are from, sits in a cavern many times larger than this. There, food is harvested, animals are raised. There, the Bec Timur and the Timur Bec'stor support an abundance of waterfowl and fish. It is brighter there and the air less ... tasty." He smacked his lips, then closed his eyes and sighed. "The rock layer—that is the Sentinel Band—that exists between the Core and the Flux here tints the light blue. In Shava El'Ruhan the light is a soft golden hue." He opened his eyes, and Lander couldn't miss the tears glistening on his lashes.

Castor cleared his throat. "On the far side of the El'Ruhan Cavern are two tunnels. The Bec Jekesh and the Bec Timur flow through them connecting the El'Ruhan Cavern with the Al'Wisan Cavern. Shavah Al'Wisan sits on the banks of the Bec Jekesh. The chamber there is about twice as large as this one and air there is tinged red. It is the city of your mother's clan, Lander, and the seat of politics. There the clan leaders and elders meet when decisions must be made."

Desma clicked her tongue. "Castor." She shook her head and turned around to face Lander, Becky, and Michael. "Let me explain. For starters, s*hava* means city. So, Shava Deklakh is city of the Deklakh clan just as Shava El'Ruhan is city of the El'Ruhan clan and Shava Al'Wisan, is the city of the Al'Wisan clan. *Bec* translates as river. Bec Jekesh means River Jekesh and Bec Timur is the Timur River. You will need to be aware of these names."

"This isn't what I expected." Becky's gaze roved over the city. "I thought it would be all dark and dreary and ... I don't know ... scary. This is magnificent. It's like visiting a new country or a fairy land, not exploring a cave."

"Please." Desma huffed. "You can't compare the vast caverns of the Core with some shabby, Surface *hole in the ground.*"

Lander agreed with Becky. Though his thoughts over the past few months included the possibility of coming to the Core, nothing had prepared him for the actual experience.

They continued walking for a time without speaking. As they approached the rock stairs leading to the first raised level, a man and a woman dressed in simple sky-blue garments, walked down the steps and stopped before them. The two stared for a minute, then the woman said something in Corish.

Lander understood the words 'Desma' and 'you', but the woman spoke so fast, he couldn't catch anything else. Desma nodded, said something in return, and opened her arms. The excited lady fell into Desma's hug and the two of them rattled off in Corish again.

The man approached, a hesitant smile flitting across his rugged face. He and Castor gripped each other's forearms in what Lander suspected was a greeting. He spoke in a measured pace and Lander had no problem understanding his words. "Castor El'Ruhan. I never thought I would see you again."

Shock set Lander's nerves sparking, and a weight dropped into his stomach when Hunt pushed between Becky and him and greeted the man in Corish. The Core Dweller nodded, then said in halting English, "You are ... first visitor ... Aurelius Hunt. You return." His eyes flicked over the group before settling back on Castor. "Where is your Stone Sovereign? Chancellor Morrison ... has ... a ... a ... waited Aurelius Hunt's return many ... years. Where is Abiasaphel'ian Deklakh? The one you call Ian?"

Hunt grabbed the man's arm, mirroring Castor's greeting. "Excellent. Excellent. Mr. Morrison has been awaiting my return?"

The man stepped back and nodded; confusion flashed across his face followed by a guarded expression.

Ignoring the man's obvious discomfort, Hunt continued. "And whom am I addressing?"

The man's brow crinkled for a moment, then relaxed though his manner remained cool. "Ah." He nodded. "My name Benam El'Ruhan. My…" He inserted a Corish word, then turned to Castor, a hopeful look on his face.

Castor patted his arm and addressed Hunt. "Benam doesn't know the word for wife. His wife's name is Orpha."

Benam spoke a rapid run of Corish to Castor and Castor translated, his eyes hard and fixed on Hunt. "Your man Morrison, and his associate Jenkins, appear to have somehow gained control of the Core. Benam wants us to follow him to *Vice Chancellor* Jenkins's home."

CHAPTER 3

Hunt's smile of superiority set Lander's flesh to crawling. Benam bowed to the man and a premonition of coming trouble sent chills up Lander's spine. A small sound near his shoulder drew his eyes to Becky. She grimaced at him and mouthed the words, *Let go. You're crushing my hand.*

His gaze shifted to their clasped hands. His fingers were twisted around hers. He released his death grip and mouthed back, *Sorry.*

Lander slid his attention back to Hunt as the man cleared his throat, pulled back his shoulders, and rubbed his hands together. A look of glee lit his face. "Ah … yes. Very good. It seems my old associates have done well for themselves. Of course, it's been more than sixteen years—far longer than any of us expected." He glanced over his shoulder. "Mr. Talen, please keep an eye on our young friends. I'd rather they not get into any mischief."

Hunt turned and fixed his attention on Castor. "I expect you to fill the role of interpreter. Though I understand Corish rather well, I am not fluent. But make no mistake, if I suspect you are deceiving me or mistranslating my words, I will not hesitate to take punitive action. Do you understand, Castor?"

After waiting a moment, Hunt shifted his gaze back to Benam. "And now, if you would, please lead the way."

The heavy air sparked with electricity as Castor's face turned a mottled red and he threw a dark look at Hunt. For almost a minute, he stood without moving. With a snort, he walked past Hunt, took Desma's arm, and waved for Benam and his wife to lead the way.

An uncertain smile flitted across Orpha's face before she scurried to Benam's side and the two set out, their quick steps a muffled shuffling in the still air. Castor and Desma followed at a slower pace with Hunt at their heels.

Lander bristled when Talen positioned himself behind Becky. Lander's fingers curled into fists and the muscles in his arms flexed.

Michael leaned in and dropped a hand on Lander's shoulder. "Keep cool." He sent a quick look behind them, where Hunt's other guards pressed forward. "Now's not the time. Becky's okay. Right Becks?"

She nodded.

"We need to stay calm and stick together. If you do something, they might get the idea to separate us. Not good."

"Michael's right, Lander." Becky grabbed his hand again. "We can't take them all on. Especially since Hunt has your Stones. Just keep cool. Look around. This is where your parents grew up. Take it in while you can. Who knows how long we're going to be here."

Lander swallowed the anger that threatened to spew out in reckless action. He let go of Becky's hand and wrapped his arm around her shoulders. With a warning look directed at Talen, he turned to follow the path up the cut rock stairs.

Becky and Michael were right. He needed to focus on the

sights before him, not get embroiled in a confrontation with Talen at this point.

The last month and a half seemed like a dream: Pop-pop Ian's death, Lander's time on Zephryn Island, his mother, traveling through the Vortex, breathing the air of the Core. He slowed and scanned his surroundings as the path leveled off.

Talen's shove came without warning, and Lander clenched his jaw, set to spin around and face the man when Becky stumbled.

Becky's arm shot up in front of him. "It's okay, Lander. Don't let him get to you. He's provoking you, trying to get you to react. Don't give him the satisfaction."

A soft chuckle from behind gave credence to Becky's words. Talen chuckled again. "Try it, boy, and let's see how much pain that girlfriend of yours can take. Come on…" He shoved Lander again.

Michael stepped between them, glared at Talen, then turned and prodded Lander and Becky forward. Castor and the others were already partway down the winding path leading to the next set of stairs, so they picked up speed, putting distance between themselves and Talen, and closing the gap.

Lander breathed hard as he struggled to climb the steep steps. Becky climbed at a steady pace before him as if she clambered up this rise every day.

"You're still weak from healing me, aren't you?" Michael's voice came from behind. Becky must have heard Michael's soft words because she stopped, reached back and took hold of Lander's hand.

"'Kay, Core boy … come on. I'll pull. Michael, you push. We've got this."

Despite the circumstances, a smile spread across Lander's face. Becky flashed him a quick grin in return and, once again, he marveled at her beauty, and at the thought that this remarkable young lady could care for him. The heavy, damp air had plastered strands of dark hair to her face and drawn droplets of sweat out on her chocolate skin. She practically glowed with health and vitality in the blue-tinged light. Lander grasped her hand tighter and soaked in her emotional support. Michael let loose with a kung fu scream and shoved Lander from behind and together they sprinted the rest of the way to the next level.

The final path brought them to a series of steps leading down into an underpass the length of two football fields. Climbing the stairs up from the passageway, they emerged onto what looked like a street lined with lighted lamps. Lander pulled in a sharp breath at the multitude of buildings lining the street. Rounded, like overgrown boulders, the majority were two or three stories tall. And though most were dark, pale light flickered from a few windows.

Lander's eyes roved the structures, looking for more signs of habitation. Seeing little, he scanned the street. *Is it night here? Is everyone asleep? How do they tell night from day?*

"Castor." Lander grabbed Becky's hand. "Castor."

Castor stopped, turned, and moved toward Lander. "What?"

"Where is everyone? Is it … like the middle of the night here or something?"

"That's a good question." Castor nodded, spun around, and walked back to Desma who had stopped when Lander called. "Benam? What hour is it? If I remember correctly, this thoroughfare is unusually busy even at Mist Fade."

Sorrow traced deep lines on Benam's face, and he looked away. "There was a …" Yet again, he struggled for a word.

"Sickness." Orpha wrapped her fingers around Benam's elbow and gave him a look of support before facing Lander. "There was sickness. Many died. Shava Deklakh lost most."

"When?" Desma asked, her brows drawing together.

"After you left." Benam's unfocused gaze roamed the group. "First just a few, then many. Time passed; many …

more died. That when Surface Dweller Morrison ... created the Company of Sovereigns ... for healing. It was new beginning. He new ruler. Call him Chancellor. Now him, Vice Chancellor Jenkins, and Company of Sovereigns rule."

"Benam!" Orpha's eyes widened. "Stop."

"What about the elders?" Desma's voice rose on the last word and the fingers of her right hand fluttered at her chest.

Fear flitted across Benam's and Orpha's faces. "Please." Benam's hands rose in a placating gesture. "We are not ... *qualified* ... to answer questions. We go to Vice Chancellor Jenkins. He will ... take charge. Come. Now."

The couple resumed their hurried pace and after several turns led the group to a grand, three-story mansion. Sky blue lights shone through several windows on the second floor. Though built of the same steel-blue stones as the other dwellings, double doors at the grand entryway were inlaid with a border of polished amethyst and sapphire gems. Two Core Dwellers wearing blue and white uniforms stood to either side. "This Vice Chancellor Jenkin's home. We cannot enter. We go now."

He and Ophra bowed, then hurried up the street.

"Well, that was interesting." Hunt stared at the retreating figures, his lips pursed, then turned and led the way to the double doors. When the guards attempted to block his entrance, he pulled up to his full height. "Tell *Vice Chancellor* Jenkins Mr. Hunt is here to see him. Immediately." He lifted his hand and signaled with his fingers. The armed men behind him moved into position, their guns ready. "Now."

The larger of the two guards spoke into his partner's ear and the young man marched to the doors, pulled one open, and slipped inside. Less than five minutes later, the young man opened both doors wide and waved the group in. "Vice Chancellor Jenkins will see you now."

Once they were all inside, the young man approached

Hunt. "Mr. Hunt, the vice chancellor asks you leave your honor guard here."

"Oh? He does, does he? Well, I suppose we will adhere to his request for the moment." Hunt waved Talen over. "Mr. Talen, I suspect Jenkins is feeling a bit intimidated by our arrival. Remain here. I will call you if there is any need." He focused on the young Core Dweller again. "We have had a long journey. Could you please arrange for some food and drink to be delivered to my people while they are waiting here?"

An uncertain expression crossed the man's face. "I will take you to Vice Chancellor Jenkins now."

Folllowing Castor, Desma, and Hunt up the grand, curved staircase to the second floor, nervous energy set Lander's hands to twitching. He missed the comforting feel of the cool weight of his Stones and began to rub his right thumb over the palm of his left hand, reminding himself he wasn't helpless without their power. Still, having them now would go a long way to calming his agitated state.

Becky, climbing the steps alongside Lander, looked over. She sent a quick wink his way and pulled his left arm to her side. They reached the second floor and headed down a wide hallway. As they passed a room on their right, the door opened and six people, four male and two female, stepped out, laughing as if in response to a joke. They stopped and stared at the travelers.

Lander slowed as he walked past. They all wore belted, cobalt-blue uniform tunics, grey trousers, and dark gray boots. The sleeves of the tunics ended in wrapped leather bands at the wrists. Sturdy leather pouches on their belts bulged in familiar patterns. *Are those Stones of Power? Nice. That's handy.*

He looked up and met the gray eyes of one of the young men. His nerves sparked with a shot of adrenaline when the youth crossed his arms over his chest and his mouth turned up at the corners in a mocking smirk.

Turning away from the Core Dweller, Lander set his hand

on the small of Becky's back, propelled her forward, and followed Desma through an open door at the end of the hall.

"What was that about?" Michael asked, leaning into Lander's shoulder as he followed him into the large room.

Lander shook his head. "No idea."

A deep, unfamiliar voice pulled Lander's attention to a desk at the far side of what looked to be an office.

"Mr. Arelius Hunt. You've returned." A tall, thin man with a military haircut, striking blue eyes, and a sharp nose walked up to Hunt, his hand held out, a thin smile on his face.

"Mr. Jenkins." Hunt took Jenkins's hand and gave it a quick shake. "You are looking well."

Jenkins's smile flattened. "Sixteen years?" He turned from Hunt and stalked across the room to a large desk that looked as if it had been fashioned out of one large sapphire. He slammed his hand on the top and turned back to Hunt. "You were supposed to come back for us in two months. What happened? I figured you got whatever it was you thought you wanted and wrote us off. Yet here you are."

He shifted his focus to the young guard who had shown them in. "Did you pass Kaleb and his team in the hall?"

"Yes, Vice Chancellor Jenkins."

"Tell them to proceed as ordered."

"Yes, Vice Chancellor Jenkins." He turned on his heel and left the room, closing the door behind him with a soft click.

Returning his attention to the group, Jenkins took a minute to study each person. His eyes focused on Castor. Extending his hand toward Castor, Jenkins said, "If memory serves me you must be Castor El'Ruhan." His eyes flicked to Castor's right. "And this is your lovely wife—what was her name? Oh, yes. Desma."

He scanned the travelers again before setting his focus back on Hunt. "Where is Ian? You could not have come through the Vortex without a Stone Sovereign."

CHAPTER 4

Hunt's gaze shifted toward Lander, and Jenkins's eyes tracked the shift. A half-smile flitted across the vice chancellor's face and he stepped up to Lander, his focus intense.

Lander swallowed and fisted his hands to suppress the tremor that threatened to expose his frayed nerves. He struggled to overcome the fatigue brought on by expending large amounts of energy in such a short time. But he met Jenkins's questioning gaze with a display of confidence: an unblinking stare, his mouth flattened into a pinched line. He shook his fists loose at his sides.

Jenkins's brow crinkled as he studied Lander. "Core Dwellers age at the same rate as humans until they get into their thirties or forties ... for some, even, their fifties. What are you? Sixteen? Maybe seventeen? You're too young to have traveled to the Surface sixteen years ago. So, who?" A light of understanding blossomed in Jenkins's eyes as they widened. "The pregnant Stone Sovereign. You're her son." He nodded. "Sixteen years ... right."

It was a statement, not a question so Lander felt no pressure to respond. He shrugged. Refusing to be intimidated—he'd had enough of that back at Hunt's complex—he wrestled down the lethargy that threatened to dull his senses, clenched his jaw, and continued to stare into Jenkins's piercing blue eyes.

"Yes. Yes." Hunt moved between Lander and Jenkins, waving his hands, and breaking the tension. He faced Jenkins, tilted his head, and looked down his nose at the taller man. "He's Cyanne's son, but she died years ago. And that is all beside the point. The point is, I have finally been able to return and take charge as planned. I want a full report from you on all you've done since I left." He stepped closer to Jenkins. "In private."

Jenkins ignored Hunt for a few seconds, still fixated on Lander, a thoughtful expression on his face. He turned his back on the group, strode across the room, and took up a position behind his desk before returning his attention to Hunt.

Jenkins pulled in a deep breath. "Yes, *Mr.* Hunt. I agree. We do need to talk. But ... that can wait." He pointed at Lander. "Your young Stone Sovereign looks like he's about to drop from over-extending himself. He needs to rest." He tapped his fingers on the desk's polished surface for a moment, his brow crinkled in thought. His gaze drifted to the window where the pale blue light leaked into the room. "*Misfadura*—what you would call night or Mist Fade Dura—is upon us and I was just getting ready for a late meal. Come. We will eat."

Jenkins waved them back into the hall and down the stairs, then led the way to a formal dining room. He waved a server over and spoke in a hushed voice to the woman. She hustled through a half door and reappeared with another man and woman who set heavy plates, eating utensils, and stone mugs for the unexpected guests.

The oblong table, molded from a block of polished gray stone with veins of blue and gold running through it, sat on soft rug woven in threads of blue and burnt orange. Chairs formed from the same worked material were arranged around the massive table, eight to a side and one on either end. Mats matching the rug were placed on the chairs, softening their appearance, and adding comfort for those who sat on the hard seats. Woven tapestries in geometric patterns adorned the white-washed, smoothed-rock walls.

Rather than the flat walls Lander was used to, these bowed out in the middle like concave lenses then curved into the ceiling above and the floor beneath, where they flattened out like a fat pancake. The image of the entire building hollowed out of one immense boulder arose in his mind, reminding him of the work that Castor did manipulating smaller stones.

Jenkins walked to the group. "Please, everyone, sit." He guided Lander to the seat at his left as he waved Castor over. "Castor. Sit here at my right. And, of course Desma next to you."

Becky took the seat to Lander's left with Michael grabbing the next one over. Hunt's face turned red. He huffed and settled into the chair at the far end of the table.

The whole situation struck Lander as absurd. Here they were, sitting down to eat as if nothing out of the ordinary had happened. He glanced over at Becky. She raised her eyebrows and shrugged.

A potent mix of anger and suppressed frustration roiled in Lander's stomach. If not for his continued weakness, he would push up onto his feet and demand that he, Becky, and Michael be allowed to leave. Though such a move might be stupid, a part of him longed to claim some level of control over the situation. He looked up to see Jenkins staring at him again and glared back. The man reminded him of a soldier with his ramrod-straight back and well-toned muscles. Though on the thin side, he was tall and carried himself with an air of authority. Like the guards who accompanied Hunt—men like

Talon—Lander suspected he would be able to inflict pain without remorse.

His face a stony, unreadable mask, Jenkins offered Lander a slow, mocking salute. "I acknowledge your power, Stone Sovereign. It must have taken quite a toll on you to have brought so many through the Vortex safely ... and by yourself. Impressive."

Lander stuffed down the anxiety the man's predatory gaze birthed in him. "C-C-Castor and Desma helped." *Stuttering? Great! Way to go, stupid!*

"Please, be at ease, Lander." Jenkins's attention shifted between Hunt and Lander, as if gauging the situation. "I assure you. No harm will come to you and your friends. I think once you understand how things work here, you will find the Core to your liking. Stone Sovereigns of your caliber are rare and, as such, command a good deal of respect. Tomorrow we will leave for Shavah Al'Wisan to meet with Chancellor Morrison. He too will be impressed by your achievement."

"Don't." Hunt glared at Jenkins. "You forget your position, Jenkins."

Jenkins's eyebrows spiked upward. A moment later, he snorted, ran his tongue across the front of his upper teeth and shook his head. "Mr. Hunt, I think it is you who does not understand his position. By now my Stone Sovereigns have taken your people into custody. I can't believe you didn't protest the order to leave them in the foyer. You've grown lax; fat, dumb, and rich. You screwed up."

He shook his head and released a sigh. "You need to understand, *Mr.* Hunt. The Core you thought we subjugated for you belongs to Phil Morrison and me. We control everything." His gaze shifted back to Lander and he winked. "And, with the help of Stone Sovereigns like this exceptional young man, we have kept things nice and orderly for years.

"It took a while to understand, but once Phil and I recognized the alternate evolutionary path here, it all made sense. We showed Stone Sovereigns the truth, gave them the opportunity to exert superiority over the lesser peoples of the Core. It's a little like we stumbled onto Hitler's Master Race, hiding here, unaware of their superiority. So, yes, we used them to seize total control of the Core."

O-kay … he's a little crazy, flitted through Lander's mind.

Desma pushed up from her chair; she pounded a fist on the table, her eyes flashing. "How dare you spread this nonsense. Who are you anyway? Where are the elders?"

Castor placed his right hand on Desma's arm and shook his head. She lowered back into her seat with a huff, and Castor said, "What Desma is trying to ask, is this; if you and your partner are now ruling here, what has happened to the elders and the guilds?"

Castor's questions piqued Lander's curiosity. Though returning Becky and Michael to the Surface was his main concern, he needed to regain his strength before attempting the Avortex. *I don't even know where the Avortex is. And … since I'm here, what would it hurt to learn more about how to control my gifts better? It just makes sense.*

Hunt's eyes focused on Jenkins like laser beams. "I'm your employer, Jenkins. I continued paying your wife your full salary for the last sixteen years. You still work for me."

Jenkins leaned back in his chair and templed his fingers. He pulled in a deep breath and released it through his nose. He met Hunt's steely eyes with his own. "Shortly after you left, we implemented the plan, Auelius. Sheer genius. Within weeks, nearly thirty percent of the Core Dwellers were sick or dead."

Desma's audible intake of breath drew Jenkins's attention for a second before he claimed Hunt's eyes again. She turned her face into Castor's chest as Jenkins continued. "Things turned ugly and, as you predicted, order needed to be restored. Phil and I—with the help of certain, cooperative, Stone Sovereigns and our *unique* skill set—took control and restored order. We made decisions, chose who lived and died. We've fought rebels and Jerr'as.

His gaze shifted to Lander. "Your fellow Stone Sovereigns were instrumental in this restoration of peace. Their ability to cure many of those afflicted by the illness, followed by … their help with a military restructuring of the Core, proved quite effective. After the Elders' Council was disbanded and the guilds dissolved, Chancellor Morrison, the Company of Stone Sovereigns, and I have ruled the Core."

Hunt's eyes glittered and he rubbed his hands together. "You did it? Set all in motion just as I planned? Excellent work, Ryan."

"No." Jenkins shook his head as a look of disgust filtered across his features. "Don't be absurd, Aurelius. Phil and I no longer work for you. That ship sailed sixteen years ago when you didn't return. We have made this our world; we are the power here, and we have no intention of turning control over to you. You have no authority here. You never should have come back."

As Jenkins finished speaking, the young man who had smirked at Lander in the hallway came in. He saluted Jenkins. "Vice Chancellor, your orders have been carried out. The Surface Dwellers have been subdued. Deolah's team is guarding them and, as ordered, will transport them to Shavah El'Ruhan at second Mist Rise."

Vice Chancellor Jenkins pushed up onto his feet. "Well done, Captain Kaleb. I have one more task for you."

"Wait just a minute." Hunt's chair scraped behind him with a sound like nails on a chalkboard. "What did he say?"

"He said your people are now our prisoners. Is that clear enough for you?" Jenkins waved toward Hunt while remaining centered on Kaleb. "He is concerned about his people. Take him to them and secure him as well. Inform Deolah we will join her and her team at the transport tunnel at Mist Rise after next. Together we will escort the Surface Dwellers to Shavah El'Ruhan."

"Yes, sir."

Kaleb pulled a Stone of Power from the bag on his belt and focused. A narrow, controlled beam of light speared Aurelius Hunt. His eyes bulged and his mouth dropped opened and closed like a fish out of water. His eyes rolled up into his head and he collapsed to the floor.

Kaleb shifted to face Jenkins again. "With your permission, sir, I would get Sovereign Siprian to help me carry out the prisoner."

Jenkins nodded and Kaleb marched back through the door. A moment later, he re-entered. A large Core Dweller with a shaved head followed. The man looked to be in his early forties with well-defined muscles and a scar puckering the corner of his left eye.

As the two bent over to lift Hunt's body, Lander jumped up. "Wait. Wait a minute." He rounded the table and dropped to his knees at Hunt's side. After a quick search, Lander pulled his Stones from a front pocket of Hunt's slacks.

A comforting warmth filled Lander as he rose, holding all four Stones of Power. Kaleb and Siprian backed away, each pulling out their own Stones.

"Kaleb. Siprian. Stop." Jenkins's command wasn't loud, but the two Core Dwellers froze, their eyes locked on Lander.

Lander backed away around the table. "I don't want to make trouble. I just wanted to get these. They belong to me."

Still sensing the icy stares of the other Stone Sovereigns, Lander returned to his chair, sat, and kept his eyes cast downward. The last thing he wanted at this point was to push the others into doing something stupid.

He looked up. Kaleb and Siprian hadn't moved. *Okay, this doesn't look good. What do I do now?*

Jenkins cleared his throat. "Captain Kaleb. Sovereign Siprian. That will be all."

Kaleb's mouth twisted. "He has four Stones, sir. No one is allowed to hoard Stones of Power. Should I take..."

"I said, that will be all, Sovereign Kaleb. I don't need to explain myself to you, do I?" The edge in Jenkins's words sent skitters up Lander's spine. The man may have said he wouldn't hurt Lander or his friends, but the frost in his voice caused Lander to question that.

Kaleb and Siprian both inclined their heads in submission, collected Hunt, and carried him out the door.

Jenkins rubbed his left hand over the stubbles of his military haircut and turned his attention to the plate in front of him. No one spoke. The servants cleared the table, then returned with mugs of tea and a tray of desserts before, once again, disappearing through the other door.

Jenkins tapped his fingers on the side of his mug. "That went well. But now it's time to decide what to do with you, Castor, Desma. You are El'Ruhan clan. What is your gift?"

"Desma isn't gifted. I am a Stone Worker."

Jenkins pursed his lips. "Pull out gems, right?"

Castor nodded.

"Can you pull out light?"

Castor nodded again, his eyes narrow slits. "I've done so when necessary. Why?"

"It's the way things work here. All who can't manipulate stone in a productive way are sent to the fields to do manual labor along with the Ungifted. The Core has no need for more fancy gems. But ... if you can produce light, you will be allowed to reside in Shavah Al'Wisan or here in Shavah Deklakh. If not, you will be placed in one of the small settlements around the fertile zone in the El'Ruhan Cavern."

"This is a joke, right?" Desma looked as if she had swallowed a lemon.

C. S. WACHTER

"No joke. You have until second Mist Rise to decide Castor. One of my people will show you to a room where you can stay until then. I will expect your answer at that Mist Rise meal."

Jenkins must have signaled in some way because one of the men who had served at the table earlier entered and motioned for Castor and Desma to follow him.

Desma huffed her protest, but Castor took her arm and they followed the man to the door. Before walking out, Castor turned back. "You caused the epidemic so you could take control of the Core, wiped out all those people just to gain power. It was Hunt's plan from the beginning."

Jenkins took his time to press up onto his feet, then strode a few steps toward Castor. He stood with his backbone stiff, his expression cold. "Yes, Castor. I should never have discussed it with him in your presence. The information you possess is dangerous. If I were you, I wouldn't mention this ... *theory* ... to anyone. At least if you want to stay healthy yourself. Do you catch my meaning?"

Castor went still for a moment, his lips pressed into a thin line, then nodded. He turned, took Desma's elbow again and followed the server out the door.

Jenkins released a sigh and paced around the table to stand behind Lander. "Now, Lander, what do I do with you and your friends?"

Lander's thoughts refused to settle as the door closed behind Castor and Desma. Too many inputs made it difficult to make sense of things. If Pop-pop Ian had told him more about the Core and how the elders—or was it the guilds—ruled here, he could figure out how things were different now under Jenkins's rule. *An epidemic? What did that mean? People died so Jenkins and that other Surface dweller could ... take control for Aurelius Hunt?* He met Jenkins's icy eyes.

"Well, Lander?" He placed his hands on Lander's shoulders

39

and pressed down lightly. "No." The word was soft. "Don't make a decision yet. I have much to show you. Next Mist Rise you and your friends will travel with me. In a few days, you will meet High Chancellor Morrison in Shavah Al'Wisan. A Stone Sovereign with your power will be welcomed with honors. For now, you three will remain here as my guests.

CHAPTER 5

ater that night—if it could be called night when the level of ambient light remained constant—Becky sat at a translucent window gazing out on indistinct stone dwellings punctuated by city lights and the glow of one of the brighter tunnels beyond. No sun, no sunrise, no sunset; just a muted light that didn't vary. Though the air was warm, she suppressed a shiver.

Traveling to the Core with Lander hadn't been her choice. Aurelius Hunt had taken that decision from her. And now, Hunt was a prisoner. Would Chancellor Jenkins let them go? Judging from the way he looked at Lander, she doubted it. The man had an agenda. The thought of being with Lander and supporting him, brought a smile to her lips even if she hadn't planned to come. He was so shy and awkward. The smile melted. Her heart hurt at the idea of not seeing her parents for … well, maybe forever. *No. I won't accept that.*

She shivered again and a tear dribbled down her cheek. Resting her head against the stone veneer that served as glass, she prayed for her family, Lander, Michael, and herself. In the end, it came down to admitting she had no control over circumstances. Neither did Aurelius Hunt or Vice Chancellor Jenkins. God was in control. She would find strength in that truth.

Turning away from the window, she scanned the room. Like the other rooms she had been in, this one looked as if it had been scooped out with a monstrous spoon, then smoothed and painted pale blue. She brushed the tips of her fingers along the rounded wall but pulled them back with a quick jerk. The stone was warm, not cool as she expected. Curiosity sparking, she touched a fingertip to one of the three-foot long, golden, glowing sticks that sat in urns like flower arrangements and lit the room. Her muscles eased at the comforting warmth and, with a sigh, she wrapped her hands around its two-foot circumference, running them over the smooth stone. She closed her eyes and imagined she was back home, rubbing the salt lamp she kept near her desk.

Turning to the bed, she examined the teal mattress. *Soft.* She pursed her lips. *Unexpected.* She picked up the delicate nightgown someone had left out for her, brushing the fabric against her cheek. Supple and smooth, the blue cloth reminded her of silk. *Silkworms? Here?* She shrugged. *Maybe.*

The need to see Lander and Michael before trying to sleep grew strong in her, like an almost physical ache. She had tried earlier, but a guard in the hallway stopped her. Hoping he was either asleep or gone, she peeked out the door. Tense muscles loosened. No guard.

"Yes," she whispered, pumping her arm.

Within seconds, she stood in front of the room Michael and Lander had been given and tapped with her knuckles. Lander opened the door and she fought the urge to fall into his arms. Beyond Lander, Michael sat on one of two narrow beds.

"How'd you get past the guard?" Michael asked.

Becky shook her head. "He's gone. The hallway is empty."

She turned to Lander. "How are you doing?" *He must be freaking out. I know I am. Come on, Becky, keep it together.*

He grimaced and his gaze darted around the room before landing back on her. "Honestly? I don't know. When those Stone Sovereigns took Hunt away, I didn't know what to think." He rubbed the back of his neck and shook his head. "I mean, Hunt…" He released a huff. "He was wrong to do what he did to me … to you." He waved toward Michael. "What he did to Michael." His hand landed on the back of his neck again. "But, to drag him off like that. That's just wrong. And what was that about an epidemic? We can't trust Jenkins and his Stone Sovereigns any more than we can trust Hunt."

"Yeah. What was that all about?" Michael sat up, his right knee bouncing. "Jenkins worked for Hunt, huh? At least that's what it sounded like. And Hunt seemed to think he'd be welcome here. And … and … that Jenkins owed him something."

"And what about Castor and Desma?" Becky shook her head. "I mean what was that? Aren't they Core Dwellers? It sounded more like they were prisoners too. Prisoners with more freedom, but not really … free. Gave me the willies."

Lander's haunted eyes met hers and Becky's heart broke for him. He looked so lost. She couldn't begin to imagine how hard this must be on him. Especially after bringing everyone safely through the Vortex. He put on a good show of being strong, but she saw the exhaustion on his pale face.

He was as confused as she and Michael were, maybe even more. Seeing his need, she stepped into him and wrapped her arms around his waist. Though her goal was to comfort him, his close warmth eased her own tension. Even now, he leaned on her as if he needed her strength to stay upright.

"I'll tell you one thing." Michael rose from where he was sitting and walked to Lander and Becky. He scanned the room, then leaned in and whispered, "Do you think this room is bugged? Can they do that here in the Core, Lander? Do they have a way of listening in while others are talking?"

Becky's mouth opened and closed without her saying a word. The idea that the rooms were bugged hadn't occurred to her. *Leave it to Michael to think of that.*

Lander released a sigh that fluttered the hair on top of Becky's head. "Your guess is as good as mine. I didn't even know there was a Core before Pop-pop died." He yawned. "And ... I'm too tired to think straight. For now, there's nothing more we can do than wait and see what happens. Since I'm a Stone Sovereign, I think that gives us some leverage."

Michael snorted. "Yeah. From what I was hearing, you're some kind of badass Stone Sovereign. That's got to count for something."

Lander grimaced. "No way. No!"

Becky sent Michael a penetrating glare.

"Oops. Sorry Becky. Won't happen again."

"Apology accepted." Becky's anger at Michael's language evaporated as she considered how much trouble they were in. She scrunched her brows together, a line forming between them. "Lander's right. You're reading too much into it, Michael. We have no idea how strong the other Stone Sovereigns are. Lander's a stranger here. And he's unexperienced. There's too much we don't know."

"Maybe things will look better in the morning, or is it Mist Rise?" Lander yawned once again. "There's one thing I do know. We need to get away from Jenkins and make it to the Vortex ... no, wait, the Avortex." He groaned. "That's going to be a problem. I don't know where the Avortex is. It might be close to the Vortex where we came in, but for all I know, it might be on the whole other side of the Core. We're going to have to figure that out before I can get you two back to the Surface."

"We'll figure it out." Becky stepped back from Lander and

looked him and Michael in the eye. "Tomorrow. For now, we all need to get some sleep. I have a feeling tomorrow is going to be a long day … or whatever they call it here."

Wishing she didn't have to leave Lander and Michael, she paced the few steps to the door, her movements heavy and slow like she was forcing her way through an incoming wave. Sheer willpower propelled her through the doorway and down the hall toward her own room. The door across from her room that had been closed earlier now stood open. Peeking through the open doorway, she pulled in a quick breath and smiled. A bathroom. *Unexpected but totally appreciated. Yes.* A stone sink, soap, and small brushes that looked like toothbrushes with bristles on the end, drew her attention. Ten minutes later, feeling refreshed, she knocked on Lander's door.

Lander's eyes grew wide when he cracked the door open. She pointed back down the hallway. "Bathroom, boys. You might want to take advantage of that." She pointed to her teeth and grimaced. "There are some toothbrushes. Strange toothbrushes, but they work well. Goo'nite."

With a lighter step, she returned to her room where the nightgown and soft bed awaited.

Lander ran his tongue across his teeth. They felt good, clean and smooth, much better than the furry scum he'd put up with the last few days. He cringed at the thought of how bad his breath must have been and how close Becky and he had gotten. A quick sponge bath and he slipped out of the bathroom while wiping the back of his neck with his tee shirt. He stared at Becky's door and debated. *No, she's probably already asleep.*

"Michael." Lander left the door ajar. "Your turn."

The brawny youth groaned. "Awww. Do I have ta?" He pushed up from his bed and vanished down the hallway.

Lander threw his damp tee on one of the stone chairs near the window and collapsed onto the springy moss pad that masqueraded as a mattress. He snuggled down; it was more comfortable than he expected considering the thin thing sat on a stone slab. *No wonder Michael didn't want to get up.*

Exhaustion hovered like a fog around him. Trying to think straight felt like slogging through a swamp filled with pockets of quicksand—not something to be attempted in his current state. And yet, his mind refused to stop churning. Laying back, he locked his fingers together and cradled his head in the palms of his hands. He stared at the ceiling, his Stones of Power hard lumps in his back pockets. Pushing upright, he twisted and pulled out the Stones.

"It's all your fault." He glowered at the four. Glimmers of red, blue, and green leaked through his fingers as he balanced two in each hand, their weight pressing down on his palms. "I wish I'd never found you." His mother's red and cream Stones were larger than his father's teal ones; more like miniature eggs in shape. They were heavier as well, not as easy to palm.

His thoughts drifted back to Castor's lesson explaining how Stone Sovereigns each kept two Stones, how they balanced one another.

Every Stone Sovereign works with two Stones. I've mentioned Stones of Protection; those are the Stones of creative power. The second Stone is a Stone of opposing power. Each Stone Sovereign must choose wisely how he or she will balance the powers in the two Stones.

So far, whenever Lander used his Stones, he hadn't thought about the opposing powers. He'd imagined the outcome he needed and then allowed the Stones to work. But seeing how Kaleb sent a bolt of energy into Hunt earlier intrigued him. Did the young man use one Stone or both? Could Lander do that? How did sending a bolt like that compare with flicking and throwing fire? There was so much he needed to learn and the only way to do that was to stay in the Core. But his conscience balked at the idea. Returning Becky and Michael to the Surface needed to be his number one priority.

Lander's eyelids drooped. Michael returned. Five minutes later, Michael's breath came and went in an even cadence and Lander's eyes slipped shut. Before he realized what was happening, he fell asleep.

CHAPTER 6

ander's eyes popped open and he gasped, his upper body springing into a sitting position. Curved blue walls and glowing light sticks brought memories racing back. The Core. He was in the Core.

You are destined. You must return to the Core and save our people.

His mother's words ricocheted around his mind like a bouncing spring. He groaned, lay back down, and threw his arm over his eyes. He closed them hoping if he opened them again, he'd be back home in Wharton, and Pop-pop Ian would be frying up bacon and eggs for breakfast. *No such luck.*

Michael shifted on the other bed and mumbled something in his sleep.

What time is it anyway? Lander had no concept of how people figured time in the Core. But there was no way he could fall back asleep now. He groaned again. *Stupid bio-clock.*

He slipped his feet off the side of the bed to the warm, stone floor, pulling the rest of his body into a sitting position before dropping his elbows on his knees. He ran his hands over the stubble on his head. Stress thrummed a painful beat at the back of his skull. How could he do what his mother asked and still get Michael and Becky home?

Pulling in a deep breath, he puffed out his cheeks, then released the air through a flutter of lips. Pushing up onto his feet, he grabbed his still-damp tee shirt and his shoes, and slipped out the door, pulling it in with a soft click behind him.

Sitting on the floor, he pulled on his shoes. Rising, he slid his shirt over his head, jogged past Becky's room, and down the stairs. Hearing voices, he slowed, listening.

"You need to give him a chance," a deep feminine voice said. "V.C. Jenkins thinks he has potential."

A masculine voice spoke in Corish. Though Lander couldn't catch what was said, he sucked in a breath when his name was mentioned.

"English, Kaleb. Remember the last time you ignored the V.C.'s orders." It was a deeper male voice speaking this time.

"Do not press me, Siprian!" Kaleb must have turned away from the door; his voice now bounced off the walls of the room. "I will not bow down to some Surface Dwelling pretender. You saw the way Vice Chancellor Jenkins looked at him when we collected that other Surface Dweller. He was practically drooling."

"Why would he not be impressed?" The female voice again. "That young man brought almost twenty people through the Vortex . . . alone . . . and controlled *four* stones. The V.C. is right. He is special. You could not have done it."

"How do you know, Rahni?" Kaleb's voice rose, frustration leaking through the words. "Chancellor Morrison and Vice Chancellor Jenkins don't trust us enough. We could do more if they gave us the authority."

"Calm yourself, Kaleb." Siprian's deep voice again. "Chancellor Morrison has made it clear; all he and V.C. Jenkins order us to do is for the good of the Core. Travelling the Vortex and

A vortex help no one. Attempting it is dangerous and forbidden. If you want to prove yourself, challenge the newcomer to a duel."

"Siprian has a point, Kaleb," Rahni said, her voice calm and low.

Lander missed what she said next as he ran his left hand along the curved, polished wall and inched closer to the open door.

"Who are you?"

Lander almost jumped out of his skin at the powerful voice behind him. Pulling upright, he turned and faced a large Stone Sovereign, gray eyes sparking, Stones already clasped in each hand. Lander took a step back and bumped into another body behind him.

"I asked you a question, Ungifted. Who are you and where do you belong?"

Lander rammed down his rising panic at the aggressive stance of the interrogator and juggled the Stones in his pockets, grateful he kept them with him. The Core Dweller reminded him of Talon. Lander didn't want a confrontation, but he wasn't going to wimp out either.

The person Lander had backed into slipped past him. Hands held out to either side, his gaze flicking to Lander then onto the other man. "Arien, glad to see you." Siprian's voice. Lander recognized him from the evening before. The large man with the scar marring the corner of one eye.

Teeth grinding, Arien growled, then pointed at Lander. "I caught him slinking around. Never seen him before. Ungifted need to be taught their place."

Kaleb stepped past Lander, taking a position next to Siprian. "Stand down, Arien. This one is not Ungifted; he is a visitor. A fellow Stone Sovereign."

Arien's nose wrinkled. "Visitor? From where? He is dressed in a strange manner and I do not recognize him."

A slight, older woman moved next to Lander. She touched his shoulder and when he glanced at her she gave him a friendly smile. "Come now, fellow Sovereigns. I think there is too much male ego happening here now. We need to welcome … Lander. Right? That's your name?" A thick, black braid hanging to her waist shifted as she took a step forward.

"Yes, ma'am."

A raspy chuckle sounded deep in her throat. "See, boys, this one has manners. Something not one of you is showing at the moment." Turning her back to the others, she grabbed Lander's elbow and propelled him into the room. "You must understand, Lander, your appearance has caused a major uproar. We Stone Sovereigns are a tight-knit bunch; we need to be to function as teams. To have a new, unknown Sovereign appear among our ranks is … disturbing. But don't judge us too harshly. Once you get to know us, you'll see. We will become like family.

"Let me introduce everyone." She waved over her shoulder. "You've already met Arien, the suspicious bully; Siprian, the scarred one; and Kaleb our team captain." She pointed toward two more men sitting on a stone couch, dressed in the same belted tunics, one cobalt blue and the other a cinnamon red, and leaned into Lander as if about to whisper a secret. "The stern-faced Sovereign in red, sitting like he has a rod up his back, is Shahan, he's with Darrius's First Team. Next to him is Tuvyam, one of our own."

Letting go of his arm, she slid past Lander to stand behind one of the most beautiful women Lander had ever seen. Gray eyes dominated her pixie face while silver hair stood up in short spikes on her head. Full, pink lips parted in a smile, revealing dimples. "Hello, Lander. I am Dena. One of Kaleb's team." Her voice, smooth as honey, flowed across the room.

"And for what it is worth, our Dena is as sweet as she sounds," Rahni said, resting her hands on Dena's shoulders.

"Unless you come face to face with her in the sparring ring." Tuvyam snickered. "Then she is as sweet as Prickly Plums from the outer tunnels of Shavah El'Ruhan."

Tension bled from the room as everyone laughed.

Dena's lips flattened. "Prickly indeed. But only in a good way, right Tuvyam? You like my *prickly* abilities when we face rebellious Ungifted or thieving Jerr'as."

"I need to go." Sovereign Shahan's deep voice broke through the banter as he stood, brushing the wrinkles from his maroon tunic. "Captain Deolah reported a number of Jerr'as were spotted in the upper tunnels between here and El'Ruhan. It might mean trouble. She asked that I leave at this Mist Rise to scout the route before she and her team pass the area with the prisoners."

"Smart." Kaleb nodded. "We are going to be traveling with Vice Chancellor Jenkins and the Surface Dwellers as well so if you need any help, you'll have it"

Shahan dipped his head. "Thank you, Kaleb. It is good to know you have my back."

Shahan walked out the door and Lander felt all eyes turn toward him.

"And now, what do we do with you?" Kaleb gave Lander an appraising look. "Vice Chancellor Jenkins says you can use all four of those Stones of Power you carry. Is this true?"

"Well, mostly…" Lander shuffled his feet. "I guess. Castor helped me control things when we came through the Vortex." He closed his eyes, pulled in a deep breath as the silence of the room pounded against his eardrums, then he spoke in a rush. "I've never been taught. Don't know how to do much. Didn't even know about the Stones or what I was until … well … Pop-pop Ian died—"

"Ian is dead?" Rahni sucked in a breath. "What about the others? Cyanne and Jerod, are they … are they dead too?"

Lander nodded.

"And are you truly their son?"

Lander looked up to meet Rahni's eyes. "Yes."

"That explains a lot." Rahni turned to Kaleb. "You know the stories, Kaleb. Cyanne and Jerod were heroes. Lander is their child, a melding of two strong Stone Sovereign lines. Think about it. Ask V.C. Jenkins to assign him to our team."

Kaleb shook his head. "By his own admission, he knows nothing. He hasn't been put to trial and we have no idea what he can do."

Rahni snorted. "Think Kaleb."

Dena's honey sweet voice drifted over the room. "Vice Chancellor Jenkins said Lander and the other Surface Dwellers will travel with us to Shavah El'Ruhan at second Mist Rise. If we see Jerr'as we can test him. With us near, he will be safe."

Kaleb nodded. "Good idea, Dena."

"I don't know." Siprian shook his head. "If he has no training . . . no. He needs to pass trial, but not against Jerr'as, at least until we know what he can do."

"What are Jerr'as?" Lander suppressed the urge to disappear as all eyes turned to him, but if he came face to face with the beasts, he wanted to know what he was getting into.

"Creatures of darkness that snuck into the tunnels with our ancestors during Noah's flood. Nasty killers." Arien's mouth twisted as if he had eaten a lemon.

"Very like us, they are, but only so tall." Rahni held a hand at chest height. "Two arms, hands, six fingers with sharp, curved claws. Two legs and wide feet. They have pale, translucent skin. Poisonous fangs. Oh, yes, and their skin is smooth as a rock . . . no hair."

"And they are strong," Kaleb added. "Vicious and cunning." He met Lander's gaze. "You do not want to run into them alone."

Lander tilted his head, his thoughts racing. "But didn't Shahan say he was scouting alone."

Laughter and snorting filled the air. Kaleb shook his head, pressing his lips together as snickering filtered through the crack. "Shahan is…" Another snort broke through.

Rahni's voice rose over the mirth. "What Kaleb is trying to say, is that Shahan is our most experienced scout and warrior. He has been hunting Jerr'as for over two-hundred years and is well able to take care of himself."

A slight youth dressed in shabby, pale-blue trousers and a too-large shirt, appeared in the doorway. "Sovereigns. It is near to Mist Rise." He ducked his head, one eye twitching in a nervous manner, turned, and sprinted away.

Kaleb approached Lander and held his hand out. "It is good to meet you, Lander. Please excuse us for any offense we might have caused in our ignorance of Surface Dweller customs. I hope you will consider joining us. I look forward to travelling with you."

Lander scanned the faces around him and allowed a soft smile to emerge. Repeating Castor's hand grip from earlier, he clasped Kaleb's arm. "No offense. I mean . . . none taken. I too look forward to traveling together." He paused and fought the urge to bow. "I have much to learn and I hope you and your team are willing to teach me."

"Well said, Lander." Dena's eyes sparkled as she pushed up from her chair and gifted him with a full smile. "It is a sign of wisdom that you are willing to admit what you do not know, ask questions of others, and learn from those more experienced. I hope to have a hand in your training."

While she was speaking, Dena walked over to stand in front of Lander, her movements smooth and graceful.

Lander swallowed as she reached out and took his hand in both of hers. "I am certain you will surprise us all."

"As am I," said Rahni. "But for now, you should return to your room and rest while you can."

CHAPTER 7

Becky watched Lander from the corner of her eye as he walked next to her, disquiet churning her insides. In the wee hours of what would have been early morning on the Surface, unable to settle, she wondered at the sound of soft footsteps slapping past her room. Peeking out, she had caught sight of him descending the stairs. Nearly an hour later, comforted by his return, she finally fell into a soundless sleep.

Later, when they woke and had tried to go downstairs, they were told to remain in their rooms and meals would be brought up. After the servant left, she snuck down the hallway and spent the day in Lander and Michael's room. Lander's behavior had been unusually quiet, even for him. Being stuck in the room all day had been bad enough, but when she asked Lander when he planned to talk to Jenkins about returning to the Surface, his response sent prickles of foreboding up her spine.

"Becky, please try to understand," he had said as he played with his father's Stones of Power, his eyes locked on their glowing surfaces. "If I return to the Surface, I might not be able to come back. And since we're already here, and Hunt's no longer a problem, why not meet Chancellor Morrison. I can see the other cities and learn more from Kaleb and his team before I lose the chance." His eyes had flicked to her for a moment before returning to the Stones resting on his palms.

"I mean, for all we know, the Avortex may be on the other side of the Core and we might do better going to Shavah Al'Wisan and meeting Chancellor Morrison first. It'll just be for a few days, okay, Becky? Then I'll ask Jenkins about going home. In the meantime, why don't you think of it as an adventure? You know, like Michael here."

"Hey, don't put me in the middle of this," Michael had said. "Though I do love me a good adventure."

Lander's focus shifted back to Becky. "Please?"

She had sighed, finding it hard to deny him the chance to find his roots.

But now, nearly twenty-four hours later, after leaving Jenkins's place and walking through the silent city for what seemed like forever, doubts resurfaced. Everything Lander did here in the Core affected her and Michael. She struggled with a growing tightness in her chest. The feeling that Lander was blowing off her concerns hurt.

"I'll be back."

Becky startled out of her thoughts at Lander's unexpected words as he sprinted ahead. A pang shot through her at his desertion. Uncertain if she was more hurt or angry with him, she ground her teeth.

"What's up Becks? You look like you just sucked on a lemon." Michael bounced on the balls of his feet as they slogged up a steep hill leading out of the city toward the immense, misty blue tunnel they had noticed when they arrived.

Michael took up a position next to her, his eyes tracking Lander's movements as their friend approached the band of six

Core Dwellers dressed in matching thigh-length, cobalt blue tunics and cloaks, and snug dark-gray trousers.

Walking behind Vice Chancellor Jenkins, Castor, and Desma, the fine material of their thin cloaks fluttered in the light, sporadic breeze and skimmed the top of knee-high, charcoal gray boots. *Stone Sovereigns.* She recognized two of them as the ones who had taken Aurelius Hunt away the day before yesterday.

Each had an oiled, tooled leather bag with a stylized stone etched in the surface on his or her belt where she suspected they secured their Stones of Power.

Lander slipped in among them as laughter filtered through the group. One of them, the young man Jenkins had called Kaleb, slapped Lander on the back as if he was greeting an old acquaintance.

"Looks like he's found some new friends, Becks."

She glanced to her right, taking in Michael's expression. "Now who's eating sour lemons?"

"Huh? Oh, yeah." Michael shrugged. "Should we join them?"

Becky chewed her lip and shook her head. "Honestly, I don't know. I suspect we wouldn't be welcomed."

"We should try anyway."

"Yeah, you're right, Michael. Nothing ventured; nothing gained, as my granny says."

They increased speed at the same moment Aurelius Hunt, Talen, and Hunt's other guards trotted in from a small side street on their right. Bound, and herded along by a second group of Stone Sovereigns, the influx forced Michael and Becky to shift to the far side of the lane.

When the incoming group came abreast of Jenkins and the others, several members of the team Lander walked with split off and joined ranks with those guarding Hunt and his people.

Houses thinned then were left behind when the street

widened and rose in a steep incline. Becky's breath wheezed through her teeth and her thigh muscles burned with the effort of the climb that seemed unending. She glanced in Lander's direction. He walked alongside a tall, stunning Core Dweller with short, spiked hair.

"Humph." Becky's eyes narrowed.

"Don't." Michael shook his head. "You know how Lander feels about you."

"Yeah, right! Come on Michael." Breathing hard, Becky struck out at a faster pace.

Chuckling, Michael set his palms against her back and pushed her forward. "That's it. Keep it up Becks. You can do this."

"Shut up, Michael."

Huffing, her lungs burning, Becky drew up alongside Lander. "Hey ... Lander." Huff. Huff. "Who . . .'s . . . your . . . nu . . . friend?"

Lander's eyes grew wide and he reached out to take her arm. "Becky. What are you doing? Are you okay?"

She glared at him. "Do I look okay, Core boy?"

The willowy, silver-haired goddess turned to face Becky. "Core boy?" A musical chuckle tinkled on the air. "That is cute. I am going to remember that.

"You must be Becky." Gentle, gray eyes met Becky's. "Not much farther. We are almost to the level."

"Hi! I'm Michael." He shuffled forward and grabbed Becky's other arm.

"Great way to look like a dork!" Becky growled. Five minutes later, they crested the rise.

Becky shook Michael's and Lander's hands from her arms, straightened her spine, and brushed back the hair that had fallen into her eyes. She froze when she noticed the goddess watching. "What? Do I have something on my face?"

Light laughter sounded again. "No, nothing on your face.

Never have I seen anyone with such beautiful, dark skin, except the one prisoner and you. It does not exist in the Core. Do many on the Surface have this color skin?" A soft smile surfaced. "I am sorry. I should introduce myself. I am Sovereign Dena Al'Wisan. Of Captain Kaleb's team.

"May I?" Dena reached out to run the back of her hand down Becky's cheek. "So soft."

Becky opened her mouth to protest, but it was too late.

"I am sorry." Dena's gaze dropped to the ground. "I have stepped over my bounds."

"Overstepped," Becky mumbled.

"What?"

"You have overstepped, not stepped over," Becky said. "But it's okay. It's not a problem."

By now the rest of the travelers had gathered on the level. Becky looked back the way they had come. The shimmering beauty spread out before them took her breath away. The hair on Becky's arms rose and a tingle worked its way up her spine as energy filled the air, reminding her of the time a bolt of lightning had struck near where she stood on her grandparents front porch watching a summer storm.

The glowing lights of the city twinkled like living flames as a translucent, blue mist rose. But it didn't just rise from the ground, it drifted down from the dome far above, like sparkling sapphires, light as dandelion down. Becky sucked in a breath. *This must be what it would be like to live in a snow globe with glitter snow. Magical. Spellbinding.*

Lander stepped to Becky's side, warm and familiar, his focus locked on the swirling curtains of mist. "Wow! This is incredible."

"That's for sure." Michael's voice sounded over Becky's shoulder.

"It's . . . enchanting . . . like we're in some kind of fairy tale," Becky whispered as a scent similar to rain hitting hot pavement permeated the air.

"It is Mist Rise." Dena spoke so soft only Becky, Lander, and Michael could hear. "It happens every day . . . *day* . . . *dura* in Corish. It was *misrisdura*, but Chancellor Morrison forbids us to use the Corish. We speak Surface words now."

"Mis-ris-dura. That's musical. It seems to fit the beauty of this moment better than Mist Rise . . . though Mist Rise isn't bad." Becky couldn't look away. As the mist continued to tumble up and down the two motions came together, swirling faster, thickening. As if burdened by its own weight the ephemeral dew began drifting downward again, covering everything in a layer of shimmering blue-green droplets.

Warm, soft moisture dripped onto Becky's face and she looked down to see her hands covered with the glistening liquid spheres. The soft hush of millions of tiny drops falling on stone whispered in her ears.

All too soon it was over. Becky pulled in a deep breath and released it with a sigh, already missing the transient beauty. The Core couldn't be all bad if every day began like this.

"I have missed this." Desma's voice cracked as her words carried on the air. The woman walked over to stand next to Lander. "This is what I meant." Her eyes shifted to Lander. "Remember? When you read in your mother's journal? About that day in the library . . . and the storms. This soft beauty is what my spirit longed for then." She pulled in a breath through her nose and released it while she looked back out over the city as Castor approached from behind and wrapped his arms around her waist.

Jenkins's piercing, authoritative voice shattered the peaceful moment. "Deolah. Kaleb. Move."

Jenkins pulled a rifle from where it hung on his shoulder—Lander recognized it as one of the Mossberg MMRs taken from Hunt's men—and waved Castor and Desma over. "You might not understand the threat Jerr'as now pose since they rarely ventured into the major tunnels and weren't aggressive before you left. They became destructive and violent after so many Core Dwellers were lost in the epidemic, leaving sections of the caverns uninhabited.

"Traveling isn't safe without Stone Sovereign protection or something like this." He held out the rifle. "And no, I'm not going to arm you people." He shifted the Mossberg, the sling settling it onto his back again. "Just stick close. If you two can't keep up, I'll leave you behind. Do you understand?" Without waiting for a response, he turned. Long strides propelled him across the hard-scrabble slope toward the massive tunnel entrance.

"Go. Go. Go." Captain Deolah called, pulling her Stones of Power from her pouch and shoving Talen forward.

Kaleb nodded at Lander and his friends, then pointed toward the tunnel. Less than a minute later, the level of light increased as Hunt, his people, Castor and Desma, and Lander, Becky, and Michael jogged toward the blue-tinged tunnel.

CHAPTER 8

The vast tunnel they had entered upon leaving Shavah Deklakh shrank over time as they traveled farther in. After three hours of steady walking, the ceiling still soared several hundred feet overhead, though the sides had tapered into a narrow passage.

Muted, deep blue light filtering in from the Flux above now shown in sparkling shafts of mixed pale blue and gold. Beneath their feet the same colors dominated in an almost imperceptible glow.

Waist high, bioluminescent grasses grew in large clumps along the curved sides of the tunnel. Vast patches of moss and lichen in varying shades of blue and green, taller than any varieties Lander had known on the Surface, covered the rocky terrain that bordered the smooth path that ran down the center of the tunnel. A scent that reminded Lander of wet mushrooms hung heavy in the air. Periodically soft breezes wafted through, disbursing the fragrance for a few minutes before it settled again. Scattered pools of collected moisture dotted the tunnel, and, from time to time, the sound of dripping water echoed.

They walked through the day, if it could be called day, taking short breaks every few hours. Almost twelve hours later, they set a camp. After eating a meal of goat cheese and dried meat washed down by warm water, Lander laid out the blanket Kaleb had given him on a clump of shorter moss, next to where Michael already snored. The moment his head hit the blanket, the scent of soft, moist growth permeated the air around him and within seconds, he was asleep.

The next *morning*, Mist Rise filled the tunnel with a layer of fog that seemed alive as it rose and fell at the same time, performing its dance and leaving droplets on everything. An hour later, the mist disappeared, though it left the air heavy. Sweat beaded on Lander's temples and ran down the sides of his face.

His gaze roamed over his shoulder to where Becky and Desma lagged behind everyone else, talking. Michael had walked with the two for the last few hours. Now, however, catching Lander's eye, his typical level of excess energy sent him sprinting up to Lander where he introduced himself to Kaleb and his team.

Over time the company became strung out along the path with Deolah taking point, Hunt's men behind her, flanked by Stone Sovereigns. They kept pace without protest, as if they had learned yesterday that any defiance under the circumstances would be useless.

Hunt, however, dragged his feet and protested. "Mr. Jenkins. How dare you treat me like this. When we get back to the Surface I'll have you arrested for kidnapping. You will not get away with this."

Lander admired Talen's patience as he shifted to his boss's side offering quiet support even when Hunt berated him. "You, too, when we get back, find yourself another job. Useless waste of oxygen." Talen walked alongside the man, without a word, his focus ahead and his lips flattened in a severe line.

Though Talen's presence still sent shivers up his spine, Lander had to admit the man was loyal.

Everyone ignored Hunt's verbal attacks as if they didn't hear them, and, eventually, he gave up and walked in silence. Whenever Deolah sprinted ahead to scout, however, Hunt leaned into Talen and whispered, but one look from the Stone Sovereign captain as she walked back, her Stones of Power in hand, put an end to his murmuring. *Yep, she must have made her point with him yesterday.*

Though it seemed strange to Lander, Jenkins and Castor conversed as they walked together between the prisoners and Kaleb's team. Lander shrugged, wondering what common ground the two had found that was so interesting.

Glancing back again, he slowed, allowing Kaleb, his team, and Michael to continue on without him. When Becky and Desma caught up to him, he came alongside Becky, setting his pace to match theirs.

He glanced to the left, met Becky's angry gaze, and quickly lowered his to the smooth, blue rock of the path. Abandoning her to walk with Kaleb's team hadn't been his wisest decision and he swallowed the lump of guilt sitting at the back of his throat.

"Well?" Becky asked without looking at Lander.

"Ah ... well ... what?"

A very unfeminine snort sounded from beyond Becky. "What young man leaves the lady who willingly put her life in danger for him, to walk with a group of strangers?" Desma snorted again. "I thought you appreciated this precious friend ... apparently not!"

Lander's shoulders sagged. Desma was right. He should have stayed with Becky. But the desire to learn about his heritage pressed down on him; and to do that, he needed to talk with others like himself. A fracture opened within his heart and confusion poured out.

"I know, Desma. You're right. But I'm here now. That should count for something, right?"

"I don't know," she replied. "You'll need to ask Becky that, not me. Besides, I should check on Castor. He's spent far too much time talking to that snake of a vice chancellor." Desma hurried ahead, leaving Lander alone with Becky.

Silence rode heavy on Lander as he walked beside Becky.

Five minutes passed and Lander pulled in a breath, preparing to speak, when Becky said, "I'm sorry I got so angry, Lander. It's just ... I ... I'm afraid. You're meeting people like you here, but Michael and I are outsiders. Michael, well, you know what he's like, he'll fit in anywhere. It's not so easy for me."

"Don't say that, Becky. You're one of the nicest people I know. I promise I won't leave you alone again." He scanned her profile as she continued staring forward. "You met Dena. She's nice, right? I'll introduce you to the others and they'll see what I see ... a beautiful, caring, incredible girl."

"Girl? Did you just call me a *girl?* Lander you have a lot to learn. I am a woman ... a young lady. Six-year old females wearing pig-tails are *girls.*"

Lander chuckled. "Yes, ma'am. Ms. Rebecca! I'll never call you a *girl* again. You are waaay toooo old for that."

She pulled to a stop, turned, and punched Lander's arm. "Sometimes, Lander, you are worse than Michael. And that's not easy to accomplish."

Lander pulled Becky into himself and wrapped his arms around her. Her head tilted back, and her eyes closed. He leaned in, savoring the warmth of her body, his focus on her luscious lips. The sound of dry leaves rattling in a strong wind filtered down the tunnel, pulling his attention.

He straightened and Becky's eyes popped open. "What's the matter, Lander? Lander?"

"Do you hear that?"

She shook her head, her brow crinkled in concentration. Her eyes widened. "Oh. Yes. What is that?"

Lander shrugged. "I don't know."

He took Becky's hand and together they approached the closest Stone Sovereign, Arien, the muscular man who had questioned Lander's appearance in Jenkins's manor.

"Arien," Lander called.

The sovereign turned cool eyes on Lander. "Yes, Surface Dweller. What?"

Lander stiffened when Arien's gaze moved to Becky. His eyes roamed up and down. In response, Lander stepped between them forcing Arien's attention. "That sound. We weren't hearing it until now. What is it?"

Arien tilted his head in an attitude of focused attention. A grimace surfaced. "What sound..." A look of understanding replaced the sour expression. "Oh, that sound. You must get used to it, it will grow louder as we come closer to..."

Lander motioned with his hand for the irritating sovereign to continue.

"The joining."

"Yes? The joining?" Lander prompted again.

"It is Bec Jekesh." Kaleb walked up. "Arien, I will handle this."

Arien sent a self-satisfied smirk in Lander's direction before striding ahead.

Kaleb watched him walk away then turned back to Lander. "Walk with me, Sovereign Lander. I will explain. Sovereign Arien does not know you. He does not trust. And Surface speech does not come easy for him."

Lander and Becky hiked alongside Kaleb. He didn't speak for a few minutes, then said, "The sound you asked about, it is getting louder, is it not?"

"Yes. At first, I thought it sounded like dry leaves blown along the ground by a strong wind ... in the distance. But now

... it sounds more like ... like a growl or a roar. A river? Here in the tunnel?"

"Yes." Kaleb nodded. "You are correct. Bec Jekesh flows into this tunnel. Our path joins the bec ... umm ... no, river ... all the way to Shavah El'Ruhan."

"Is it safe?" Becky asked. "The river doesn't flood the tunnel, does it?" She leaned past Lander to catch Kaleb's eyes. "You said *joins the river*. What exactly does that mean?"

A smile flitted across Kaleb's face. "You will see soon. Not far ahead now, our path will open onto *Becavan* ..." He shook his head. "I mean the *river cavern*. It is a remarkable sight." His face clouded. "However, as there are many unused tunnels there, Jerr'as often attack unwary travelers along the river. Though it is beautiful to walk with the river, it is also very dangerous. We Stone Sovereigns are frequently called upon to accompany and protect those who transport goods between Shavah Deklakh and Shavah El'Ruhan."

"Walk with the river? That sounds interesting." Lander smiled at the thought. Judging by the increased volume echoing from ahead, he suspected the Bec Jekesh must be fast and wild— fierce. A sight worth seeing.

Lander's thoughts fled when Sovereign Shahan sprinted around a bend, his breathing heavy and one arm cradled at his chest. Seeing the group approaching, the scout pulled to a stop for a second then sprinted toward them. "Jerr'as. Behind me. Hurry."

Kaleb sprinted to his team while Shahan joined Deolah and her team. Deolah shouted, "Kaleb, we'll set the barrier, get your team ready to send shocks on my signal."

Kaleb nodded. "Got it. Siprian, Arien, Rahni, Dena spread out."

Rahni's voice echoed. "Kaleb. The side tunnel we passed."

"Shiviah-zor." Kaleb's gaze flashed to Lander. "You, Surface Dweller. Can you set a barrier?"

"Yes."

"Good. Go back to that cleft in the right wall we passed not long ago. Make sure nothing comes through. Nothing! Go!"

Lander grabbed Becky's arm; his focus intense. "Stay here with Michael. He'll keep you safe."

He looked up and scanned the tunnel. Jenkins stood near Hunt and his people, his rifle up and ready. Michael had taken up a position near them, his hands fisted, his expression alert.

Deolah and her team shifted to positions on either side of the tunnel with calm, practiced movements. "Now," she called. Instantly, a thick, translucent barrier filled most of the opening. Kaleb and his sovereigns stood in a line across the tunnel behind the barrier, glowing Stones in hand prepared to fire bolts of energy.

Lander nudged Becky. "Go."

Turning on his heel, Lander sprinted back toward a fissure in the rock wall about two-hundred feet behind. Before he reached the spot, his eyes widened and he stumbled to a stop. In the half-light along the inner wall of the tunnel, two deeper shadows moved through a clump of grass toward him. Their moves slow and stealthy, they approached like hunting cats. He swallowed back bile. Jerr'as. They had already entered the main tunnel and the only one between them and his unsuspecting companions behind him—between them and Becky—was Lander.

He squelched his rising panic and pulled his father's Stones.

No. Use mine.

Lander almost dropped his Stones when the voice he had heard back on Hunt's island—his dead mother's voice—spoke inside his head. But with no time to consider the consequences. He slipped his father's blue Stones of Power back into one pocket and pulled out his mother's red ones. They ignited, warm and bright, their intense gleam drawing the Jerr'as' attention.

The Jerr'as stopped, noses lifted, sniffing with loud snorts. Large, pale luminous eyes fixed on Lander. He stared back, frozen. No taller than his waist, the Jerr'as appeared human in shape. They wore ragged shreds of material like clothing. They growled and sharp, canine teeth glittered red in the light of Lander's Stones of Power. *Human like but not human. Definitely not human!*

Lander flexed his fingers around his mother's Stones. His knuckles turned white. He set a barrier. He had no idea how the Jerr'as fought, but he vowed to do whatever was necessary to stop the creatures before him. Since a strong barrier infused with fire wreaked havoc on Hunt's guards, Lander hoped it would do the same against Jerr'as. With a thought, the Stones flared crimson and the barrier ignited. He pushed the flaming wall of energy toward the Jerr'as.

With what sounded like screams, the Jerr'as threw up their arms, blocking the sparks that flew off the barrier. The larger of the two growled again and flung itself at the point where the barrier curved inward.

Lander's heart rate spiked. The stench of burning flesh infused the air as the thing fought to work its way around the edge. Seconds felt like years as it screamed and clawed the air between the wall and Lander's shield, bending it, but not breaking it.

Bile rose as the sound of claws against stone shredded the air.

Unable to worm past, the Jerr'as stopped and turned glowing eyes on Lander. It breathed in heavy pants, its tongue lolling to the side like a dog's. Drops of yellow liquid clung to the exposed, razor-sharp fangs. With a growl, it flung itself bodily at Lander, crashing into the shield with brute force.

Lander jerked back at the impact, but the Jerr'as hung,

unable to move, pinned to the side of the barrier like a stuck bug, until the second Jerr'as pulled it away, its skin smoldering.

After a series of deep growls, the two turned and darted back to the crack. As they disappeared though the opening, Lander dropped his shield and sprinted after them. Too large to fit into the opening and uncertain if following them wouldn't be a huge mistake, Lander pulled to a stop, bent over, his hands on his knees, and sucked in deep breaths as the trembling in his body subsided. When his heart rate dropped to a semblance of normal, he turned and sprinted back up the tunnel.

CHAPTER 9

Lander raced back to the others. Coming around a slight bend he slowed, approached Becky, and touched her shoulder. With a soft squeal, she turned from Michael, Castor, and Desma, and wrapped her arms around Lander's waist. "Thank God you're safe," she murmured into his chest. "I was so worried."

"We all were," said Castor.

Lander nodded to the others, then pulled Becky in closer. His chin resting on the top of her head, he scanned the tunnel. The battle must have been one-sided. The bodies of six Jerr'as smoldered on the ground where the barrier had been set. Deolah and Kaleb stood over them. Lander startled and a chill swept through him when the two sent shafts of fire into the bodies, incinerating the remains.

A few minutes later, Vice Chancellor Jenkins approached Lander. Deolah and Kaleb followed. "Did you run into any Jerr'as?" Jenkins asked.

Lander nodded. "Two."

"Did you think to dispose of the bodies? Probably not. We'll have to go back and fry them."

Lander forced down a surge of discomfort at the look on Jenkins's face. "I didn't kill them. They disappeared back into that crack. I couldn't follow, so I just came back here."

"Shiviah-zor." The word Kaleb had used earlier erupted from Deolah and Lander had the feeling it was a Corish swear word by the tone of it. Jenkins turned to Deolah and glared. "Corish? In front of me?"

"Sorry, sir. It won't happen again."

"See that it doesn't." He turned back to Lander. "In the future, do not hesitate. If you face Jerr'as, put them down. Otherwise people get hurt." He waved to where Sovereign Shahan sat on a rocky ledge, his upper garments resting on the rock next to him. Sovereigns Rahni and Siprian stood next to him, focusing their Stones of Power at four long, deep gashes that ran from his right shoulder blade to his waist.

"That wound on Sovereign Shahan's back was from a Jerr'as claw. Not pretty, is it? And their bite is poisonous. They show no mercy; neither do we. Remember that."

Jenkins turned his back on Lander and strode toward where the remaining Stone Sovereigns stood over the prisoners who now sat in a group on the ground. "Get them up. We're moving."

As Aurelius Hunt was pulled to his feet, he elbowed Sovereign Arien, breaking his hold, and rounded on Jenkins, his face twisted into a snarl. "Ryan. Enough. I demand you let my men and me go now, or I promise you there will come a time when you will regret this foolishness."

Arien reached for Hunt's elbow again, but Jenkins waved him away. "Aurelius, stop acting like a fool. Of course, I'll let you and your people go. In time. For now, accept the situation. When we meet with Phil, we'll discuss the terms of your return to the Surface."

He walked over to Hunt and dropped an arm across Hunt's shoulders. "Think of it this way, I'm keeping you safe from the Jerr'as and the rebels your plan created."

Jenkins patted Hunt's cheek and Hunt's face warmed to a mottled red. "That's right. I'd forgotten your temper." He slapped Hunt hard enough to make him stumble back, but then leaned and whispered something in Hunt's ear.

Talen moved forward to step between the two, but Sovereign Arien grabbed his elbow. Even with his hands bound, Talen levered a sweeping kick at Arien's calves, dropping him to the ground. In a second, Kaleb, Deolah, Dena, and Tuvyan had Stones of Power pointed at Talen.

"Enough!" Jenkins shouted.

But it was Hunt's soft words that brought the conflict to an end. "Let it go, Emmet."

Fire smoldering in his eyes, Talen stood as if frozen for a moment, then dropped to his knees. "I concede."

Fifteen minutes later, the group moved past another slight bend and the tight confines of the tunnel opened on their left, exposing a vast cavern. From the landing on which they now stood; the ground dropped in a sharp, vertical incline for fifty feet to where a churning river rushed through a narrow, rock-strewn channel—the source of the sound Lander had been hearing.

"The Bec Jekesh." Desma's soft words filtered to Lander over the roar of the water.

Lander sucked in a breath, gasped, and coughed as the moisture-laden air filled his lungs. His senses tingled at the overload of sight and sound. The ubiquitous Core light now shown with a warm, golden tinge. The path they had been following continued on into the distance; a vertical wall rising to its right and a steep drop off to the river on its left.

Here green trees and shrubs supplanted the blue flora of Shavah Deklakh. Immense trailing vines twisted among the shrubbery, covered the vertical inclines, and hung from the ceiling three hundred feet above, their yellow flowers like beacons in the muted light.

Ahead, the churning water dropped through a series of falls before flattening into a smooth wide flow as the edges of the river spread out.

Heavy scents of flowering shrubbery and moss permeated the warm, humid air as Lander, Becky, and Michael stood like fixed statues, staring in slack-jawed wonder.

"Quite a view, isn't it?" Castor asked, his voice rough.

Jenkins and the Stone Sovereigns already had the prisoners moving forward along the ledge where wet vegetation slicked the smooth surface.

Following the others, Lander took Becky's hand, helping her to stay stable on the slippery path, while Castor did the same for Desma.

A short while later, Kaleb and Rahni dropped back to walk with Lander, Becky, Michael, Castor, and Desma.

"Shahan told us he found the remains of a Jerr'as attack ahead. That was where the Jerr'as took him by surprise." Kaleb's eyes flicked to Becky before settling on Lander. "You should see this, but you might want your friend to stay back until we have cleared the area. Jerr'as do not leave bodies in one piece."

Becky's gasp went right to Lander's heart. Regret at not returning her and Michael to the surface before now soured Lander's stomach. His decision to not confront Jenkins when they first arrived had been petty and selfish. In his desire to learn more of his legacy, he had placed his friends in true, life-threatening danger. But he couldn't change the past; all he could do now was try to keep them safe. The Core was turning out to be so much more than he expected.

"You go." Desma dropped her arm over Becky's shoulders. "I'll stay with Becky."

"I will stay as well," Rahni said, earning a nod of thanks from Lander.

Desma steered Becky and Rahni to a seat near the wall and the three sat together on the moss-covered rock.

Lander's eyes met Becky's. "I'll be right back." His focus shifted to Michael. "You coming?"

"I think I need to see this too." Michael's unusually serious gaze bored into Lander. "Looks like Becks and I are stuck here for now." He waved his hand out over the river. "We should know what we're dealing with."

For the first time, Lander sensed Michael's disapproval. It hurt, but he understood where his big friend was coming from. Lander had betrayed his and Becky's trust. He ran a hand over the back of his neck smearing droplets of mist, turned back to Kaleb, and pulled in a breath. "Okay, Kaleb. Lead on."

Michael and Lander followed Kaleb behind a waterfall where the path widened into an alcove carved into the rock. Scattered drops of dried, brownish blood marked torn up vegetation, and trampled moss and lichen spoke of a struggle. Beyond the splashing water, Tuvyam and Siprian stood guard over Hunt and his people.

Swallowing back his dread of what he would see, Lander moved toward the back of the recess where Jenkins and the other Stone Sovereigns stood. Sovereign Shahan knelt next to something on the ground. Two steps later, Lander swallowed back bile at the sight of the remains. He wished he'd never looked because now those images would be with him the rest of his life. Michael gagged, then turned and shuffled away.

Jenkins hand on Lander's back propelled him closer. "This. You see this? This is why we need your help as a Stone Sovereign. And this is why we never let Jerr'as escape."

Lander pulled away from the man and glared at him, anger at the situation setting his gut to churning.

"Think about it." Kaleb stepped up to Lander. "You can

help, be a part of what we're doing to prevent tragedies like this."

"I won't pressure you anymore, Lander," Jenkins said. "But remember this when you think about returning to the Surface."

Lander stumbled out the far side of the waterfall, his mind spinning, and moved to stand next to Michael. "I'm sorry, Michael. It's my fault Becky and you are here. I…"

"No." Michael gave a firm shake of his head. "I don't blame you. Hunt is the reason we're here … not you. And, because we decided to follow you. It was our choice."

"But—"

"No. I'm angry about how we got here and being stuck. But … I have to admit, it's incredible … the adventure of a lifetime. We've seen things that are so amazing no one would believe it. But I'm scared too. Scared for me and for Becky." He grabbed Lander's elbow and turned Lander to face him. "But I don't blame you. Don't take that on yourself. Just promise me you'll get us back to the Surface as soon as you can. Okay? Will you promise me?"

"You have my word, Michael."

Michael nodded. "That's all I need. I trust you."

The stench of burned flesh lingered in the still air after the Stone Sovereigns burned the victim's remains.

Fifteen minutes later, as the path leveled off in a small clearing next to the river, Jenkins called for a break. Up until now they had only stopped for short spells along the way, while Sovereign Rahni handed out trail snacks and Sovereign Arien passed around water jugs. Now, they stopped for the night.

Dena disappeared into some dense shrubbery with Desma and Becky. They returned a few minutes later, much to Lander's relief. While Shahan and Siprian headed off to hunt, the remaining sovereigns established a camp site and started a cooking fire. A rope was passed through the bonds of the prisoners, then tied off on one of the larger trees.

By the time Shahan and Siprian returned with several rodent-like animals, the fire had settled into hot coals. They cut up the carcasses, seasoned them, placed them in small, sealed cylinders, and buried them in the coals. While the meat cooked, Dena and Kaleb foraged for edible plants to add to the menu.

Lander, Becky, and Michael sat a short distance apart from the others on a moss-covered outcropping overlooking the chuckling river. Soon Castor and Desma joined them. Soft conversation laced the air, but Lander remained quiet, wrapped in his own thoughts. Several large groups of travelers passed their campsite. Though Lander expected them to stop and talk with Jenkins and the Stone Sovereigns, the groups avoided them, hugging the other side of the pathway and hurrying past.

"What do you make of that?" Michael asked. "Looks like they don't like their Vice Chancellor or Stone Sovereigns much."

Desma snorted. "It's a good indication of how most of the people must feel. I suspect neither Vice Chancellor Jenkins nor Chancellor Morrison is well liked."

"They did take over the Core in what must have been a brutal manner," Castor whispered, his eyes locked on Jenkins and his Sovereigns.

Desma nodded, her gaze following her husband's. "And fast. Here we are only sixteen years later, and everything has changed. Good grief, we had lived here for thousands of years with no major changes and now… Well, all I can say is, it's a good thing Ian died before he saw the end results of his *friendship* with Aurelius Hunt."

Lander resented how Desma talked about his grandfather with such disdain, but he understood. That fateful meeting of Ian and Aurelius had caused so much harm. And Lander suspected as they continued to travel in the Core, more would come to light. Thinking of Aurelius sent Lander's gaze to Becky and the Wasp still fastened to her ankle. He shifted his focus to the one on his leg. He toyed with the idea of trying to remove the two himself but discounted it. He didn't have enough control of his gifts ... yet. But just fifty feet away sat several Stone Sovereigns who had spent their lives learning to control their Stones and their powers.

"What are you thinking? You zoned out there." Becky's dark eyes probed Lander's.

"I'm thinking it's time we got rid of these." He pointed to the Wasps.

"Can you do that?" she asked.

The trusting expression on her face, seared Lander. He wanted to say yes, to be capable of freeing her himself, but reality mangled the thought. In his mind, he saw again the drawer of Hunt's desk exploding when he sent a fine stream of fire into the lock.

"No. I can't. But I know someone who can. Wait here."

Pulling in a deep breath, Lander pushed to his feet and walked to where Jenkins and the Stone Sovereigns sat.

CHAPTER 10

Dena, Deolah, and Siprian followed Lander and Kaleb to check out the Wasp on Becky's ankle. Kaleb knelt next to Becky, examined the device, and nodded. "This is not a difficult task." He pulled two Stones from his pouch and the familiar blue-green light thrummed to life.

"No." Lander stopped Kaleb. "Remove mine first. Just in case."

Siprian huffed and Dena's gentle laugh rose above the soft chuckling of the river. "You must trust Kaleb, Surface Dweller. If he says he can do this, then he can do this."

Lander squirmed but held his ground. "Me. First. It's not that I don't trust you, Kaleb, it's just that … well … you've never seen anything like this before and if something is going to go wrong, I want it to go wrong on me, not on Becky."

Kaleb pushed back upright and approached Lander. "I will remove your device first. Sit."

Five minutes later, Kaleb stood at Lander's side by the Bec Jekesh as Lander flung both Wasps out into the wide flow.

"Can you teach me?" Lander asked, keeping his focus on

the rushing water rather than turning to Kaleb. After Jenkins's comments about Lander's abilities, he suspected Kaleb might just laugh in his face.

A sigh of relief passed his lips and the tension gripping his muscles eased when Kaleb said, "I would be honored to teach you."

Lander's muscles seized once again when Kaleb added, "But you will need to join my team as a cadet. That is how Stone Sovereigns are taught. We learn through training as cadets. It will take time."

Once again, Lander faced a choice. Did he stay and learn, or return to the Surface with Becky and Michael ... and, maybe even Castor and Desma. They had also asked if he would take them through the Avortex. He could, of course, return after escorting the others back, but he suspected once he reached the Surface with Becky, he wouldn't be able to leave her again.

"Well?" Kaleb's question hung on the air.

Lander looked back over his shoulder to where Becky sat with Michael, Desma, and Castor. Her expression serious as she listened to Castor, her eyes wide.

Kaleb cleared his throat, pulling Lander's attention back to him. "Look, Lander. If Vice Chancellor Jenkins is right, you have the potential to be a great asset to my team." His lips flattened into a firm line and his eyes narrowed. "My team is one of the best. I do not need to ask Stone Sovereigns to join; they usually seek me out. But I will ask you. Please join me. Together we could wipe out the Jerr'as and quell the rebellion that threatens our stability. We can bring peace back to the Core."

A light flutter twisted Lander's stomach. "Rebellion?"

Kaleb growled. "Yes."

Lander's gaze flicked to the river, a knot of uncertainty twisting his gut. "Um ... thanks Kaleb. But..."

Kaleb's hands formed into tight fists. "Your choice,

Surface Dweller. Think about my offer. You will not get a better one. And if you choose to not join a team, your Stones will be confiscated to be used by those who do. Think about that too." Kaleb stalked off to join his friends.

Lander kicked at a pile of regular stones. He reached down and grabbed a couple promising ones, stepped closer to the river, and began skimming them. His anxiety subsided in the familiar motions. From the time he was a child, skimming stones had been a release when his emotions threatened to overwhelm him. He bent and grabbed several more of the right size and shape. As he came upright, he startled.

Not five paces away, Becky stood with her hands on her hips. "Are you going to tell me what that was all about?" She waved her hand toward where Kaleb stood, deep in conversation with Jenkins.

Shrugging, Lander turned back to fling another skipper.

Becky stepped up behind him. "I know you, Lander. You think you have to hold everything inside. Well, you don't. I'm here for you. Just remember that. Now, tell me what happened between you and Mr. Team Leader there that caused him to lose his cool."

Lander closed his eyes and let his breath hiss out between his teeth, then turned to face Becky. He struggled with the words that wouldn't come. As if she understood, Becky came forward and took the remaining two stones from his hand. A moment later, one after the other sailed across the water, skipping at least ten times each.

"Wow! I didn't know you could do that, Becky."

She gave him a sly look. "There's a lot about me you don't know yet, Core Boy. Don't underestimate me. I'm stronger than I look. So ... trust me, okay?"

He twisted his lips and nodded, seeking to rein in his stampeding thoughts. "I trust you. I just don't want to see you get hurt. Especially if I'm the reason."

"I know. But I'm okay. Now, tell me what happened."

Becky moved onto a huge, flat-topped rock that hovered over the water. She sat, dangled her legs over the rippling stream, and patted the smooth surface next to her. "Come on, Core Boy. Tell me all about it."

A soft chuckle surfaced, and Lander allowed it to escape in the form of a smile. He loved that, even now, Becky could get him to relax. He sat by her and she scooted over so their shoulders touched.

Telling Becky what Kaleb had said proved easier than Lander had expected; sharing his feelings, however, was much harder.

"So, you feel caught between keeping your promise to your mother by learning more about your gifts and how to help your people, and the promise you made to Michael and me to return us to the Surface."

"Yeah. That about sums it up."

"But it's more than that, isn't it? Otherwise you could just get us home and then return. What's the problem?"

Lander ran his tongue over his lips. "I'm afraid Jenkins isn't going to just let us leave."

Becky chewed her bottom lip and nodded. "You're probably right about that. But if you don't ask, you'll never know."

"True. But, I guess, it's easier to not say anything, than to find out I'm right and you and Michael won't be allowed to leave. At least this way I can ... you know ... keep hope alive."

Becky scrunched her nose at him. "That sounds like false hope to me. Isn't it better to know the truth and deal with it."

Lander chuckled. "Yeah. It is. And thanks for not saying what you feel."

"What?"

"You know ... that I'm a coward."

"A coward would not have run back down that tunnel to face Jerr'as by himself. But you did without even questioning it. Your problem isn't courage, your problem is not having the confidence to make a decision."

It struck Lander like a bolt of lightning. *Becky's right. I'm so afraid of making the wrong decision that I can't make any decision. I need to think on this.*

"Lander?"

"Huh?"

"Why don't we pray about it."

Rahni's call broke through the peace surrounding Lander and Becky. "The food is ready."

Lander helped Becky to her feet. They walked over to the fire, where everyone else had already gathered, hand in hand. The peace that filtered into Lander while he and Becky prayed had strengthened him and he approached Vice Chancellor Jenkins. "Sir. We need to talk."

"I know. Sovereign Kaleb already told me what he said to you. Have you decided?"

"I want to keep my promise to Becky and Michael first. I want to head back to Shavah Deklakh now and take them to the Surface. Desma and Castor too, if they want." He swallowed a growing discomfort at Jenkins's blank expression. "And ... after that, I promise to come back and join Stone Sovereign Kaleb's team and learn how to use my gifts. That's all I've got to say."

Jenkins didn't speak, just stared at Lander for so long, Lander began to fidget. Even if Jenkins would scream at him, it would be better than this silence.

Jenkins's breath pulled in and rushed out through his nose as he clasped his hands behind his back. "I think not. If I'm right ... and I believe I am. Your gifts are too important to ignore. You could be just the asset we need to help turn things around down here. And, as a Core Dweller, this is where you belong.

"It is unfortunate. Your friends do not belong here and

yet cannot return home. They have no choice. As infiltrators, they will be assimilated into the community at Shavah El'Ruhan along with Aurelius Hunt's people. And since Castor has chosen to not use his gift for the community, he and Desma will remain there as well.

"You, however, have a choice. You will either agree to join one of the Stone Sovereign teams and use your gifts for the good of the Core, or you will adapt to life without your Stones of Power in the community at Shavah El'Ruhan along with your friends. You have until we meet with Chancellor Morrison to choose. I suggest you think hard about what you want. Here in the Core, Stone Sovereigns are highly honored and compensated. The Ungifted at Shavah El'Ruhan are … treated … not so well." A sly smirk surfaced. "And that is all *I have* to say."

A lead balloon dropped into Lander's stomach and breathing came hard. His worst nightmare had come to life and now he faced a decision that was no decision at all, no choice. In fact, it was an ultimatum. The thick air pressed in on him and his hands trembled as his eyes sought out Becky's.

He blinked back moisture and turned away. He understood what he needed to do. There was only one choice that would allow him the freedom to escape with his friends when the time came; but still the decision loomed like a dark cloud over everything. *What if?*

He still had time to think things through. Maybe another way would present itself before they met with Chancellor Morrison. *Maybe … just maybe.* In the meantime, Lander looked up and locked gazes with Jenkins. A quick shake of the vice chancellor's head told Lander what he needed to know. *I have no choice.*

Lander squared his shoulders and approached Kaleb. "What must I do to join your team?"

"Lander. No!" Becky's cry almost destroyed his new found resolve. The shocked hurt on her face, the red fury on

Michael's as he stared at Lander from over Becky's shoulder, was more than he could bear.

He choked back the scream that raged behind his locked teeth, seeking escape. He erected an internal wall to block out Becky and Michael ... their need, their security. He knew he couldn't protect them—or Desma and Castor—while trapped here in the Core. Jenkins had just made that clear. But Lander would find a way to get them all—*all*—back home ... soon.

He wasn't certain why his mother had told him to travel to the Core, but he promised he would. Now he had promised to protect his friends and get them back to the Surface. The conflict within him threatened to tear him apart. But neither of those things mattered anymore. He was hemmed in and the only way he could move was forward. Right into Kaleb's team. He would trust God and take that step. Even if it meant accepting his friends' hostility for the time being. He would learn to use his gifts; and, when the time came, he would use them to keep both his promises. No matter what it took.

CHAPTER 11

eolah's and Kaleb's teams took turns guarding the campsite while everyone else slept or tried to sleep. Lander's mind continued to churn in a dizzying spiral. Unable to relax, he propped up onto his elbows and glanced over to where Becky and Michael had bedded down with Castor and Desma. Low-growing trees and thick bushes reduced the muted light further and he couldn't make out anything more than lumpy shadows scattered on the ground between the two to three-foot tall mosses and lichens.

"Here." Lander turned and blinked, then reacted as Kaleb tossed him one of the team's water jugs. "If you cannot sleep, join me on watch. We can talk."

Lander swallowed a gulp of warm water then pushed to his feet and handed the stone vessel back to Kaleb.

"Come," Kaleb said.

Without a word, Lander followed the team captain as he walked back along the path to a grouping of huge rocks scattered in a haphazard manner like they had been dumped by some giant between the path and the vertical wall. Approaching the tallest, Kaleb reached up, pushed his fingers into all but invisible indentations, and began climbing. When he reached a level ledge about fifteen feet off the ground, he turned and reached back to pull Lander up beside him.

"Aren't you supposed to be guarding the prisoners?" Lander asked, stifling a yawn.

"Others are guarding them. We are watching for Jerr'as."

Lander nodded, his focus set on the distant point where the cavern collapsed into the shadowy tunnel they had come through. A shiver ran through him. Facing Jerr'as again was not something he wanted to do. His mind replayed the moment the Jerr'as tried to force its way between the edge of the shield and the wall. If it had breached his shield, would he have been able to kill it? Visions of the mangled bodies from the Jerr'as attack not far from where he now sat flashed across the back of his eyes.

His imagination sent his thoughts reeling in illusions born of nightmares. Becky lying there, her body twisted and torn. He grunted as bile blocked his throat and the need to protect her surged.

"Are you okay?" Kaleb's voice pierced Lander's mental fog.

Lander scrubbed his face with his hands, as if the action could erase the frightening images. "Yeah. I'm fine." He swallowed again; moist droplets of sweat dotted his arms. He needed to change his focus. "How do I join a Stone Sovereign team? Officially?"

Kaleb's silver eyes sparkled in the golden light and his white teeth gleamed in a wide smile. "Tell me something first." Kaleb cracked his knuckles as he turned his head from side to side while scanning the cavern floor beneath them. "What is the Surface like?"

Lander blinked. The question took him by surprise. He

thought about what he should say as the sounds of the rushing river and dripping water echoed off the walls of the vast cavern.

"It's different than here. A lot brighter … and bigger … I mean we have the sun and continents … and whole countries. Sometimes the weather is hot or rainy or cold."

"Sun? Weather? Rain? I do not understand these things."

Lander's thoughts drifted back to his mother's descriptions of Desma's fear of things on the Surface, and stuff he'd learned in World Geography class.

"Well … the Core is the center of a huge—really huge—ball; and the Surface is all the outside of that ball. Here things are … stable … predictable. The light stays the same, day or night."

"Day? Night? Different light?"

"Yeah. Well sort of. You know. Mist Rise is like morning . . . the beginning of day. On the surface the sun—that's an even bigger ball of burning gasses—rises. Well … actually it doesn't rise, the earth rotates, and the sun's light heats the air on the Surface."

The next hour sped by as Lander struggled to answer Kaleb's seemingly endless questions.

When Kaleb finally paused, probably trying to digest all Lander had said, Lander again asked, "So, how do I become part of a team?"

Kaleb huffed. "You are a Stone Sovereign. That is the most important thing. You already spoke about joining my team. But you do not get to decide that. Chancellor Morrison and Vice Chancellor Jenkins assign team members. If you are as strong as Vice Chancellor Jenkins says, you will probably be assigned to First Sovereign Darrius Deklakh's team. They guard the chancellor and the Al'Wisan Cavern. Lesser teams guard the Ungifted who work in the El'Ruhan Cavern."

"Why do they need to be guarded?"

Kaleb pursed his lips and sent his focus out over the river.

"Ah. Good question. The Jerr'as make trouble there. There is always trouble in the El'Ruhan Cavern. And the Ungifted do not always want to work."

Lander let that last statement go. He got the feeling now wasn't the time to press the matter. Shifting gears in his mind, he raised his gaze from where he scanned the path to Kaleb. "You said no one *is allowed* to have four Stones of Power. Will Chancellor Morrison try to take my Stones?"

"What can you do with four Stones that you cannot do with two? Nobody needs four. Besides, no one can handle four Stones of Power at one time—it has never been done. Except for once … maybe. Some say it happened when Cyanne Al'Wisan did it almost two-hundred years ago to drive off the last large band of Jerr'as. But there is no proof it really happened. Many think it was a lie put forth by the Al'Wisan Clan to claim more glory for themselves."

Lander's breath caught at his mother's name. *Mother? Of course. Castor said Mom and Dad were strong . . . and brave. They died protecting others.*

Greater love hath no man than to lay down his life for another.

Anger bubbled up at the voice in his head. Once again, circumstances were spinning out of control and Lander resented being caught in the middle of things he didn't ask for and couldn't understand. Kaleb's words belittling Lander's mother's actions churned within him. Though telling the team captain about the Surface had momentarily eased his anxiety, his feelings of good will were now buried beneath a layer of resentment and fear. *What if they don't allow me to train with—or keep—my parents' Stones? They're my Stones of Power. How can I help Becky and Michael if I lose them?* The need to move sent his foot thumping against the rock. He fisted his hands. "I'm done with this."

Stifling the urge to punch Kaleb, Lander pushed off the

ledge. Air whooshed from his lungs as he landed, his knees bent to take the impact. He allowed his momentum to propel him a few steps forward. He aimed a final glare up at Kaleb then stormed to the bank of the Bec Jekesh where he paced as though he wanted to wear a path in the rocky shoreline while he struggled to make sense of both the voice in his head and an overwhelming need to cry. He ground his teeth and, with the back of his hand, swiped at the tears that leaked out.

His energy finally spent, he stopped pacing and crossed his arms in a hug of self comfort. "I'm going nuts. That's what's happening. The only reason for this voice in my head. I should never have listened to it in the first place. Now look what I've gotten Becky and Michael, and even Castor and Desma.... mixed up in. He shook his head, turned away from the gurgling water, and stumbled back to where he had left his blanket.

He sneezed as he mashed down a clump of moss and lichen and covered it with his blanket. Though his tired, scratchy eyes dropped shut the minute he collapsed onto the blanket, and the warm, moist air soothed his muscles, it took a long time before his breathing evened out and he relaxed enough for sleep to claim him.

It seemed like only minutes had passed when Dena shook him. "Lander. Wake up. We are moving."

While Rahni handed out strips of dried meat that tasted like spicy beef jerky and Arien passed around a water jug, the other Stone Sovereigns packed up the camp. In less than twenty minutes, the company was on the move, strung out along the path heading toward the El'Ruhan Cavern.

Mist Rise enveloped them once again as they approached the far side of the Bec Jekesh cavern. Layers of moisture swirled over the river in thick coils, like heavy fog flowing in a soft breeze, blanketing the water. Vapor dribbled down from the ceiling far above, sparkling like millions of diamonds in the hazy, golden light. Beads of it collected on clothing and packs. The stone path turned slick in places as if coated with a thin sheet of ice though the ambient temperature remained warm. The scent of decay blended with the fragrance of damp moss, filling the saturated air and lodging in noses and throats.

Vice Chancellor Jenkins and Sovereigns Shahan and Deolah took the lead while Deolah's team flanked Hunt, Talen, and their men. Lander trudged along behind Kaleb and his team, trying unsuccessfully to ignore the otherworldly beauty that surrounded him. Thoughts and theories battled an unending loop of questions within him.

Soft, warm fingers circled his hand and he swallowed hard when he looked down into Becky's deep brown eyes.

His mouth hung open, yet no words came. He gulped. "I thought you hated me now."

Her gaze shifted away from him to where the cavern shrunk back into a tunnel in the near distance. "No. I think I understand. Michael, Desma, Castor, and I had a long talk then prayed about it before we went to sleep. I'm angry … and hurt. But I don't hate you. Castor thinks with the way things are now, our only real chance to escape the Core is if you go along with Jenkins and train with the Sovereigns. At least for now. He says things are very different from when he and the others traveled to the Surface and we need to … as he put it—" She formed air quotes. "*Gauge the situation*—before we make a move."

Uncertain what to say, Lander nodded and rubbed the back of his neck. "Yeah … sure. I guess. That makes sense."

Becky glanced over at Lander from the corner of her eye. "What makes sense is for you to pay attention, learn what you can, and then get us out of here. I mean, I've already lost so much time at school. Winter break is almost here. We're probably going to miss Christmas with our families." A soft sniffle floated up to Lander. "Mom and Dad are probably going nuts wondering about me and where I am. And ... I don't want to miss any of my last semester of high school if I can help it."

"Is everything alright here?" Kaleb had slowed his pace to fall in line with Lander and Becky. Without waiting for an answer, he pointed to where Michael, Castor, and Desma lagged behind and said to Becky, "You should join the other Ungifted." Shifting his focus to Lander, he said, "Come. Siprian is giving us pointers on how to handle larger groups of Jerr'as."

Lander blinked as a droplet of water dribbled off his right eyelash and into his eye, stinging it. He wanted to tell Kaleb to go take a flying leap, but in his moment of hesitation, Becky squeezed his hand.

"It's okay, Lander." She scowled at Kaleb. "Just be careful ... and watch your back. Remember who your real *friends* are." She flipped her ponytail, turned on her heel, and strode back to walk next to Michael."

"That was rude," Lander said. "Becky's my friend and I won't let you treat her like that."

Kaleb's eyes went wide. "I am trying to be your friend. You are no longer on the Surface. You are here now, and in the Core, Stone Sovereigns are not friends with Ungifted." He patted Lander on the back. "You will learn; then you will understand what I say. Come. I want to hear Siprian's advice."

CHAPTER 12

Becky glanced over her shoulder and winced. As Lander watched her, Kaleb reached an arm around Lander's shoulders and turned him around. Together, they caught up to the other Stone Sovereigns. A weight settled in her stomach. *Please Lord, let him be okay. I know he wants to learn what they can teach him—keep his promise to his mom—but I have a bad feeling about Jenkins and ... well, this whole idea of one group of people lording it over everyone else... Lander's faith is so fragile. Please help him. And please help us to get home.*

Michael walked up with Desma and Castor following. Desma's frown plowed deep lines on either side of her flattened mouth. "Mark my words, Castor. Once that boy gets a taste of what Jenkins is offering, he'll forget all about his *Ungifted friends.* Just you wait; you'll see."

Castor's gray gaze lifted to where Lander, Kaleb, and Dena walked behind the rest of Kaleb's team. He shook his head. "You don't know that, Desma. I hear what you are saying but give Lander a chance and he might prove you wrong. He is Cyanne and Jerod's boy ... and Ian's grandson."

"We'll just have to wait and see about that, won't we Castor? But things don't always work out the way we want them to. I wished to return here for so long; and now that I'm here, everything is different. All I want to do is go back to our boys, our home. I'll even be more patient with Violet. How I miss her. Her energy and the way she always slammed the door whenever she left the house."

Desma leaned into Castor as they walked. She chewed her lip and her chin trembled. Her words brought thoughts of her own family to Becky's mind and she allowed a couple tears to track down her cheeks. Then Michael was beside her, pulling her left arm through his right and settling it in the bend of his elbow like an old-fashioned gentleman.

"Do not fear, my lady. I will be your knight in shining armor, or some such nonsense, and see you safely home. Even if I must kidnap yon scalawag and compel him to do your bidding."

Becky pulled away and punched Michael in the arm.

"Ow! What did you do that for?" His eyes widened at the soft smile she aimed at him.

"Thanks, Michael. You are my best friend in the whole world . . . and now, at the center of the whole world too."

Michael's back straightened and he lifted his chin. "You got that right, Becks. And don't you forget it."

Becky couldn't suppress the light chuckle that burst out at Michael's upbeat attitude.

Castor dropped a large hand on Michael's shoulder and leaned forward to catch Becky's attention. "It is good to hear you laugh. This trial will not seem as harsh if you can keep your sense of humor."

"Do you think we'll ever get home again, Mr. Elm?" Becky tried to keep the tremor out of her voice but still the question ended with a quaver. The reality of how impossible the situation was, almost robbed her of breath. She needed to be brave, but she wanted to see her parents … her friends … school … and Pastor Stevens. She missed his kind wisdom and advice.

"I believe we will." Castor's deep voice growled. "I don't know what's going to happen in the meantime, but something tells me it will be an adventure; and, in the end, we will get home. Don't lose hope. We'll stick together and when the chance comes, I'd bet money on Lander doing everything in his power to get you safely to the Surface."

"He's probably right," Desma said. "I hate to admit it; but, he's usually right."

Becky's gaze drifted ahead to Lander again. His black T-shirt and jeans standing out among the blues of the Stone Sovereigns' uniforms.

Castor's and Desma's words comforted her and yet, she couldn't dismiss Murphy's Law, that anything that can go wrong will go wrong. So far, this whole *rescue* had been one wrong thing after another. The words repeated over and over in her head like some kind of sick mantra and she tried to block them out as she watched Lander and his new friends. *Wrong. Wrong. Everything will go wrong.*

They approached the end of the vast cavern where the walls closed in around them again. The ceiling dropped and the path descended into a shadow-drenched tunnel. The Bec Jekesh, forced back into a tight channel alongside the narrow path, thundered over a series of small falls, its echoing roar preventing any further conversation.

A chill pimpled Becky's arms and, without thought, she ducked her head though moist warmth pervaded the thick air and the ceiling hovered more than fifty feet above.

They had been hiking for several hours with a short stop for lunch, when the light filtering through the tunnel grew bright enough to see that the surrounding rocks were green with golden veins running through them.

"Look at that." Michael whistled. "Gold. Thars gold in them thar hills, son. Gold, I say."

"You are correct." Castor chuckled. "Wealth here in the Core is measured very differently from on the Surface. Though I am a Stone Worker and can pull precious gems from apparently plain stones, my work was always prompted by a love of beauty, not wealth. It was only when we escaped from Aurelius and needed to survive on the Surface that we began to appreciate the value our gifts represented to Surface Dwellers."

The sound of rushing water increased to a mighty roar that echoed through the remaining tunnel as a third of the river branched off, dropped through another series of waterfalls, then flowed under the ledge where the path ran. The sensation of falling oozed through Becky's stomach as the swirling, thundering water disappeared beneath her feet. The balance of the river continued straight, growing wider as it flowed off into the distance.

Beyond the tunnel opening, the rushing water calmed, its surface spreading and shining in a mix of green and gold like an impressionist painting as it flowed out into a radiant brightness. The narrow confines of the tunnel gave way to a vast expanse flooded with creamy yellow light.

Becky blinked. An intense glow in the distance hurt her eyes. Though it was no brighter than a cloudy day on the Surface, her eyes had grown accustomed to the muted light of Shavah Deklakh and the Bec Jekesh Cavern.

The group spread out as they exited the shaft. Becky's arm shot up to cover her eyes with the back of her hand. Tears leaked, but she blinked them away and, as soon as she was able, she gazed out on a scene that took her breath away. They stood on a rise that overlooked a golden valley surrounded by low hills and small groves of green trees. The portion of the Bec Jekesh that had disappeared underground resurfaced fifty yards beyond the tunnel entrance, took a bend to the right, then flowed off in that direction.

Next to her, Michael gasped. "Holy ... wow! This is ... unbelievable."

Realizing she had been holding her breath, Becky sucked in a gulp of air. The fragrance of fresh mown barley, sweet and unexpected, filled her lungs. She gazed out over a vast expanse of golden farmland and gently rolling, mint-green hills. *How is this even possible?*

As if reading her thoughts, Castor said, "This is where the Bec Jekesh gives birth to the Bec Timur. The Bec Jekesh flows through the El'Ruhan Cavern and into the Al'Wisan Cavern where it passes Shavah Al'Wisan. The branch we just crossed over is the Bec Timur which flows past Shavah El'Ruhan before it spreads and becomes the Timur Bec'stor, a great lake. This is where crops are grown, and livestock are raised. It is the Cavern of Bounty."

He pointed to a collection of stone buildings spread out along the shore in the near distance. "Ahead is Shavah El'Ruhan, the City of Bounty. Here the rock barrier—what we call the Sentinel Band—that protects the Core from the heat of the molten rock of the Flux is thinner, so the light is brighter and the air warmer, the energy stronger."

"The El'Ruhan Cavern." Desma stepped next to Becky. "Beautiful, isn't it? Perfect." Her eyes twinkled with unshed tears. She raised her hands and covered her mouth before dropping them back to her sides. "This is the heart of the Core. Our home. Where we were born, where we lived. This ... this is what I've yearned to see for so long." She released a long sigh. "The Surface may be my home now; but this will always be my first home."

Becky shifted her gaze from Desma to the idyllic panorama before her. She looked up to where the upper limit of the cavern vanished into heights she could only imagine. "This is impossible. How can we be underground and yet feel as if we're on the Surface?"

Jenkins's voice drew her attention as the man walked over, Lander and Kaleb trailing. "It is all in the scale. A cavern this immense will appear to be no cavern at all, but a typical valley on the Surface. Or, in this case, a series of valleys. The only difference is the light. It never gets darker here, but also never any brighter. Though at Mist Fall, the sparkling of the vapor makes the light appear more *luminous*. Or so I've been told." He huffed. "Enough lessons. We need to keep moving. I want to sleep in a bed tonight." He waved his hand in a circle over his head then pointed toward Shavah El'Ruhan, signaling for the company to move out.

When Becky looked up, she met Lander's eyes. He stood staring at her. His mouth opened as if he wanted to say something but then snapped shut. He turned to follow Kaleb.

"What was that about?" Michael asked.

"I don't know." Becky chewed the side of her lower lip for a few seconds. "Maybe he's having second thoughts?"

"Or feeling like a traitor. Come on Becks, let it go. I want to see this Shavah El-whatever place."

"Shavah El'Ruhan." Castor's gravelly voice sounded over loud in Becky's ear as he strode up to walk next to Michael and her. The big man made a show of drawing in a noisy breath. "Ah, yes! Breathe that in. The El'Ruhan Cavern has the lightest and purest air in the Core."

"You're right," Michael said, sucking in a loud gulp of his own. "That feels much better than that yuck in the river cavern."

"Well, I wouldn't exactly call it yuck, Michael," Becky said. "Thick with moisture, sure, but not yucky."

"Call it whatever you want, Becks, it doesn't change the fact that it was hard to breathe in there and now my lungs are thanking me for the change."

Michael turned in a circle, thumped his chest and let loose with a full-on rebel yell. Becky's eyes popped open and she couldn't suppress her laughter. Jenkins, however, turned; a frown drew lines of displeasure on his face as the Stone Sovereigns yanked Stones of Power from their pouches and moved into defensive postures. Even Lander reacted, his father's Stones shimmering a light blue on his palms as he spun around.

"Um, Michael ... you're crazy, you know that. This isn't some game." Becky's eyes flicked from Michael to Jenkins and the Stone Sovereigns now approaching. "I don't think you should have done that."

Michael shrugged and managed to produce a sheepish grin. "Yeah! I sorta get that." He waved in a broad gesture over his head. "Hey guys. Sorry. I just got carried away. You know, breathing in this amazing air."

Jenkins scrubbed his hands over his face. "Do something like that again, and I'll tie you up with Aurelius's people. Do you understand?"

For once Michael didn't have a ready retort and Becky thanked the Lord that he kept his mouth shut and just nodded.

Becky reached over and grabbed Michael's hand. "He won't do anything that stupid again, Sir. I'll make sure."

She trembled when Jenkins's cold gaze swept over her. "See that you do."

Spinning on his heel, he strode off at a rapid pace on the dirt path heading toward Shavah El'Ruhan. The others fell in behind him.

As the trail wound around the borders of several fields, Becky noticed groups of workers. Some were harvesting while others were planting. Small flocks of sheep wandered through other fields. Though it seemed odd, she figured without needing to follow the changing of seasons, Core Dwellers weren't confined to a time to sow and a time to reap like farmers on the Surface. But as each group they passed stopped working, gathered, and stared, tension laced the air. Several Sovereigns pulled Stones of Power from their bags.

Jenkins yelled across the fields, "Back to work people. There is nothing to see here." As the clusters of workers began to drift apart, Jenkins warned in a softer voice, "Deolah. Kaleb. Control your people."

Jitters scurried up Becky's spine and pimpled her arms. *Not good! Definitely not good!*

CHAPTER 13

Shavah El'Ruhan sat along a bend in the river, surrounded by a series of slight, rolling hills. Hundreds of small, round stone houses lined an ordered succession of paths that followed the curve of the river. Beyond the tightly packed, tiny houses a fold of land rose. There, larger dwellings spread out among stands of small trees and bushes.

As the company approached the first of the tiny houses, a contingent of what must have been city leaders hurried out to meet them.

"Greetings, Vice Chancellor Jenkins. Your presence honors us. What can we do for you?" a tall man who reminded Becky of Castor called out as he strode ahead of the band of inhabitants who had come out to greet the travelers. As the man reached out to grasp Jenkins's hand, his gaze drifted over the group and he froze, his eyes locked on something behind Becky. He took a step back and shook his head. "Castor?" He grabbed his chest. "I thought ... we thought you were dead."

Castor slipped past Becky and made his way around Jenkins and the rest of the group, Desma following on his heels. "Enoch, my brother." A huge smile lit Castor's face as he pulled Enoch into a bear hug, tears filling his eyes. "It is good to see you again."

Desma stood at Castor's back and Enoch's wide eyes grew even larger when he caught sight of her. "And Desma. This is a wonder." He released Castor and pulled Desma into a tender hug.

Jenkins shifted into a position at Enoch's shoulder. He cleared his throat. "Now that we've acknowledged who's here, Enoch, we need food and lodgings." He waved toward Hunt's people, his gaze pinning Hunt. "See to these prisoners. They will be assigned to tunnel clearing. I will send other Sovereigns to take control of them once I reach Shavah Al'Wisan. The old one there," he pointed at Hunt, a slight grin raising one side of his thin lips, "will be coming with us when we leave at Mist Rise. Until then, guard him with the others."

"Castor and Desma will stay here in the El'Ruhan Cavern along with those two Surface Dwellers. See that they are given housing and proper clothing. Make sure they understand how things work here. Assess their abilities and see that they are given duties where they can be supervised."

His gaze sliced to Castor. "Don't make me regret allowing you to stay here with family. I would hate to see any of them harmed." Castor bristled, but Jenkins ignored him and shifted attention back to Enoch. "Now, about that food."

Several of the men who had followed Enoch took charge of the prisoners, herding them off on one of the small side paths while Enoch acknowledged Jenkins with a nod and took off at a brisk pace down the main road.

Becky caught Lander's eye when Kaleb and the rest of the team turned to follow Jenkins, the conflict roiling within him palpable in the way he shifted his feet and stared back at her before, finally, turning and hurrying up the path after the others.

Castor and Desma stood, talking in hushed tones, as the

others passed. Enoch nodded to Castor before joining Jenkins and the Stone Sovereigns as they made their way through the lower level of the town.

Michael and Becky stopped alongside Castor and Desma. "What does this mean?" Becky's eyes narrowed to slits and she asked, "What did Jenkins mean when he said that we're staying here and not going on to Al'Wisan? Aren't we going with Lander?"

Castor turned to face Becky and Michael head on. He ran stiff fingers through his unruly beard. "I'm not certain, but from what Jenkins said, it sounds as if we are now part of the Ungifted population while Lander will be received as one of the chosen and given great honor."

Becky licked her lips. "Unless Lander . . ."

"Yes. You are a Christian, right Becky?"

She nodded.

"Then pray that Noah's God touches Lander's heart and strengthens him when the temptations come. Pray that he remembers you and his promise to get you safely home."

Becky watched Lander, her brow crinkled in thought, then followed as Castor took Desma's arm and proceeded up the path.

Old men and women, and young children, dressed in dull, beige shirts and trousers, stared with bland expressions as Becky, Michael, Castor, and Desma, trailed Enoch, Jenkins, and the Stone Sovereigns. The main path climbed the gentle slope toward the large, domed houses.

As they approached one of the largest of the rock dwellings, Desma gasped. "Castor. He's taking us to our own home."

"Stay calm, Desma. Remember, we've been gone for sixteen years. They thought we were never coming back. This is no longer our house. Accept whatever happens with the dignity I know you are capable of showing."

Desma's eyes narrowed. She flicked her focus from Castor

to the rock structure and back again. She pulled in a deep breath through her nose and released it with a huff. "I will try."

He gave her a soft smile and a nod. "I know. You will do fine."

Michael's hiss drew Becky's attention from the couple. Following his line of sight, she wondered what caused his reaction. Then it hit her. The house Lander and the others had entered was gold. Not painted gold or covered in gold, but an unbelievably huge orb of a golden-hued gem with green and tan veins tracing throughout. It had to be at least forty feet tall and even wider. *That's just impossible.* She stopped, her mouth hanging open. At that moment, two ladies came running around the side of the golden dome.

"Desma," the older of the two called. "It is you."

The three ladies came together in a tearful, group hug. After a minute, they broke their hold and the woman who had spoken grabbed Castor's and Desma's hands. "You must not go in there." Her gaze shifted to Castor. "You might be fine, Castor, you are a Stone Worker. But Desma is Ungifted. Vice Chancellor Jenkins and those shiviah-zor excuses for Stone Sovereigns have no use for Ungifted."

"Follow us," the younger woman who looked to be in her early twenties said. "They will not miss you. Come."

Just when Becky thought things couldn't get worse, circumstances had conspired to separate her from Lander and any hope of influencing him. She chewed her lip and swallowed past the burning lump in her throat.

"Are you coming?" Castor waved toward Desma and the ladies, already hurrying back down the pale-yellow, stone path toward the lower town.

Becky looked up at Michael, a fog of disappointment clouding her mind. "What do you think? Maybe Jenkins would let us go with him if we asked? I'd rather stay close to Lander; you know what I mean? Make sure he doesn't forget his promise.

But, maybe, it would be better to just stay here with Castor and Desma?"

Michael's mouth opened and closed a few times like a fish trying to breathe air.

Come on Michael. You've always been strong for me. Don't fail me now.

His eyes hardened and he snarled in an uncharacteristic exhibit of anger. "We follow Castor and Desma. Lander's a fricken jerk. We'll find a way out of here without him."

Ten minutes later, a skittering of apprehension climbed Becky's spine as she followed the others into a small tunnel that ran parallel to the river. They passed several doors on either side before the passage opened onto a series of rooms lit by the same glowing stone sticks she had seen in Shavah Deklakh.

Warmth radiated from light sticks and the many bodies. Becky swiped at sweat dribbling down from her right temple as the heavy heat pressed down on her. She and Michael sat together on a ledge that ran around the perimeter of the room while Castor and Desma spoke at length in Corish with several people. Becky noticed glances thrown in her direction and shifted closer to Michael.

When two little girls and a boy approached her, she smiled. "Hi. Do you speak English?"

"Everyone must speak English," the smaller girl said, her words slow and precise. "I have spoken English since I was little."

Becky stifled a chuckle.

"Are you always that color or are you dirty?" the little boy asked as he ran the back of his hand under his nose.

"I am this color all the time. What do you think?"

"I think you are pretty," the smaller girl said. Then, with a light tinkle of laughter floating on the air behind her, she ran across the cave and disappeared.

"Welllll . . ." The boy drew the word out. "You are different.

But maybe you are pretty too." He took off after the girl and with a shy smile, the other followed them.

Becky picked at a tear in her capris as the minutes ticked into hours. At one point, the younger woman who had led them here brought Becky and Michael mugs of water and pieces of dried fruit.

After downing his water, Michael chowed down on his dried fruit. Becky chuckled as his eyes scanned the crowded room. "Not enough to fill you up, is it?" She held out her remaining pieces of the sweet snack.

"No. It wasn't enough. Not anywhere near." Snatching the fruit from her hand, he stuffed another piece into his mouth. "This is really good."

"Yes. Sort of like apricot; but—I don't know--there's something different about it too."

Michael nodded as he finished the last piece and wiped his hands on his thighs.

Finally, Enoch came. The ongoing conversation turned heated and Desma's voice rose as her hand chopped the air.

"So much for English only," Michael muttered.

"Yeah. I wish I knew what they're going on about."

Michael's soft chuckle bled some of the tension from the back of Becky's neck.

Castor approached. "Enoch had to return to the house. Tomorrow he will assign housing for us. We will also receive food rations and clothing according to the work we are assigned."

"Assigned?" Michael asked, pushing up onto his feet, his muscular shoulders hunched. "What does that mean?"

Castor ran fingers through his scruffy beard and released a sigh. "It means, as Ungifted, we do what we're told and do not create problems for these people." His eyes bored into Michael's.

Michael's brow furrowed. "I thought you were *Gifted*."

"I have chosen to accept the label of Ungifted so I may stay with Desma. At least for now."

The large youth paced for a minute. Catching Castor's eyes, he released a huff, nodded and sat back down. "If you think that's best ... for now." Becky couldn't miss the glint of a challenge in her friend's eyes.

"It could be worse," Castor said. "That tunnel clearing Jenkins mentioned, means clearing rubble from tunnels where Jerr'as have been sighted. It is dangerous work, and hard."

The meeting broke up and Core Dwellers filtered out of the tunnel. Michael left with Castor. A few minutes later, Desma and her friends took Becky to one of the small houses. Though six young, unwed ladies were quartered there, and things were tight, the well-scrubbed floor and walls shone as if polished in the glow of the one, lonely, well-worn light stick. Everything was clean, neat, and orderly.

Desma's young friend introduced herself with a shy smile. "I am Acasia. I am happy you will be part of my team, Bec'kash."

"Becky . . . my name is Becky."

A soft pink suffused the Core Dweller's cheeks and Becky felt bad for saying anything.

"I am sorry. I will try ... Becky."

"Yes. Thank you, Acasia."

Though exhaustion stole her ability to focus, Becky's heart warmed at the gentle ways of the other young women as they shared their meager meal with her. After cleaning the dishes and the kitchen, Acasia showed Becky to a room crowded with stone beds like the one she slept on the night she had arrived.

Acasia pulled back a cream-colored blanket to show Becky the layer of long-leaved moss beneath. "This is good. You will like?"

"Yes, thank you." Becky fought a wave of impatience as Acasia lingered in the doorway. The young Core Dweller had been kind and Becky prayed for patience, but at this point, all she wanted was to lie down, close her eyes, and drift off into the oblivion of sleep. "Thank you Acasia." *Please get the message.*

"Sleep well, Becky. May Mist Rise find you rested and well."

Becky vowed she would be kinder to Acasia in the future. Every muscle ached as she collapsed onto the soft moss. *Please, Lord ... keep us safe. Help us to go home ... soon...*

CHAPTER 14

uilt settled like a rock in Lander's stomach as he followed Kaleb into the golden dome house in Shavah El'Ruhan. He struggled against the need to turn around and run to Becky. Back to where he had left her behind with Michael and the Elms in a run-down section of town. Not far from where Hunt's men were turned over to another team of Stone Sovereigns. He feared if he even glanced back, his feelings would reduce his logical decision to nothing more than empty words. *What was I thinking? What if I never see Becky again? Am I wrong?* Pain seared his chest as the reality of his decision threatened to rip his heart in two.

Struggling to keep his doubts at bay, he put one foot in front of the other and kept his eyes focused on Siprian's back as he trailed the scarred Sovereign down a hall and into a large dining room. More than a dozen yellow and green light sticks rose out of green stoneware pots set at regular intervals around the perimeter of the room. Their light reflected off the walls, ceiling, and floor. Lander blinked at the unexpected brightness.

Like in Jenkins's house, the walls and ceiling looked as if

they had been carved out with an immense scoop then buffed to a high gloss. It reminded him of gold. He approached one of the concave walls and examined it, running his hands over the smooth, polished finish alongside a wall hanging depicting a flock of wooly gray sheep. He sucked in a breath. *Gold? No.* It wasn't gold. It shone with the depth of a precious gemstone. And warm to the touch, like the other dwellings he had been in. Thinking back to when he visited the museum with Becky, a name came to mind: Golden Beryl. *That's it. It's supposed to be really hard too.*

A solid, rectangular block of green stone with amber striations, set on four legs of the same stone, filled the role of table. Placed in the center of the room, it had seating for more than twenty. Jenkins settled in one of the matching chairs while the Stone Sovereigns stood in small groups, talking.

After overseeing the placing of a buffet of warm and cold dishes on the table, Enoch excused himself. "My staff is available, Vice Chancellor Jenkins. Please make them aware if you have any needs. I will return shortly." The man bowed at the waist and backed out.

When Kaleb and his team joined Deolah and hers at the table, Lander took a seat as well. Though his natural inclination was to sit alone, he pushed it down and lowered into the chair next to Shahan, who, himself sat at the far end of the long table. The old scout had recovered from his injuries and Lander hoped to gain some honest information about the Core and what was involved in being a Stone Sovereign. Kaleb and his teammates were eager to answer Lander's questions, but he couldn't sluff off the feeling that they weren't being completely honest. And he didn't need the unavoidable pressure to join their team.

Uncertain how to open a conversation, Lander ran a hand over the prickly stubbles growing back on his head, after Hunt's people had shaved it, and contemplated the man with a sideways gaze. Shahan, his maroon uniform hanging in the back where the Jerr'as had slashed him, wore his gray-streaked black hair in the cropped military style favored by the Sovereigns Lander had met.

Shahan turned and his icy, silver eyes speared Lander's. Startled at being caught staring, Lander swallowed.

"Well." Shahan's deep voice rumbled in his chest. "Did you want to ask me something, or do you normally stare at people you have just met?"

A shiver traced its way up Lander's spine at the Sovereign's intimidating manner. Lander opened his mouth and forced out words. "I . . . I . . . just wanted to . . ."

"They say you are Cyanne's and Jerod's son. Is this true?"

Lander nodded.

Shahan pursed his lips. "They are good friends. Why did they not return with you?"

Lander's gaze dropped to his hands as the aroma of roast lamb drifted up from one of the platters. Fingers twined in and out as he wondered how much Shahan really knew. But, when he looked back up, he couldn't miss the concern etched in the lines on Shahan's face.

"They died when I was a baby."

"I am sorrow to hear that."

"Sorry." Lander cringed at correcting the intimidating Stone Sovereign's choice of words. It seemed Shahan, like Dena, confused English terms.

Shahan's eyes crinkled in question.

"I am sorry ... not sorrow."

"Yes. I am sorry."

Lander nodded again. He chewed his bottom lip for a moment, then asked, "Did you know them well?"

"Jerod was a Deklakh like me. I traveled up the Avortex with him and Ian a couple times. Is Ian also dead?"

"Yeah."

"How they died?"

Lander jumped when Jenkins dropped a hand on Shahan's broad shoulder. "It is better if these things are discussed when we meet with Chancellor Morrison."

Shahan stiffened and pulled his mouth into a severe line. "Yes, sir. I understand. If you will excuse me." He pushed up from his chair, turned to face Jenkins, dipped his head, then left without another word.

"That one can be troublesome. Captain Darrius should keep a tighter rein on him." Jenkins's mumbled words drifted to Lander. He suspected the man underestimated his hearing. *Friction? Wonder what that's about.*

Jenkins dropped into the chair Shahan had vacated. He drew in a stiff breath and released it through his nose as he studied Lander. "You may have potential Lander, but you have much to learn. When Chancellor Morrison asks you, remember you committed to join Captain Kaleb and his team. If you were to choose to renege on that commitment, you will gain enemies. A Stone Sovereign who makes enemies, even an unusually gifted one, can find himself in … unpleasant circumstances."

A wide smile spread across Jenkins's face, but his eyes held a frigid cast. "Just a friendly piece of information, my boy. Though Captain Darrius serves directly under Chancellor Morrison, Captain Kaleb's team would be a better fit for you.

"Eat up, my boy. We leave before Mist Rise tomorrow, so you need to eat then get some sleep."

After Jenkins left Lander's side, Lander released the breath he had been holding and closed his eyes. Another breath out, in. A third. He blinked his eyes open. The aroma of roast lamb drifted to him again, his stomach rumbled, and his mouth watered. But Lander feared if he ate anything, it would just find its way back up. *And I thought Dena's pressure was bad. I guess I'm going to be part of Kaleb's team whether I want to be or not.*

Praying his stomach would settle, Lander filled a plate. After a few sips of Akh'umm, the Corish equivalent of sweet tea Dena recommended he try, Lander's attention turned to the food. His fears dissolved when the first mouthful set his saliva to flowing as he chewed the seasoned, succulent lamb. The limp, overdone greens weren't a favorite, but years of Pop-pop drilling him to eat his vegetables pushed him to swallow the unappetizing mass. He had just finished sopping the meat juices off his plate with a heel of brown, whole grain bread when Dena and Arien dropped into the empty chairs to either side of him.

Lander cast his gaze back and forth between the two as he gulped down a mouthful of Akh'umm. "Do you want something?"

"We do not," Arien said, his tone formal.

"Vice Chancellor Jenkins tell us to show you where you are to sleep." Dena's soft smile warmed Lander. Though she had been pushy about the team; she had also been kind. And, truth be told, she was pretty to look at. Lander didn't try to stifle the grin that worked its way out onto his lips. Especially when Dena's smile broadened, and her eyes sparkled.

"Are you done?" Arien said, pushing back up onto his feet. "We are all done."

Lander dropped his focus to his well-scoured plate. Looking back up at Dena, he nodded.

"Good." Dena rose with grace and, taking Lander's hand pulled him to his feet. "Come. Before we rest, we drink."

"Whoa!" Lander cocked his head. "Did you say ... drink? As in *drink*?"

Lander followed Dena's tinkling laughter up to a second story where she and Arien led him into a room where Kaleb and the rest of his team sat. Deolah, the only member of her team present, sat next to Kaleb. Lander scanned the room. Shahan was also noticeably absent.

"Vice Chancellor Jenkins and I welcome your decision to join my team," Kaleb said, sloshing a bit of clear liquid from the mug he waved at Lander. "Though your status will be that of a cadet until you prove yourself, we welcome you. Tonight, we toast."

"Thank you for inviting me," Lander stammered. "But Vice Chancellor Jenkins said I needed to get right to bed after eating. You know … something about leaving before Mist Rise."

His protests went unheeded as Dena pressed a mug into his hand, guided his hand to his mouth, and upended the contents. Though it looked like water, the liquid burned its way down Lander's throat while the others looked on laughing.

Someone began chanting, "Initiation. Initiation."

Others joined in and the contents of a second mug slid down Lander's throat.

The rest of the evening blurred into a hazy fog as Lander downed at least a couple more mugs of the potent brew. Laughter filled the air. Talking.

The next thing Lander knew, Kaleb was standing over him. "Surface Dweller. It is time to leave."

Sitting up, Lander leaned forward and propped his bowling ball of a head on the palms of his hands. It occurred to him that it must have been used to knock down pins for most of the night the way it felt now. A soft groan leaked through his clenched teeth.

Kaleb threw a pile of clothing on the bed next to Lander and dropped a pair of boots at his feet. "I think these should fit you. They are Sovereign Arien's and he is your size. Get dressed. We must leave within a short time."

Trying to keep the contents of his head from shifting, Lander changed into the uniform. It fit better than he expected. When he pulled on the boots, however, his feet sloshed around in them. He scanned the room and caught sight of a cloth similar to the towel he'd used back at Jenkins's. Tearing it in two, he wrapped his feet and slid them back into the boots. *Perfect.*

He took a few steps. Running his hands down the front of the cobalt-blue tunic, he wished for a mirror. He'd never worn anything so fine in his life. He smiled, imagining Becky's expression when she saw him wearing this. The smile faded and the drumming in his head intensified.

"Come," Kaleb called as he strode past the room and sprinted down the stairs.

Not wanting to leave his own clothes behind, Lander pulled the blanket from the bed. He set his things in the middle, twirled both ends as tight as he could, then tied them off. If he'd had a knife, he would have cut off the extra fabric but, with a shrug, he pulled one thick end over his shoulder and tied it to the other at his waist. *Not great, but it'll do.*

Walking with a stiff gate to avoid jarring his brain, he followed Kaleb down the stairs. The sound of voices drew him out the front door.

CHAPTER 15

onfusion filtered through Lander when the company
headed back the way they had come, backtracking through
town, then up along the Bec Timor.

Coming up from the rear, Lander caught sight of Jenkins
and Kaleb in the lead, followed by Kaleb's team. Behind them,
three to a side, Deolah's Sovereigns marched beside Aurelius
Hunt. No longer bound, the man walked with his head held
high. Scruffy, his linen suit now dirty and torn, his hair ragged,
and his once fine beard overgrown, the billionaire carried
himself like he was in charge and the Sovereigns were his
honor guard.

Glancing in Lander's direction, Hunt snagged his focus.
The man's charisma was still a powerful draw; Lander stared
for a moment before dragging his gaze away and settling it on
Kaleb's back. Brushing off the effects of Hunt's attention,
Lander speed-walked past Hunt and Deolah's Sovereigns.

Breaking into a sprint, he passed Kaleb's team and caught
up with Captain Kaleb and Vice Chancellor Jenkins. "Why are

we going backward?" He huffed, falling into step with the two.

"We need to go back to the split and follow the Bec Jekesh to Dock Village to get boats," Kaleb said, his gaze fixed forward.

"Boats? We're going by boat?"

Kaleb turned his head and shot a mocking smirk in Lander's direction. "Boats? Yes, boats. How else could we take the river."

"Yeah, sure." Lander scrubbed the back of his neck. *Yeah. Stupid question. Way to impress the guy you hope will train you to get better control of your gifts.* "Of course. I just didn't think there would be boats here in the Core. I didn't even know you had rivers until a few days ago."

"True." Kaleb's eyes shifted forward again. "Vice Chancellor Jenkins and I were discussing just that fact before you joined us. He thinks you and I should work together as partners within the team. What do you think?"

"Okay." Lander drew out the word as the idea settled on him.

"This way I will train you personally. If you are not as gifted as the vice chancellor believes you are, I will discontinue your instruction. Of course, Chancellor Morrison will need to give his permission first."

A deep, aborted laugh rumbled through Jenkins. "Oh, he'll agree. I'll see to that." He glanced at Lander, then returned his attention to the wide, dirt path that meandered along the river to the left and fields growing a variety of produce on the right. "I look forward to seeing what the two of you can accomplish together. I have high hopes. In fact, there is a nice, level meadow just outside Dock Village. We will take a break there. I want to see what you can do on your own, Lander, before you start training."

Three hours later, Lander stood alone in the middle of an

empty field. Several goats watched him with apparent interest from a second pasture beyond. Jenkins and the others waited at a dry rock wall that lined the road.

Jenkins leaned forward, his hands braced on the waist-high wall, his eyes bright with anticipation. Kaleb and his Stone Sovereigns sat on the wall to Jenkins's left. Deolah, her team, and Hunt, stood watching from Jenkins's right. As usual, Shahan stood alone, observing from a short distance farther up the road.

"Okay, Lander, show us what you've got," Jenkins shouted.

Lander closed his eyes and pulled a breath deep into his lungs. He released it and dragged in a second. Remembering Pop-pop Ian's instructions, he focused on becoming invisible and debated how much he should show Jenkins.

Exclamations of surprise drifted to Lander from the road.

Keep it simple. Don't give away too much. With a thought, he flicked fire on his fingertips then grew the sparks into balls on the palms of his hands. Blinking his eyes open, he flung the balls, exploding them on two separate boulders, sparks skidding across the field.

Pride of accomplishment swelled in him as he heard more shouts of support from the onlookers. He chewed his lower lip. *You liked that, huh? Well watch this.* He pulled out his father's Stones of Power. Maintaining invisibility, he set a barrier between himself and the road.

He thought for a moment, then, cupping his father's Stones in one hand, he pulled the stronger of his mother's two from the pouch on his belt, leaving the weaker Stone in the bag.

Heat flared from the powerful Stone and Lander used it to flick fire again. Gritting his teeth, he sent glowing embers into the barrier and created a wall of oily, red flames. He pulled in another deep breath and prepared to propel the blazing inferno toward Jenkins.

No. Two must work together. Stop.

Lander's blood ran cold at the words. He lost invisibility and everything collapsed; the fire sputtered out, leaving no trace except blackened grass.

Voices grew in Lander's awareness as Kaleb and his team bounded across the field.

"Invisibility!"

"That was incredible."

"You are truly gifted."

"Can you teach me that?"

Lander looked up to find Kaleb, Dena, and Arien standing in front of him. The captain reached out and mock-punched Lander's shoulder. "Why did you lie about being trained? Invisibility? No one has done that since ... well, it has been a long time."

"It would have been impressive if that wall of flames hadn't fizzled." Jenkins's scowl pierced Lander as the man strode up behind Kaleb's team. "What happened? You lost it at the end, didn't you?"

Lander's gaze shifted to the vice chancellor. How could he explain that he heard his mother's voice in his head? Memories of Hunt's testing room and how Hunt didn't listen when he tried to defend himself played like an old black and white movie in Lander's mind. He swallowed down his resurging fears, locked them behind a wall of bravado, and shrugged. "It was nothing ... I ... stopped because ... well. You saw what you needed to see. I didn't need to keep going."

Jenkins studied Lander with narrowed eyes for a full minute. "No. There's something more. You stopped for another reason. You may not want to tell me now, but in time." He turned his back on Lander. "Let's go."

Leaving the meadow of testing behind, the group followed the trail down a shallow slope into town.

Villagers scurried in various directions at their approach,

many disappearing into huts, others moving off to stand at a distance, anger and fear infusing the air around them. Women grabbed children, whisking them out of the path of Jenkins and the Sovereigns.

"Why are they running?" Lander asked as he watched a man with a pronounced limp struggle to avoid the company. "You're Stone Sovereigns. Don't you heal and protect them?"

"We do," Deolah said as she marched forward, her face a mask of disdain. "Many of the Ungifted are superstitious and suspicious of what they do not understand though. You will see."

Siprian released a huff of breath. "In time you will learn to ignore the Ungifted. Unless we are called on to—as you say, heal and protect—they treat us as outsiders. That is fine by us. In truth, they are—"

"Enough." Jenkins's words, though not shouted, carried the weight of a command. "This conversation ends now."

For now. It ends for now.

The street emptied and Lander shifted his focus to the river. Wider than where it exited the tunnel, it flowed in a lethargic manner. Several small fishing boats bobbed in the distance. On the opposite shore, a strip of small trees grew. Beyond them, vines like those in the Bec Jekesh Cavern climbed upward until they vanished from sight. *The end of the Shavah El'Ruhan Cavern.*

Lander joined his team watching the yellow-green water roll by while Jenkins spoke with a man who had exited a small hut built on one of the docks.

Downstream, a series of small, round huts sat. Stone pillars anchored to bases hidden beneath the water supported enclosed porches that extended out over the chuckling stream. The vines Lander had taken note of across the river grew over porch roofs, covering them with lime green leaves and yellow flowers. Peaceful and beautiful, the tiny village spoke to

Lander. Visions of spending time here with Becky filled his wandering mind with daydreams and he smiled. *Becky would like the vines. Their fragrance reminds me of Lilies of the Valley.*

Stupid. Stupid. Put Becky out of your mind or you'll never be able to help her. Focus on what you need to do Lander. But before he knew it, Becky once again filled his mind; her laughter, the tinkling of the bells in the tiny braids she liked to wear, the scent of her favorite perfume.

He ground his teeth and scanned the river. Tiny flashes above the water caught his eye and he squinted, trying to make out what he saw.

Rahni moved in next to him. The older woman closed her eyes and let out a sigh. "I love the vines here. The flower smell."

Lander glanced at her. "Do you mean the flowers smell nice?"

A soft growl from her throat surprised Lander. "Yes. Yes. My English is bad. It is because I am older. Shahan and I still struggle at times. I am sorry."

Lander's gaze returned to the air above the gurgling flow. "Nothing to be sorry about. How long have you spoken English?"

"Let me think. It will be fourteen cycles. No. That is wrong. It will be fourteen *years* next fluxon." She shook her head, then glanced back over her shoulder. "Next season. Please do not tell Vice Chancellor Jenkins about my mix up of words. Only English is allow … allowed."

"I won't."

Lander caught sight of the sparks again. "What are those?"

Rahni's eyes tracked where Lander was pointing. She chuckled. "Do you not have insects on the Surface?"

Lander's mouth hung open a few seconds. "Uh, yeah. Yeah. We do. We have bugs … lots of bugs … insects. I just didn't expect any down here.

"It's all so different from what I imagined. Even after reading my mom's journal, I still thought it would all be dark and … I don't know … different." He shrugged. "I never expected so much beauty and variety. Bugs … rivers … farms." He chuckled. "Goats."

"Someday you must share what you read in Cyanne's journal. Many of us older, surviving Stone Sovereigns knew her and Jerod. We would hear more of the story."

An unexpected lump formed at the back of Lander's throat. He struggled to swallow past it but almost choked when one of the sparkling creatures flying over the water zipped up to him, stopping inches from his nose.

Smaller than a damselfly, the insect hovered as if staring at Lander. Its wings glittered a variety of colors ranging from deepest blue to pale yellow as they whirred, holding aloft a green body with a yellow stripe down the center.

Lander watched in wonder as it continued to linger before him. A moment later, it rocketed away in a sharp arc.

"Rahni. Lander. We are ready." Siprian waved toward the second dock where Deolah, her team, and Hunt juggled for positions on five benches in the largest of the gray boats tied there. "Vice Chancellor Jenkins has secured four boats."

Lander followed Siprian and Rahni. Stepping onto the dock, he pulled in a sharp breath at the realization it was a solid block. He stopped, knelt, and ran his hands over the green stone. *Whoa! The water never freezes so it won't crack! Cool!*

"Lander. Come." Kaleb motioned to Lander from one of the vessels still tied at the dock. Smaller than the boat taken by Deolah, it bobbed on gentle waves as they slapped against the stone dock. It reminded Lander of a canoe, but wider, stockier.

Noting only Kaleb and Shahan in the craft, Lander wasted no time jumping in and plopping down next to Kaleb. A sigh of relief slipped through his lips as Jenkins joined Dena, Tuvyam, and Siprian, leaving the last and smallest craft to Arien and Rahni.

With just the three of them alone in the small boat, Lander hoped he might be able to get Kaleb and Shahan to talk more openly.

Already caught in the swift current, Deolah's boat sped past the edge of the village as the boatman threw the end of the rope into the bow of Lander's boat, releasing them. Kaleb and Shahan grabbed paddles, pushed away from the dock, and propelled their stone craft toward the center of the river with strong, even strokes. Lander looked for another paddle, but there were only two. He felt the shift once they entered the main current and the little boat picked up speed.

Kaleb and Shahan paddled without a break, hour after hour, as the river flowed past a verdant landscape of fields and small orchards on the right and a thin band of vine-covered, stunted trees to their left. Lander huffed his frustration as he watched the dragonfly things zipping around him.

So much for my plan to get information out of these two. I need to do something.

"Can we talk?"

Kaleb and Shahan stopped paddling. Shahan shook his head, then turned on his bench to face Lander and Kaleb. "What is it you want to know?"

Kaleb maneuvered his paddle across his knees and scanned the uninhabited left shoreline as they floated with the current. "I will keep watch.

CHAPTER 16

Shahan's gaze flicked to Lander before shifting to Kaleb. "Our new friend noticed our lack of welcome in Jekesh Village, Kaleb. We—no, you—need to explain to him how things work here."

The big Stone Sovereign's eyes caught and held Lander's, and though he didn't say anything more, Lander got the impression he had more to say—much more—just not now and not in front of Kaleb. Shahan gave a quick nod, then closed his eyes. "I am nap."

"What do you want to know?" Kaleb asked as he continued scanning the banks of the Jec Bekesh.

Lander's mind scrambled to frame his question, but what passed his lips was the thing he couldn't let go. "Why were those people so angry ... and fearful?"

Kaleb snorted an aborted chuckle, his silver eyes still roaming, though Lander thought they narrowed in irritation. "You heard Deolah, The Ungifted fear us because they are not like us. And those who run from us today will be the first to call us for help when the Jerr'as are killing their livestock or raiding their farms … or someone has gotten sick or injured. And then, if we cannot help, they blame us and grow angry. Perhaps Jerr'as attacked and no Stone Sovereigns were near to help so Ungifted died. You will see. I give you one full cycle. By then, you will have learned to ignore the Ungifted."

As Kaleb's words sunk in, Lander caught movement along the left bank of the river. He blinked, uncertain if he was imagining things. A deeper shadow ducked from tree to tree, following the boats.

"You have good sight." Shahan's soft voice pulled Lander's focus.

"I thought you were sleeping."

"I was. But I set a thin barrier to sense movement between us and the cavern end. It triggered."

His breath catching, Lander shifted his attention from the moving shadow to Shahan. "A barrier? Like the one I used? How can you make it … sense things? I need to learn that. Everything I do is wild, like I can't control it. Can you help me?"

One of Shahan's eyes opened, and he yawned. "Ask Kaleb. If you are to be his, he must teach you."

Lander shifted on the bench to face Kaleb. "You can do that too?"

"Of course. It is one of the first things we learn as cadets. How is it you can control four Stones of Power, travel the Vortex, and yet not know how to set a sensor sweep?"

The urge to mouth off at Kaleb burned through Lander, but he got the feeling if he wanted to learn from Kaleb, he'd need to control his anger. Instead, he took a deep breath before answering. "Pop-pop Ian didn't explain a lot and then he died. There was no one else to teach me."

"You are friendly with that Stone Worker, Castor, why did he not teach you? Oh … that is right. He is not a Stone Sovereign.

And now he has chosen to remain with his Ungifted wife. Foolish. It is best you learned nothing from him. You have a strong gift. But with the inadequate training you have had so far, I am not certain your bad habits can be corrected. And I begin to think I am not the one to help you."

Lander's leg bounced and he bit back the words he wanted to throw at the conceited Sovereign. Instead, he set his gaze back on the shifting shadow that still tailed them.

"Hey, Surface Dweller. Now is your chance. Take down that Jerr'as following us. If you have the guts to do that, I will reconsider."

Pulling his mother's Stones from the pouch on his belt, Lander considered how to kill the Jerr'as from this distance. But as he formulated a plan, visions of the guard he had killed back on Aurelius Hunt's island invaded his mind. The urge to vomit climbed his throat. He shoved it down. There was no way he would let Kaleb think he was weak. Besides, this was just a Jerr'as, not a human. Just an animal like the ones he and Pop-pop killed for food.

He glanced at Shahan, hoping the man would give him a hint at what to do, but Shahan's focus remained glued on the Jerr'as.

Lander licked his lips and followed Shahan's line of sight to the creature. The Stones of Power glowed red on his palms. Stuffing down the memory of the dead guard, Lander pulled up thoughts of hunting with Pop-pop. He could do this. Prove to Kaleb he was worth training.

He'd never flung a fire ball so far but thinking about how Kaleb had destroyed the Wasps with just a controlled jolt of energy, Lander concentrated on forming a small but powerful ball rather than a barely controlled sphere. When his ball felt right, he set his focus back on the Jerr'as and plotted a trajectory then let the flickering orb fly.

Jumping from the bush where it hid, the Jerr'as screamed,

beating at the flames that encased it. It sprinted to the river where it plunged below the surface. Lander watched the spot where it disappeared until the concentric circles flattened and vanished in the current.

"Woo hoo!" Kaleb pounded Lander on the back. "You killed your first Jerr'as. There is hope for you yet."

Lander caught Shahan staring. "Well done, Lander. You learn by watching Kaleb, no? Not so powerful but effective, controlled."

Unexpected warmth filled Lander at the praise. Perhaps training with the Stone Sovereigns might not be so bad after all. Becky's face rose in his mind, churning the feelings he kept submerged. He set the image aside, reminding himself the best way to help her was to do exactly what he was doing. "Thanks. I see what you mean, Shahan. That's what I need to learn, control."

Kaleb nodded, his eyes bright. "And when you learn to be consistent with that, we will go Jerr'as hunting with Siprian. He loves a good hunt. It will be fun."

Deolah's voice drifted back to them from far ahead. "What are you doing? Get moving."

Kaleb chuckled, picked up his oar, and held it out to Lander. "Feel like helping?"

A sense of belonging filled Lander. He took the oar and smiled back. *Kaleb's right. It's like Deolah said. The Ungifted just don't understand.*

Hours later, the river roared into a channel that ran down the side of another tunnel. The light weakened and turned a pale red as the rock walls merged into shades of maroon and pink. Kaleb whooped his delight as he moved to the rear seat and they maneuvered around rocks, the rushing, frothing water spraying into the boat as it dipped and rocked. Once again Lander was shocked by the unexpected warmth of the river as streams of water dribbled down his face and arms.

"Pay attention," Shahan growled as they bounced sideways into a rock before slipping past.

"I am," Kaleb shouted, his face lit with excitement. "Stop being a sour ball."

A thrill raced through Lander. He had always wanted to try white water rafting and it was the last thing he expected to do in the Core. Grateful Kaleb had been paddling rather than him when they entered the tunnel, he sat back and enjoyed the ride which ended a few minutes later as the river poured out into the cavern, spreading and slowing.

Not long after, Lander caught his first sight of Shavah Al'Wisan. As far as he could see, a multitude of round buildings of every size and description spread out along the riverbanks. The trees and vines on the left bank had been replaced by strange, red-tinged vegetation that struggled to live on bare rocks ranging in color from pale pink to deepest maroon.

The round boulder dwellings resembled those he had seen in Shavah Deklakh and Shavah El'Ruhan. Tiny huts crowded together along the river's edge. To his right, large mansions that looked as if they had been constructed of multiple boulders climbed a hillside that rose behind the smaller dwellings and overlooked the Bec Jekesh from manicured landscapes.

Kaleb and Shahan angled the boat toward a series of docks. Once they touched one of the blocks of stone, Shahan tossed the man who waited there the rope. He secured it to a post then reached out to pull the boat parallel to the dock before helping Shahan, Kaleb and Lander disembark.

Rubbing his arms against a sudden chill, Lander looked back down at the tiny craft. Leaving the Bec Jekesh felt like losing all connections to Becky and a surge of guilt tried to tear away at his new-found sense of fitting in, but he refused to allow the negative self-talk to plunge him into a well of doubts. He'd made his decision and he would see it through.

Stepping off the stone slab dock onto the street that fronted the river, Lander's muscles ached and all he wanted was to collapse. He hoped Vice Chancellor Jenkins didn't plan to meet Chancellor Morrison until after Mist Rise. But as Jenkins gathered everyone to him, Lander's wish evaporated.

"Though it has been a long day, I sent a messenger ahead to Chancellor Morrison informing him we will arrive before *Misfadura*." He pursed his lips. "What you would call nightfall, Lander. Of course, here there is no nightfall just Mist Fade Dura."

They traveled up the road that bordered the river and were turning onto one of the many bridges that tied the two banks together when a slight, young man pulled to a stop in front of them, panting. "Chancellor Morrison ... sends his ... regrets." The messenger leaned forward, his hands on his knees and drew in a couple deep breaths. "He asks that you come after Mist Rise as he cannot meet with you now."

"Shiviah-zor." Jenkins hissed the Corish oath through clenched teeth. "Change in plans. Deolah, you and your team take the prisoner to the Cadet Quarters. They should be able to accommodate you there." His eyes fixed on Captain Deolah. "Watch him. We will meet up at Mist Rise.

"Kaleb. Come."

Relief flooded Lander when Jenkins finally stopped on a raised platform in front of a collection of stone dwellings.

"What kind of place is this?" he whispered to Kaleb.

"A place for travelers to rest."

"Oh, the Core equivalent of a hotel?"

Kaleb turned to face Lander; his brow wrinkled. "What is a *ho-tell?*"

Lander waved at the grouping of domes. "That is."

"I see. We will rest at this ho-tell until Mist Rise."

"Good," Lander said. "I'm ready for some sleep."

Laughter erupted from several of the Stone Sovereigns and Dena whispered, "Who said anything about *sleeping?*"

After speaking quietly with the woman in charge, Jenkins

said, "Your rooms have been arranged. I will meet you back here at Mist Rise and we will go directly to meet with Chancellor Morrison." With a brief nod to Kaleb, he strode off in the direction they had come.

Kaleb moved to open the door of the building he, Lander, and Shahan had been assigned, but Shahan reached out and stopped him. "I too must leave. I have other commitment. Tell Vice Chancellor Jenkins I will see him a time other."

A scowl flashed across Kaleb's face. "He is not going to like you leaving before we meet with Chancellor Morrison."

"I must report to Captain Darrius. He will excuse me to Chancellor Morrison." He turned to face Lander. "It has pleasured me to meet you, Sovereign Lander. I hope to speak with you again."

Lander reached out to shake his hand, but Shahan's eyes widened at the gesture.

"Like this," Lander said. He grabbed Shahan's wrist. At first the older Sovereign tried to pull away. "It's okay. This is just a greeting and a way to say goodbye." Lander stuck his hand into Shahan's and pumped a couple times before releasing his grip. "I, too, hope we can talk again."

Shahan bowed, turned, and walked away. A surprising emptiness at his absence filtered through Lander as the man rounded a corner and disappeared.

"He does not party well anyway," Kaleb said as he led Lander into the spartan quarters. The small structure consisted of two rooms. The first, larger and rounded out like every other room Lander had been in since coming to the Core, contained four narrow beds and dusty-pink rock tables. The second, a bathroom, was a tiny mirror image. Both were the color of apple cider with gold veining.

"Come. Get cleaned up quickly. The others will be waiting."

Warm water and gritty soap already awaited them in the

small bathroom. It didn't take more than a few minutes for both young men to clean up. Lander followed Kaleb back out onto the cobblestone street.

While they waited for the others, Lander scanned his surroundings. Though Shavah Al'Wisan was not as dark as Shavah Deklakh, and the atmosphere here sparkled with myriad shades of red; the light here couldn't compare with the brighter, clearer light of Shavah El'Ruhan. And there were so many people. Several Stone Sovereigns passed waving to Kaleb or calling out greetings. Crowds of people walked along the street, the activity increasing as time went on. *Interesting. They don't seem angry. They don't even seem to notice us.*

Dena's distinctive laugh preceded the rest of the team as they arrived together. "Come," she said. "I know just the place." Her silver eyes shifted focus to Lander. "A perfect place to initiate Lander."

She led the team across one of the bridges and down the road paralleling the river. A short while later, Dena stopped in front of a dome with a large, outside eating area built onto its side. Light from myriad light sticks, loud voices, and laughter rose on the warm air.

Dena slid her arm through Lander's and smiled up at him. "After Mist Rise, you will meet Chancellor Morrison and official join our team. For now, we party!"

Lander shifted, uncomfortable at Dena's nearness. He wished he could flee back to Shavah El'Ruhan and Becky. But Dena pulled him along as the others surrounded them, clapping him on the back. Exclamations of welcome settled like the moisture of Mist Rise, coating Lander's misgivings with a layer of forgetfulness.

CHAPTER 17

Rushing to wash and dress, Lander blocked out Kaleb's discordant commands to 'hurry'. He had no idea what time they returned to their rooms, but the lack of rest sealing his eyes with grit alerted him to the fact it must not have been long ago. His body screamed for more sleep but that would need to wait. They were due at Chancellor Morrison's. At least he had avoided drinking anything more powerful than *ah'sim*—the ubiquitous, tea-like drink he was beginning to favor—last night, keeping his mind clear.

Jenkins's arrival moments ago set the whole place to jumping. "Move it. Move it. Move it."

The Vice Chancellor's shouts pierced Lander's consciousness like a well-placed spike as he pulled on the trousers and boots Kaleb lent him. If all went well today, he would have his own uniform soon. The thought froze him in his tracks. Uniforms entailed commitment. *How do I keep my promise to Becky— and Michael—while committing to my team?* **My** *team? Owl scat. What did I get myself into?* But he couldn't let go of the warm feeling that being part of something bigger than himself stirred within him. These were his people, other Stone Sovereigns like himself. And they wanted him.

"We are leaving." Kaleb shoved out the door. Lander grabbed his cloak and slipped through behind Kaleb, letting the thin slab of rock slam shut behind him.

Lander swiped at beads of sweat and swirling moisture as he walked out into the heart of an early Mist Rise. Curtains of vapor rose and fell in their curious dance while the light of the Al'Wisan Cavern glittered in shades ranging from palest pink to deep—almost black—burgundy, within the layers of mist swirling over the Bec Jekesh. The beauty was lost on Lander as he and the other Sovereigns kept pace with Jenkins who led them at a quick march across the same bridge Dena had taken them over yesterday. Rather than turning down the road along the river, though, Jenkins went straight, marching up the slope toward the large structures made up of multiple boulders joined by covered walkways.

At the top of the hill, Jenkins turned right and a few minutes later they stopped in front of one of the largest dwellings Lander had seen in the Core. Pulling to a stop and casting a quick glance down over the river, his thoughts turned to Becky. *This is beautiful! I wish Becky was here. She would love this. I hope she's okay.* Needing to banish the distraction, Lander set Becky within a locked room in his mind, as if to keep her safe until he could keep his promise. He shook off his musings and followed Jenkins and his teammates up a cobbled walkway to a set of wide steps and an immense double door with guards stationed on each side.

"Chancellor Morrison is waiting for you on the Overlook, Vice Chancellor Jenkins," the younger of the two said as he pulled one door open. "Please join him there."

Jenkins responded with a slight nod. "Cadet."

Kaleb leaned into Lander after they walked in. "Cadets are Sovereigns by birth and gifting but are still in training. They are assigned to teams but have not yet achieved official standing. In fact, that is probably how Chancellor Morrison will assign you, as a probationary cadet. Be warned. The other cadets will see you as a rival and hate you for receiving comparable status without working for it. Especially since word will spread that you appeared here wearing the uniform of a full Sovereign."

Lander's gaze swept back to the entryway where the cadet stared at him, open hostility burning in his eyes as he closed the door. *Oh great! Just what I need, another complication.*

By the time Jenkins and the team made their way up a grand staircase, Hunt's unmistakable voice caught Lander's attention. Reaching the first of a series of doors that lined the right side of the hall, Lander peered out on a flagged patio that overlooked the city and the river. If the staircase was impressive, the patio and view were magnificent. *Must be the Overlook.*

The final layers of rising and falling moisture twisted in the familiar closing patterns as Mist Rise came to an end, leaving the world beyond the Overlook alive in droplets that sparkled in a rainbow of red shades. Boats plied the waters of the Bec Jekesh in both directions. The only thing missing to Lander's way of thinking was a sunrise. *And Becky. No! Don't go there!*

Deolah and her team stood in a line, their backs against the dwelling; they didn't look happy. A thigh-high wall of dusty, burnt sienna stone rimmed the Overlook. Olive trees bordered one side, trailing off in lines down the slope to where a small orchard of fruit trees sat.

"You need to handle this, Phil." Hunt's voice filled the heavy air. "I left you in charge. Jenkins is out of control. Look at me. Just look at me. These barbarians treated me like a criminal. They need to be held accountable. I don't even know what they've done with my security people." He turned to wave at Deolah's team and caught sight of Jenkins. "You! How dare you even show your face in my presence. You'll pay for what you've done."

He spun back to Morrison. "Make this right, Phil. I made it right for you, continued paying your wife benefits. I'll reward you handsomely when we return to the Surface."

Morrison pushed up onto his feet, his focus on the grumbling Hunt. "Mr. Hunt, I am in charge here, not you. Ryan was out of line—I'll give you that—but also within his rights as vice chancellor. And these Stone Sovereigns ... obeyed orders like they are trained to do."

Hunt opened his mouth to protest but Morrison raised a hand. Hunt stuttered to a stop and Morrison pulled in a breath then scratched his chin. "You offer to reward me when we return. You assume I want to go back." He tilted his head, his pale blue eyes flashing. He pulled in a deep breath and released it with a loud huff. "Perhaps I do." His gaze drifted to the olive trees and he shook his head before setting his attention back on Hunt. "I don't know. After sixteen years, I doubt I have much to return to. And, even if I did, you do not have the ability to traverse the Avortex without a Stone Sovereign." Morrison waved at Deolah's team then toward Kaleb's. "I doubt any of them would be willing to help you since, from what I've heard, the last Sovereigns who did are now all dead."

"He will." Hunt pointed to Lander. "He wants to go. He'll do anything to help his friends."

Lander stepped back wishing he could melt into the solid stone behind him as Morrison's intense eyes turned their laser focus on him. Though not as tall as Jenkins, Morrison was bulkier, his face broad, with heavy jowls. Older, his gray hair cut in a short military style, Morrison had a bearing that spoke of control and power without him needing to say a word. If Jenkins made Lander uncomfortable, Morrison's presence sent Lander's heart rate up a notch. His demeanor demanded respect and Lander stifled the urge to salute.

"Is this true? Vice Chancellor Jenkins had informed me

you requested a position on Kaleb's team. Are you ready to desert your teammates so quickly?"

Though spoken softly, Morrison's words sent a shaft of guilt into Lander as the man took a step closer. "No. No, sir. I…"

"So, you will break faith with your Surface Dweller friends instead?"

"No … no … I…"

"You are a boy who doesn't even know his own mind." Morrison waved his hand as if chasing away an annoying insect. "But Kaleb has petitioned to have you on his team. I don't understand how he can trust you to have his back, if you abandon one set of friends for another without thought."

Lander swallowed, heat washed through him and his fingers curled into fists as he resisted the impulse to go invisible. "Stop. You don't know me. Don't know what I've been through … or what I'm thinking. You need to … just…" Lander lost steam and shuffled his feet. "You know. Back off."

The urge to pull his Stones from the pouch at his waist and teach the man a lesson washed through him, but after flicking his eyes to Kaleb who shook his head, Lander let go of the idea and gritted his teeth.

An almost-smile turned up one side of Morrison's mouth for a second and he nodded. "You are right. I do not know you. Vice Chancellor Jenkins thinks you have potential. And you have proven your ability to control Stones of Power by successfully bringing so many through the Vortex unharmed. But I must decide; do I send you back with Aurelius and your friends now or assign you to a team." He turned to face Hunt again. "And it is my decision. Your return—*when* or *if* it happens—will be determined by me.

"Ryan, what is your recommendation?"

Jenkins faced Lander. "You're all screwed up inside because you can't decide which promise to keep. I'm going to do you a favor and take the choice away. For now, you will join Captain Kaleb's Stone Sovereigns team as a cadet. On probation. If you prove yourself and are loyal to me … Chancellor Morrison, and your team, perhaps, in time, you will be given official Stone Sovereign status and permission to accompany your friends back to the Surface. For now, they will serve with the other Ungifted working in the El'Ruhan Cavern."

He shifted his gaze to Morrison. "Does that meet with your approval?"

Morrison nodded and his eyes narrowed as he studied Jenkins. Lander's pulse quickened at the obvious tension between the two. Morrison nodded again. "With the current level of unrest among the Ungifted population and the increase in Jerr'as raids, it is a practical decision. I agree."

His focus shifted to Lander. "Cadet Lander, you are now, officially part of this team. Honor your teammates, protect them at all times, and remember your duty to your superiors." He scanned the room. "Stone Sovereigns, you are dismissed. Aurelius. Ryan. Join me for breakfast. We need to talk."

Relieved the decision had been taken out of his hands but struggling under a weight of residual guilt, Lander followed the others into the hallway and down the steps where they congratulated him and pounded him on the back.

"Celebration!" Dena shouted. "Back to Wisan's Haunt."

"Come, join us, Deolah," Kaleb added.

Captain Deolah waved her team forward. "We will help you welcome your newest member."

Trailing his companions, Lander caught sight of Shahan watching from down the hill. Lander raised his hand to wave, but without returning the gesture, Shahan turned and headed back toward the bridge.

CHAPTER 18

Two Months Later...

Myriad voices mingled with the clang of stone pots and dishes to fill the heavy air of the dining hall with a now-familiar racket. Becky brushed a trickle of sweat away from her eyes with the back of her hand then placed a serving ladle into a large pot of steaming lamb stew, the spicy aroma setting her mouth to watering. Though Desma had cut Becky's hair into the Core equivalent of a buzz cut within days of their arrival in the Core, she still struggled to get used to the sweat that now dribbled its way from her scalp to her face.

After checking the long table and rearranging a couple platters, Becky returned to a position near the kitchen doorway alongside Acasia to await more dishes. Glancing up, her gaze caught on several men entering the far door of the dining area. Michael and Talen walked in front; Hunt's twelve guards a strong presence behind them. Sweat dampened stone dust coated their clothing, hair, and every exposed portion of skin, giving them the appearance of animated golden statues rather than living beings.

A Stone Sovereign Becky didn't recognize trailed them, his

hands resting on the pouch holding his Stones as if preparing to pull them, his eyes darting around the room as more Ungifted filtered in for the evening meal. *Another cadet.* With a nervous twitch in his left eye, the young man ran his hands down the front of his crisp, new uniform.

"Ohh ... a new cadet." Acasia's stage-whisper grated on Becky's nerves. The girl seemed infatuated with every Sovereign that appeared in their camp. She wasn't the only one either. Stone Sovereigns were like the rock stars of the Core even though they viewed Ungifted as lesser beings. In the last few months, Becky had heard rumors of Stone Sovereigns raping and beating girls and other stories that seemed too evil to be true. Despite the stories, most of the young ladies from the camp still drooled over the narcissistic Sovereigns.

Skitters of foreboding tracked up Becky's spine. She scanned incoming faces to check for other Stone Sovereigns as the noise increased with the steady influx. *Only the newbie. That's good at least.* The other Sovereigns and Gifted guards tended to avoid the Ungifted meal hall and chose to walk back into town to eat at one of the finer houses where Vice Chancellor Jenkins had made arrangement for lodging. They would return later to count heads and make certain all the Ungifted were present and locked in for the night.

"Becky. Acasia." Desma handed the two serving trays mounded with fresh, still warm, rounds of barley bread and bowls of white, goat-milk butter.

As Becky made her way to one end of the long serving table, Michael came up next to her. His teeth shown bright white against the deep gold of his skin as he cracked a wide smile and waved his fingers in the air. "Ready to get painted, Becks? You'd look cute with a gold line right down your nose." He chuckled, raising one digit, and holding it inches from her face.

She twisted away, balancing the tray between them.

"Michael! Stop that." She nodded a cool greeting to Talen and his men before returning her focus to Michael and shaking her head. "Why do you insist on breaking the rules? You know you're supposed to clean up before entering the dining hall. You're just lucky your new *babysitter* doesn't know better. Besides, Castor is waiting out by the *stream.*"

Michael winked. "Keep the newcomer busy, Becks, okay?"

The youthful Stone Sovereign walked up, his widened eyes still sweeping the busy hall.

Returning Michael's wink, Becky raised her voice. "Get out, you Ungifted ruffians! Clean up before coming in to eat. You know the rules." She shook her head and clicked her tongue. "I've already sent quite a few slackers to the trough already, so if you want to get something to eat before *Misfadura*, you had better go down to the stream to wash."

"Yeah, right. Mist. Fade. Dura. Evening, right? Remember your English, Becks."

"Shut up and get out of here." Becky turned her back on Michael and flashed a bright smile at the Stone Sovereign. "Oh hi! You are new, aren't you? Would you like some warm bread?" She looked down at the tray in her hands and feigned a disgusted look. "Oh ... not this rough stuff. Just wait here one minute." She scurried to place the tray on the table and returned. She pulled in a relieved breath that the young man hadn't moved but stood rooted to the spot, staring as if uncertain what to do next.

Folding her fingers around the crook of his elbow, she caught sight of Michael and the others disappearing out the side door. Becky pasted the smile back on her face. "Come with me. I have fine bread in the kitchen for one such as you."

"B-b-but my orders are—"

"Don't you worry about your charges. By now they are too tired and hungry to care about anything except cleaning up and getting back in here to eat.

"What is your name? Mine is Becky. Well, come along. The bread is going to get cold."

Entering the kitchen, the youth in tow, Becky caught Desma's attention. "Sit right here. You haven't told me your name. Oh look, my friend has brought the special bread ... and fresh butter too."

While the remainder of the staff focused on their duties, Becky sat with the Sovereign until his eyes drifted shut and his head lowered to the table.

"What is going on?" Acasia stood in the doorway, her hand covering her mouth.

Desma hissed and grabbed a tray from one of the heavy, stone worktables. "Nothing to concern yourself with."

"Is he ... dead?"

"Oh my goodness, of course not." Desma pushed the tray into Acasia's hands. "He will be just fine." Her eyebrows lowered and she set her mouth. "You have seen nothing here, Acasia. Do you understand." With her hands on her hips Desma projected stern authority and Becky stifled the urge to smile.

Acasia nodded, her eyes wide. She turned and sprinted into the dining room.

Pivoting back to Becky, Desma shook her head while wiping her hands down her apron. "Castor has to stop calling meetings at mealtimes or we are all going to pay the price for his lack of planning."

"I know, Desma, but it's not his fault that the plans have changed and now we're meeting tonight not tomorrow. He has to let everyone know somehow."

"But drugging a Stone Sovereign? I don't care how young or inexperienced he is, this is asking for trouble."

"He looks like he can't be more than thirteen." Becky studied the pale face. "It must be true. They are losing Sovereigns to the Jerr'as."

"And to the rebels." Desma snorted. "Too young. They lack training and discipline. But it does work in our favor."

Becky nodded. "He looks like he'll sleep for a while. I'm going to the stream. Can you cover for me?"

"Don't I always? Just be quick."

"Of course." Becky skipped out the back door and sprinted to one of the groupings of vertical boulders near a small stream that passed through their work camp before flowing into the Timur Bec'stor, the immense lake that covered the center of the El'Ruhan Cavern. On the far side of the rocks, she slid through a narrow crack between two of the twenty-foot tall, green giants.

More than two dozen men and women, including Michael and Hunt's guards, stood together in the tight space facing Castor. Becky caught the end of what he was saying.

"...half *Misfadura*. Our friend is taking a chance coming tonight; so, we need to be extra careful. I've arranged for your doors to be unlocked. However, if any of you are uncomfortable with this change in meeting time, don't come. I'll fill you in on what is discussed after Mist Rise."

Becky moved to the side as the rebels filtered out through the crack. When everyone else had left, Castor said, "I am grateful for Hunt's men. Though they started out enemies, now they are helping us. Less than six weeks since Morrison assigned them here, and already they have done much to build confidence in our cause. They may not be Sovereigns, but they understand how to fight."

Becky nodded. "And look at you. A little over two months and already you're one of the primary leaders of the rebellion."

After pulling in a noisy breath, Castor released it with a huff. "If, three months ago, anyone had asked me what I'd be doing today..." he waved his hands at their surroundings as they emerged from the rocky alcove, "this ... would be the last thing I'd have thought."

Becky chewed her lip, stilled, and turned toward Castor, then broached the subject that had propelled her to the meeting. "Has your informant said anything more about Lander? Is he okay?"

A deep growl rumbled through Castor's chest and he picked at a broken nail. "No. I'm sorry, Becky. I'll ask him tonight. I have no idea what that boy is thinking. I can't believe he hasn't contacted you—"

"And it hurts." Becky swiped at a tear, angry that Castor witnessed her weakness. "I should just accept..." She scrubbed her hands over her face. "He's forgotten me ... and his promise. And now I'm stuck here. But I keep hoping. I guess I'm just a romantic at heart. Always holding out for the happy ending."

Castor stepped in and wrapped his muscular arms around Becky. It was a little like being hugged by a bear. "You keep believing. We all need to hold onto hope. Now, we had better get back before our absence is noticed."

Though three well-used light sticks wove sputtering glimmers through the meeting cave, deep shadows invaded the room making it difficult to distinguish faces. Warmth and the odor of sweat permeated the air as everyone stood shoulder to shoulder in the tight space, the atmosphere close and uncomfortable as more people pressed in on those already occupying the space.

Becky strained to see the cloaked form standing behind Castor. As tall as Castor, he wore no uniform, but it was common knowledge the informant was a Stone Sovereign ... and Castor had spread the news that he wasn't the only Stone Sovereign who supported the rebels' fight for equality.

She slipped past a few clumps of people. Michael followed, his hand resting lightly on her shoulder, as they made their way to the front of the crowd where he shifted into a position next to her. A few minutes later Castor raised his voice, calling for quiet and attention. As the cave settled into a semblance of quiet, the sound of dripping water echoed, lacing the cavern with its soft tinkle.

"Thank you for coming." Castor's gaze swept the gathering. "Though I have not been with you long, I have come to admire your spirit and your courage. I did not return with thoughts of leading a rebellion. In fact, I am still in awe of the trust you've placed in me by choosing me to lead this effort and pray that I do not fail you.

"When Desma and I left for the Surface, the Core was a much different place. All those who had reached the second level of kinship had a vote within their guilds; and the guilds, along with the Elders considered those votes, then implemented the rulings necessary for all to live in harmony. Neighbor cared for neighbor. Whenever the Jerr'as attacked, we banded together to drive them from our caverns. Stone Sovereigns worked alongside Ungifted and Gifted without thought." He paused as heads nodded and words of affirmation filtered through the throng.

"Now, a scant sixteen years later, Desma and I have returned to a world controlled by two outsiders and Stone Sovereigns who see themselves not as friends and neighbors, but as overseers. The Surface Dwellers have convinced them they are superior to us; that they may treat us as slaves. This should not be."

He motioned to the silent form behind him. "My friend here has informed me that many of the older Stone Sovereigns regret supporting Chancellor Morrison and Vice Chancellor Jenkins, but they are afraid to speak out. And I do not blame them. As individuals, both the Gifted and the Ungifted are weak. But … if we were to band together—unified as we were in the past—we can drive the outsiders from our world and return to a balanced rule that recognizes the worth of every individual."

Scattered applause echoed through the chamber along with several shouts of approval. One man's voice rose above the noise. "Let the Stone Sovereign speak for himself Castor. Prove he isn't playing some game, leading us on only to betray us to Morrison. Show us your face, Stone Sovereign. Speak to us. Sovereigns killed my son; tell me why I should trust you."

Bodies shifted as the shadowy figure's voice rose from within the folds of his cloak. "You must trust me as I am trusting you."

"And yet you do not show your face."

The Sovereign stood for a moment, silent and imposing. Becky pulled in a breath. Would he take offense at the Ungifted's challenge? She had seen other Sovereigns whip workers with a lash of fire for nothing more than mumbling words of anger in their presence.

A hush fell over the room. The Sovereign stepped forward to stand next to Castor. With a quick movement, he flung the hood from his head and dropped the cloak to the floor. Becky's mouth hung open. She recognized the man. Silver eyes raked the crowd and a muscle jumped in his square jaw. Murmurs flowed through the gathering.

"People of El'Ruhan Cavern, you know me. Stone Sovereign Shahan Deklakh. I am Stone Sovereign two-hundred forty years. I protected you and healed you. You are my people. I will stand with you against the Surface Dwellers. Those who have corrupted our path of life."

His gaze slid over to Castor. "My old friend Castor asked for help when I came through El'Ruhan Cavern many *Misrisdura* ago to fight Jerr'as. They are not our only enemy. I have waited long to … struggle against the invaders who stole our right to rule ourselves. I join with you." He scanned the group again. "And I am not only. Others feel as I do. They will help."

Light seemed to fill the cavern and tension bled from Becky's muscles. *Finally! Hope! I wonder if Lander is one of the* others *who want to help.*

CHAPTER 19

"Now! Lander, do it now!" Kaleb's shout bounced off the walls of the Bec Jekesh Cavern. The shrill call pierced through the rumblings of the river like the screech of nails on a chalkboard. Kaleb and Tuvyam dropped their shield. Eyes fixed, Lander sent controlled lances of fire into the Jerr'as dummies placed in various locations around the path. Lander's goal: keep his lances tight and focused while he took out the dummies on the right, Siprian took out those on the left, and Rahni smoked the ones in the center of the trail. Though it took several shots, one after another went down under the onslaught of Stone Sovereign fire.

"Do not screw up again, Lander." Laughter punctuated the comment. Lander had gotten quite a jolt and a nasty burn the last time they practiced the drill when he had inadvertently crossed lines with Siprian. A mistake he would not make again.

After practicing the maneuver for almost two months, Lander had the timing down. Kaleb raised his hand. Shield up; stop firing. Kaleb lowered his hand. Shield dropped; enemy accessible; commence firing. Again, and again. Bored with the routine, Lander yearned to erect a more powerful shield, lace it with fire, and wipe out the Jerr'as in one sharp attack. But though he wore the uniform of a Stone Sovereign it lacked the collar insignia of full Stone Sovereign status; his standing on the team was that of an untried cadet. And Kaleb kept strict control of what Lander was allowed—or not allowed—to do. That had been one of Chancellor Morrison's conditions for permitting him to join Kaleb's team without prior training. The second condition was that he promised to use only his father's Stones of Power. It rankled to leave his mother's more powerful Stones sitting unused in his pouch. But he had taken an oath.

More than half of the Jerr'as dummies had been sizzled and Lander allowed his thoughts to float free. Images of Becky rose in his mind, and his heartbeat accelerated. The need to see her flooded him like a tidal wave and a soft moan leaked through his clenched teeth. *Soon.*

Since they were hiking back through the El'Ruhan Cavern rather than traveling back by river so the team could stop at the village where Becky was posted and monitor the Ungifted there, Kaleb had promised that Lander could meet with Becky.

Guilt churned acid in Lander's stomach. When he agreed to train with the Stone Sovereigns, he never expected it to be for so long. *Becky and Michael probably think I've forgotten them.* Not a Mist Rise went by that Lander didn't think of Becky—didn't long to hold her, keep her safe, and fulfill his promise to return her to the Surface. But with each passing Mist Rise, he learned more about honing his skills. Whether working with Kaleb on precision or training with Dena healing those injured in Jerr'as attacks or accidents, his mastery of finer skills was steadily improving. Prior to this, he had used his power like wielding a sledgehammer; now he was learning to wield it like a surgeon's scalpel.

Without warning, the hairs on the back of Lander's neck rose and a chill raced up his spine. "Rahni."

She sent him a quick sideways glance. "I am busy." She targeted another Jerr'as.

"Rahni. Take my side." Her angry look caused Lander to duck his head, but he refused to ignore the premonition. Danger lurked behind him.

He turned from his team and strode back to where the path curved around a large clump of the native trees.

"Lander! Get back here!"

Ignoring Kaleb's shout, Lander continued. He slowed his approach at the point where the path bent. His eyes locked on the silhouettes of bushes and small trees before him, searching for any tell-tale signs of movement: shifting branches, changing shadows. He pulled in breaths through his nose, seeking out the distinctive stench of unwashed Jerr'as bodies.

A faint hint of breeze drifted past and there it was. Jerr'as. *Owl scat.* He ghosted into a small clump of trees, moving forward in a crouch, just like he did when he and Pop-pop hunted. He focused and went invisible. *Slow.* Reaching a break in the foliage, he peered out and sucked in a breath. Several Jerr'as squatted at the river, lapping at the water like dogs. Nearly twenty more sat on their haunches along the trail. *No way! That's a lot for one team to handle.* He backed out of the grove, released invisibility, and sprinted back to his team.

"What were you thinking?" Kaleb strode toward Lander, his hands fisted. Siprian took the captain's place holding the barrier with Tuvyam, while Dena continued smoking Jerr'as dummies.

"You never leave your team like that." Kaleb advanced, a vein pulsing in his temple. "We never turn our backs on teammates. Do you not understand the importance of this drill? If one—just one—Jerr'as gets through the barrier the whole team is at risk." Kaleb spoke the last word with a grunt as he reached Lander and slammed a fist into Lander's gut.

Lander's tail slammed into the hard rock of the path shooting pain up his spine, but he bounded back up and shoved Kaleb. "Listen to me. There's a bunch of Jerr'as around the bend. Not dummies. Real. Live. Smelly. Jerr'as."

Kaleb froze, his eyes rounded. "What?"

"Don't know if they know we're here yet, but they are going to be coming this way any second now, Kaleb. How do you want to handle it?"

"*Shiviah-zor.*" The Corish curse hung in the air. Kaleb grabbed the front of Lander's tunic. "Can you set a barrier and infuse it with fire?"

Lander nodded.

Breath hissed out between Kaleb's lips. "Okay." Kaleb's mind raced, his eyes flashing. Lander knew he was running possible scenarios by the way his eyes shot back and forth. The Stone Sovereign captain hadn't gotten his own team at only twenty-five years old by being a slouch. He was a master tactician.

"Siprian, you and Dena hide on the river shore. Tuvyam, Arien, Rahni take the opposite side of the path. Stay concealed and wait. You will be outside the barrier, so timing is everything. Mess up, you die."

Lips pressed into thin lines the five responded with firm nods.

"We're going to try Lander's approach. He and I will be the bait. The Jerr'as should focus on us and clump together when they reach the barrier. Once Lander's ready, he'll create a wall of fire and drive it into the Jerr'as. When you see the flames advancing, and the Jerr'as begin to retreat, fire at will. If this does not work, at least it will even the odds." He scanned the team. "Go!

"Lander. We need to get back up the trail some to give the team room to work."

Lander sprinted alongside his captain, adrenaline flooding through him like a drug, his cloak flapping behind.

A minute later, Kaleb pulled to a stop, turned, and scanned the path beyond where the team hid. He nodded. "This is good." He faced Lander. "I know what Chancellor Morrison said, but I'm not going to lose any teammates because you held back. Use all four Stones of Power and make this work."

Heavy air pressed down on Lander. Rivulets of sweat oozed from his hairline to dribble down his face and drip from his chin as he scooped out the four cold, dark Stones. An instant later they warmed, beams of red and blue light shifted and flickered on the surrounding vegetation. A gasp escaped Lander as the power of the Stones flooded his senses.

Snarling and barking echoed through the chamber. The Jerr'as loping down the trail slowed at the juncture where the team hid, sniffing the air, until they caught sight of Lander and Kaleb. Fixated on the two, they inched forward, suspicion evident in their controlled movements and raised muzzles.

"Are you ready Surface Dweller?"

Without voicing a reply, Lander focused. Like a section of the protective bubble he had held during the journey through the Vortex, the barrier blossomed into existence, strong and demanding.

"Do not fire it yet."

Unable to speak, Lander nodded his understanding. Kaleb wanted the Jerr'as close and packed together for maximum impact when Lander fired and launched the shield.

The Jerr'as slowed and spread out as they approached Kaleb and Lander. Dropping down onto all fours, they padded around the edge of the shield, sniffing and growling, reminding Lander of a pack of wolves. Lander swallowed hard and licked his lips, his mouth suddenly dry. Though he'd fought Jerr'as a few times, he'd never seen them behave like dogs—or like a unified pack. His vision blurred and an image rose. Becky running, being pulled down by a pack of Jerr'as. Screaming in silence.

"Get ready." Kaleb's hissed warning pulled Lander from his mind with a gasp.

"Now, Lander! Fire it now!"

A moment's hesitation, then fire ignited on his fingertips. He focused and the curved shield between him and the Jerr'as burst into a wall of blue and red flames. The image of Becky, terrified and bloody, still fresh in his mind, Lander propelled the flames into the Jerr'as.

Yelping and biting at the sparks singeing their bare skin, they turned and ran into the rest of the team's crossfire.

Fury coursing through him, Lander lost all sense. He rammed the shield down the path, moving with swift steps while pumping more threads of sparks into the inferno, intent on killing every Jerr'as. His mother's Stones, hot and demanding, burned with radiant light, searing the palm of his right hand. Beyond caring, he embraced the power surging through him.

Hands were pulling at him; fingers wrapped around his arms. A voice broke through his fog. "Lander. Stop. You're going to hurt someone."

Kaleb? Where... Lander shook his head and released his focus. *What did I do?*

Reality swarmed in on him. "Kaleb?"

The Sovereign captain took a few steps back as Lander turned to face him. "Kaleb? Did I ... hurt anyone?" Lander pivoted and scanned for signs of his teammates, his eyes smarting from the stench of burning flesh and smoky air.

Kaleb moved to Lander's side and thumped him on the back. "That was awesome!"

A moment later, the entire team gathered around Lander and Kaleb.

"A few escaped, but we killed most of them." Siprian, his

eyes burning with intensity, nodded his approval. "You must teach us to do that, Lander. It was … impressive."

Lander smiled and received praises as the others gathered around him. His trembling hands hidden at his back, he struggled with the truth that his mother's Stones of Power almost overwhelmed his ability to control them. Even more disturbing, the image of Becky pursued by Jerr'as hovered in his mind.

Pulling himself together with a physical shake, Lander pushed past his teammates and confronted Kaleb. "I want to see Becky … and Michael. Now!" He waved his arm in the general direction of the El'Ruhan Cavern. "They're in the workcamp we're supposed to visit and it's not far from here. We can make it in two Mist Rises if we leave now."

Kaleb mumbled something and Lander grabbed the front of his tunic, his eyes boring into Kaleb's. "I want to see Becky. Don't give me any excuses. I've waited for two months. If you won't go with me, I'll go alone."

Kaleb's gaze dropped to where Lander still held his tunic. "Let go." The words were spoken soft and slow, but Lander caught the undercurrent of promised violence.

Lander released his hold. *Get a grip, Lander. Don't be stupid.* "Sorry, Captain. It won't happen again." He held his hands up, palms out, conceding Kaleb's authority.

Tension bled from Kaleb and he nodded. "No problem. You are still worked up from the encounter. No harm."

Releasing a breath, Lander pushed out a half grin. "Still friends?"

"Friends and colleagues. Come. Let us clean up this mess. After it is done, we will take rest in our camp. At Mist Rise we will head to the workcamp outside Shavah El'Ruhan."

"And I'll get to see Becky?"

Kaleb shifted to stare out over the Bec Jekesh and thought for a moment. "Vice Chancellor Jenkins will not like it. His orders were to keep you away from the other Surface Dwellers.

They are not a good influence. But … after what you just did, I do not think it will be a problem. You are indeed one of us now."

After burning the Jerr'as remains, the team hiked back to their camp. Set within a small grove of trees on a slight rise, the site allowed them to monitor the trail at the point where the cavern dwindled down into the tunnel while, at the same time, sheltering them from the gaze of curious travelers.

"We will rest here until Mist Rise." Kaleb pulled a stone and flicked fire into the kindling and wood he had stacked before they left for the training exercise.

Dena retrieved several bottles of sweet fruit wine, some goat cheese, and rounds of barley bread from one of the packs. "Lander has done well. You agree, do you not, Kaleb? We will celebrate."

Siprian laughed. "Not with those. I have just the thing." He rummaged in a smaller pack. "We must celebrate Lander's transformation from Surface Dweller to full Corish Stone Sovereign and teammate." Siprian pulled out a dark red, stone crock with a lid and moved next to the now flickering camp-fire.

Lander tried to back away, but Tuvyam and Arien pushed him toward Siprian. "We drink. Now."

Rahni laughed and threw an arm around Lander's waist. "Do not fight this. I know you do not like to be drunk. But this . . . in-in-inciation you cannot avoid."

"Initiation?" Lander's eyes met the older women's sparkling orbs.

"That is what I said."

Another round of laughter floating through the camp was cut short as Tuvyam stumbled then fell unconscious to the ground behind Lander and Arien.

"*Shiviah-zor*." The swear broke from Dena's lips. "Look at his arm."

Tuvyam's cloak had slipped to the side revealing bloody puncture wounds on his right arm.

"*Shiviah-zor*," Kaleb repeated as he dropped to his knees next to Tuvyam. "Why did he hide this? Stupid."

Rahni slipped into position next to Kaleb. She pulled a knife from her belt and sliced the sleeve open exposing the torn flesh. She shook her head, her eyes seeking out Kaleb's. "I cannot heal this here. It is a bite. Poison. We must get him back to Shavah Al'Wisan without delay."

Lander leaned in over Rahni's shoulder. "I though you could heal anything."

"Not this." Rahni's attention dropped to Tuvyam's still form again. "I can heal what has been damaged. But I cannot disappear the poison without cleansing plants."

Kaleb pushed up onto his feet. "Siprian, make a frame to carry him; Dena you help him. Everyone else, pack up. If we leave for the docks now, we can be in Al'Wisan by late Mist Rise."

CHAPTER 20

The trip back to Dock Village tested everyone's patience and endurance. When they reached the small village, the team followed Kaleb as he strode out onto one of the docks where a bent figure worked. "You. Ungifted. We need a boat. Now. One large enough to carry us all. Make it ready immediately."

The man rose, chomping on a bit of bark, eyeing them with mistrust, and Lander recognized him as one of the boat tenders they had worked with in the past.

The crusty old man shook his head while wiping grimy hands down the front of his dirty, tan tunic. "No. Not possible. Nothing that size available."

Kaleb growled his frustration, flinging his arm toward two larger craft on the next dock over. "What about those."

The boat tender shifted his gaze to the boats and released a sigh of resignation before turning his attention back to Kaleb, his mouth flattened into a tight line. "Well … *sir*, they need some repairs. I suppose I *could* make one ready in…" He pursed his lips, his brow wrinkled in thought. "A couple hours."

"A couple hours?" Kaleb snorted. With exaggerated movements, he pulled his Stones of Power from the pouch at his waist. "Make it one hour."

The man chewed on his bark like it was chewing gum for a few seconds, then spit the brown mush out near Kaleb's feet.

"*Shiviah-zor.*" Kaleb's Stones ignited.

"We do not have time for this, Kaleb. Patience. We need him to ready the craft." Rahni reached out and placed a calming hand on Kaleb's arm.

"One hour, Ungifted. Any longer and I will sear you." Kaleb's threat had the desired effect. The boat tender's eyes widened but he nodded and yelled into the closest hut for help. Soon two Ungifted and one young man dressed in the better-fitting garb of a Gifted swarmed over the craft.

Rahni and Siprian set Tuvyam's litter on the dock, hunkered down, and pulled their Stones. Taking care, the two watched over him and did what they could to keep his condition stable as they waited.

With nothing to do while waiting, Lander wandered out onto the dock to watch the men work. He had heard the rumors spreading through the Stone Sovereign teams about dissatisfaction among the Ungifted, even some attacks on lone Sovereigns. But the boat tender's disrespect had taken him by surprise. He hoped for a chance to talk to the workers, but other than a few glares thrown in his direction, they went about their tasks and ignored him. Less than an hour later the three helpers walked away and disappeared between two huts farther down the road. The boat tender approached Kaleb and without a word gave him a stiff nod then turned and followed his friends.

Other than sighting a few Jerr'as along the far bank of the Bec Jekesh, the trip to Al'Wisan passed without incident. Lander helped Siprian carry Tuvyam to a healing station then requested permission to get some rest.

By the time Lander returned to his room in the Stone Sovereign Cadet Training Quarters, all he wanted to do was collapse onto his bed and catch up on some sleep. He had taken a turn helping Rahni keep the Jerr'as poison from spreading in Tuvyam while on the river, but like the older Stone Sovereign had said, they could not neutralize the poison itself.

He washed and changed into more casual attire, a simple blue tunic, representing his Deklakh roots, and loose-fitting tan slacks. Then, grateful there were no other cadets in the room, he lay down on his bed. He needed time alone to think. Interlocking his fingers behind his head he stared up at the pale pink ceiling and began to pray for Tuvyam.

Since leaving Becky and Michael, and joining the team, he had avoided praying, but Tuvyam's still, unconscious form left an imprint Lander couldn't release unless he sought God's help for his friend.

Prayer for Tuvyam slipped easily into prayer for Becky. Again, the vision of her being attacked by Jerr'as arose within him, stirring fresh fear and guilt. He chewed his lower lip.

Kaleb's plan to visit the village where Becky and Michael were stationed went south when Tuvyam collapsed. And Lander chaffed at the delay. Anger churned his stomach at the thought that another two months might pass before he got the chance again. He shifted on the bed. Though his body was tired, his thoughts made him twitchy and unable to get comfortable.

"Okay. What do I do, Mom? You told me to come here, but I still don't know why. I've betrayed my friends—betrayed Becky—and for what? What. Am. I. Supposed. To. Do. I've learned a lot, so the time hasn't been wasted. But I'm no closer to any answers than I was when I got here." He gritted his teeth, jaw cracking with the pressure. "What do I do?"

Silence surrounded him. *Great. You tell me to come here. Now I'm here and I don't know how to help.* His thoughts still churning, exhaustion finally dragged him into the depths of slumber.

The quiet sounds of the cadets' even breathing filtered into Lander's consciousness. He rose and peeked out a window. *Misfadura* was ending and the early signs of an imminent Mist Rise met his gaze. *No sense in trying to get back to sleep now.*

He donned a clean uniform, leaving his dirty one in a heap on the floor for the staff to clean and press. A minute later, he breezed out the door and down the hallway. As he reached the bottom of the stairs, a young cadet raced up to him. "Sir, I have orders to bring you to Chancellor Morrison."

Owl scat. "Now?"

The boy nodded, his eyes round and serious.

"Okay. Lead on."

Circling vapor turned buildings into hazy, pink forms and webs of moisture coated Lander's hair and cloak as they crossed the river. The muted chuckling of the water and the steady drip of condensation signaled Mist Rise. When they reached Morrison's mansion, the cadet saluted Lander and disappeared into fog.

Pulling in a deep breath, Lander climbed the six steps up to the front double doors where a guard pulled the thin stone slab open and waved Lander in. A servant, dressed in the common beige tunic and short trousers of the Ungifted, waved him up the stairs. "Chancellor Morrison is on the Overlook. Go right up."

Pausing, Lander stepped in close to the man. "Your name is Elam, isn't it?"

The man lowered his eyes. "Yes, sir."

"And you are Ungifted?"

His gaze bounced up to Lander, his mouth hanging open. Eyes scanned back and forth. "Please, sir. I cannot ... Please just go up to the Overlook."

The fear on Elam's face set Lander back a step. *Not just rumors. Truth.* With a nod he hoped conveyed his apology to the man, Lander turned and bounded up the stairs. He had been so wrapped in his own problems, his own needs, he missed what was right before him; the way Ungifted were being treated like slaves. *Is this what you wanted me to see, Mom?*

Voices drifted in past the crystal doors of the Overlook, set open to allow light and air to filter into the hallway. Lander slowed his pace wondering who was with Chancellor Morrison. When he stepped into the first doorway, a tremor of apprehension skittered up his spine. Captain Darrius Deklakh, First Sovereign of the Company of Stone Sovereigns, stood near the outer wall sipping from a stone mug, talking with Sovereign Shahan and Captain Kaleb. Not far from them stood Captain Deolah. Her gold uniform a stark contrast to the red and blue uniforms of the others, she stood at ease and conversed with Lander's other teammates, Siprian, Arien, Rahni, and Dena.

But the three men sitting at a small table at one of the outer corners of the Overlook arrested Lander's attention. Vice Chancellor Jenkins filled the chair to Chancellor Morrison's right. Though Jenkins had spent a couple weeks in Shavah Al'Wisan before returning to Shavah Deklakh, Lander hadn't seen him in over a month. *What's he doing here? Now?*

Even more disturbing though, was the man who sat with his back to Lander, his hand circling in the air as the other men listened, their attention focused.

Aurelius Hunt, dressed in a robe striped in maroon, cobalt-blue, and gold, that shouted to all 'I'm a privileged citizen of all caverns', laughed. No longer a prisoner, the man looked well-groomed, relaxed, and in control.

Droplets sparkled in the soft light as pale pink mist twisted over the stone wall that edged the Overlook, giving the impression that Lander was stepping into a dream. *Or am I walking into a nightmare?*

Chancellor Morrison's gaze snagged on Lander. "Here he is."

As all eyes turned to him, the familiar tug of shyness

almost drove him to step back into the hallway. But the confidence he had gained since Pop-pop's death kept him rooted to the spot. He pulled up a smile and pasted the awkward, crooked thing on his face. *This is nothing, Lander. You faced a pack of Jerr'as and survived. Breathe. Breathe deep.*

Morrison, Jenkins, and Hunt pushed upright. Kaleb began to clap and within seconds everyone followed his lead.

Morrison focused on Lander, his eyes brittle and glittering. *Something's not right.* Lander studied the man. Though he stood with the same level of confidence as the day Lander had met him, his ashen skin sagged down his cheeks and his eyes looked wrong … unhealthy.

But Lander had no time to ponder. Kaleb strode over, the soles of his soft boots whispering on the flagstones. "Welcome, fellow Sovereign. When Chancellor Morrison heard what you did, he made it official." He shook his head and wrapped an arm around Lander's shoulders. "Come, join your teammates while you can. If you keep this up, you'll leave us for your own team in no time."

Between thumps on his back, punches to his arms, and words of encouragement, Lander ended up in front of Dena. He looked down to meet her silver gaze. The skin around her eyes crinkled into laugh lines as she stood before him, slight but strong. Yet again, he stamped down the desires her beauty stirred within him despite the fact she was almost four times his age. Nothing more than physical attraction, not like what he felt for Becky, but unnerving, nevertheless. His mouth dry, he sent his tongue in search of moisture.

"Are you ready?" The fragrance of her spicy perfume drifted up.

Lander swallowed and nodded.

Dena took his arm and led him to a narrow table set against the side wall. Thick, gnarled branches of the ancient olive trees that bordered the Overlook reached overhead and the slight breeze sent droplets of water cascading from the dark green leaves. She turned him to face the group who had gathered behind him. Rising on tiptoes, she planted a gentle kiss on his cheek. "He is all yours, Chancellor Morrison."

The chancellor moved into position next to Lander as Dena took her place with the team.

Morrison cleared his throat. "You all know why we are here. This young Stone Sovereign cadet has earned the right to wear the insignia of full standing. His courage and ability made it possible for his team to confront a pack of Jerr'as and return here with only one injury. Speaking of which, I have been informed Sovereign Tuvyam is recovering well thanks to the efforts of his teammates."

The chancellor cleared his throat again, triggering a deep, harsh cough. A moment later, he pulled in a shallow breath. "And so, moving on. Who accepts this cadet into full-standing?"

Shoulders level and back ramrod straight, Kaleb took one step forward. "I do, sir."

"Excellent, Captain Kaleb. The tokens are on the table."

Chancellor Morrison took hold of the inner edge of Lander's cloak as Kaleb handed him a silver pin with a blue stone etched onto the front. After pinning it to one side of the collar of Lander's cloak, they repeated the procedure on the other side.

Lander tried staring down to see the emblem but couldn't get a good look.

Meanwhile, three Ungifted carried out trays bearing thin stone mugs. Kaleb's team received blue mugs, Deolah's mug sported a golden sheen, while Darrius's and Shahan's glowed in deep burgundy hues. Once everyone held a drink and the servants had left, Chancellor Morrison lifted his cup. "In representation of Stone Sovereigns serving across all caverns, we salute you, Lander Deklakh. Welcome. Your life is now intwined with the lives of all fellow Stone Sovereigns who serve the caverns. Your honor is their honor; their honor is your honor. Your teammates are your colleagues, your friends, and your family from this day forward. Do you accept this honor, Lander Deklakh?"

"I do, sir."

Mugs were downed to the last drop then flung to the floor where they shattered on impact with the hard stones. Lander followed as expected though the sickeningly sweet fermented drink left him feeling as if he had downed a dozen sodas.

After some more back thumping and congratulations, Chancellor Morrison lifted a envelop from the table. "Lander, in recognition of your service to the caverns of the Core, here is the address for your new dwelling. Though your team represents Shavah Deklakh, your current assignment is based here in Shavah Al'Wisan. Therefore, you will receive your permanent residence when you return there. For now, consider this small token as your home. Ungifted are already assigned there to serve you as you see fit. In addition, you will have four days of down time to acclimate yourself to your new situation."

Morrison shook Lander's hand then turned to Kaleb. "Kaleb, I dismiss you and the other Sovereigns. Go with Lander now. Help him celebrate getting out of the Cadet Quarters and into a proper house."

A broad smile broke across Kaleb's face. "Yes, sir!"

As Lander turned to follow Kaleb, Darrius, and the others to the door, he realized Shahan hung back. "Aren't you coming?"

Shahan's gaze shifted out over the river. "I do no think so. I have not been in celebration mood lately."

Lander walked over to where the large Sovereign stood and spoke in a soft voice. "We need to talk."

Shahan's attention flicked to the men at the table before fastening on Lander. "That would be good. There is someone

I think you need to meet." He spoke in a whisper and Lander leaned in to hear.

"Lander." Siprian called from the hall. "What is taking so long?"

"Coming." Lander took a step back and pulled in a deep breath. "Tomorrow, Shahan?"

Shahan's eyes narrowed. "Yes. Tomorrow. I know the house they are gift you. I will meet you at Mist Rise."

"Lander!" Kaleb's demand broke the connection between Lander and Shahan.

"Yeah. I'm coming."

With a quick nod to Morrison, Jenkins, and Hunt, who were, once again deep in conversation at the little table, Lander sprinted down the hallway.

CHAPTER 21

Lander startled awake, jumped from the bed, scanned the dark room, and grabbed for the Stones of Power in his pouch before he realized he wasn't in uniform. A knock drew his eyes to the door. Realization filtered through his sleep fogged brain. *Someone knocking? Right! My house. My bedroom.*

"What?" The word slipped out, scratchy and harsher than he expected.

"Sir? There is a Stone Sovereign here to see you."

"*Shiviah-zor!*" He stumbled to the window and swung open the light-blocking shutter, a greatly appreciated benefit of his new home after weeks of sleeping in the half-light of the Core. Scanning the grounds, he groaned. The Stone Sovereign had to be Shahan, but Mist Rise hadn't even started yet.

"Sir?"

"Yeah, I hear you. I'll be right out." He gritted his teeth while running his gaze over the room to locate his uniform and Stones.

"Do you need any assistance, sir?"

"No! Just … just go … make some *ah'sim* or something for our guest. I'll be right down."

"Yes, sir."

Grumbling, Lander grabbed his trousers from the floor before noticing a clean uniform laid out on one of the three chairs placed around a small table where a bowl fruit sat. *Okay … someone was in here while I slept?* He shook his head. *Of course. I have servants now.* He glanced back at the shutters then the fresh fruit. "Nice! A guy could get use to this."

He grabbed a couple dates and stuffed them into his mouth, pulled on his trousers, then slipped on his tunic. Whoever set out the clothing had taken time to pin his rank badges to the collar of his fresh cloak. "Nice," he said again.

He chewed with care to slip the pits out and deposited them on a small platter. With a bunch of olives in hand, he left the room and headed down the stairs. Voices drifted from one of the rooms to his left, and he followed the sound.

Shahan sat in a chair near a heavy worktable in what looked to be the kitchen. One older man and two young girls, all dressed in the drab tan of the Ungifted, were busy chopping vegetables while Shahan sipped from a stone mug.

"I thought you said Mist Rise." Lander paced into the room.

Shahan froze with the mug touching his bottom lip. His eyes met Lander's and he lowered the cup. "I am early. Is that problem?"

Though part of Lander wanted to say, *yes, it's a problem. I was sleeping … in a dark room.* He bit back the retort. "No. Not a problem."

Lander turned to shift his attention to the three servants. "Whoever left the fruit and clean uniform, thank you."

The old man nodded. "You are welcome, Sovereign Lander. Is there anything else I can do for you?"

"Well, for starters, you can tell me your names."

The man nodded again. "I am called Navid. These are Olive and Anah."

"It's nice to meet you." Lander inclined his head, first to the taller, older girl, then to the shorter, younger girl. "Olive and Anah."

The two giggled and heat rose into his cheeks. Flustered, he turned back to Shahan. "Have you eaten?"

"We must talk before we leave. We talk while we eat. We enjoy *ah'sim*."

"Um, yeah, sure." Lander turned back to Navid. "We want breakfast. Now. In the dining room."

Navid looked at Lander for a moment than his eyes lit up. "You mean Mist Rise meal?"

Lander huffed. "Yes. Yes. That's what I mean." He looked back into the hallway and paused. "Um, Navid. Where is the dining room?"

A look of peaceful patience swept across the man's face. "Come, sir. I will show you." Navid set a ladle into a medium-sized serving bowl. Nodding to himself, he picked up the bowl and turned left into the hallway, Lander and Shahan following. After passing one set of doors, he entered the next on the right.

Lander clamped his mouth shut before it could sag open. The room rivaled Chancellor Morrison's formal dining room. Though offered a tour of the house yesterday, he had refused. The truth zinged through him again. This was all his. If he decided to remain in the Core, he would be wealthy and powerful beyond his wildest dreams. A tendril of guilt wormed its way beneath his growing pleasure. *Becky! Michael! Castor and Desma! Just a little longer. What could it hurt?*

Navid left the pot of boiled grain loaded with chunks of pitted dates. Lander helped himself to a bowlful then passed the serving spoon to Shahan. Navid returned carrying a platter. Setting it on the table, he placed a mug of warm goat milk and a pot of *ah'sim*, the sweetened tea-like drink of the Core, within

Lander's reach. "Will there be anything more, Sovereign Lander?"

"No. Um. No. That's all."

Shahan and Lander ate in silence for several minutes. When his bowl was clean, Shahan poured a mug of *ah'sim*. He took a sip and sighed. "What do you think of your new home, Lander? Is it all you hoped?"

Lander snagged Shahan's eyes with his own. "I didn't know what to expect. Nothing like this."

"But you like it, do you not?"

"Yeah. I'd be lying if I said no."

"You should know. This house was Navid's. His, his daughters, and the rest of his family. They are now dead."

A vise clamped onto Lander's chest. Words jumbled over each other in his mind, seeking release. "No. You're playing mind games."

Shahan blinked. "No. I do not know games of mind. But I do not think I am playing one."

Okay, back off Lander. Let Shahan explain. "What happened?"

"We happened." Shahan pulled in a deep breath through his nose and released it with a huff through clenched teeth before a grimace twisted his mouth. "But that is not what I want to dis – dis – talk about."

"No, wait." Lander scowled and shook his head. "You can't drop a bomb like that and then just leave it."

Shahan's brows pulled down in confusion. "Bomb? What is bomb?"

"Never mind. Does this have to do with the Ungifted rebellion I've been hearing about?"

Shahan scanned the room. "Not here. We will speak on this later. Now, I must ask what you know of your family."

Lander pushed up onto his feet and paced to a window overlooking the Bec Jekesh, his hands balled into tight fists. He struggled to stifle the urge to pivot and plant one on Shahan's jaw. A virulent mix of anger and frustration churned in his stomach. "My parents are dead. End of discussion."

"No, not parents. Other family."

"Pop-pop Ian is dead, too. You already know that."

"But you have other family. Here."

Lander rotated from the window to face Shahan. For a moment all he could do was stare. The billowing anger that threatened to explode crashed against curiosity.

Shahan nodded. "Yes. That is why I came early. If we leave now, the river will get us there before *Misfadura*." He pushed up and walked to Lander. "Will you come with me? There is much you need to know."

"Family? I have family? Here?"

"Yes. Cyanne's father's mother. She wants to meet you."

Lander turned back to the window. Thin tendrils of moisture were beginning to form above the river. Mist Rise. Indecision threatened to hold him captive, frozen in emotions he refused to face. But if he didn't act now, he might miss the chance. Just like he missed the chance to see Becky. His heart hurt. He wanted her, needed her. Her wisdom, faith, and presence. By now she probably thought he didn't care.

Help your people. His mother's words spun through his mind like a class five tornado, flattening everything in its path. Was this what he needed to do ... meet his grandmother. *No. Great grandmother.* Was she the key? He shook his head. *No. That's just hypocritical. Admit it, Lander. You're still here because for the first time you feel like a somebody. Important. You have a house ... no. I have a mansion ... servants.*

The river blurred as Becky's face floated into Lander's vision. He remembered how she looked when they left Shavah Deklakh, strands of dark hair plastered to her face, droplets of sweat sparkling on her chocolate skin. So beautiful. So trusting.

The only way out is to keep moving forward. I promised I'd come back for her. Pulling himself together, Lander gulped in a breath and focused on Shahan. "Let's go."

After walking for almost two hours, Shahan led Lander to a small, private dock at the lower end of town. Warehouses filled the streets with small, rundown domes of indeterminate color scattered between.

Jumping down into the stone boat, Lander noted the light sticks fore and aft. Shahan had planned for limited illumination. Wherever they were going was separated from the light of the Flux by heavier rock formations, reminding Lander of the smaller tunnels where the Jerr'as preferred to live.

Shahan motioned for Lander to take the front bench, then thumped into the craft at Lander's back. Picking up a paddle, he pushed off. Within moments, they gained the center of the river where the swift flow caught them. Grabbing the second paddle, Lander stroked in time with Shahan and soon the last buildings of Shavah Al'Wisan dwindled in the distance. Beyond the edge of town, red rock formations dominated the landscape, stark, barren. The air grew heavier and Lander yawned, his body craving more oxygen.

Not long after they left the city behind, a second river curved into the Bec Jekesh from the right, increasing the flow, the river now running wider.

"The Bec Timur." Shahan waved toward the turbulence at the influx. "It passes near the village where your friends are."

"Yes. I know. The friends I promised to get back home."

"The young lady you care for?"

Lander looked over his shoulder, his eyes flicking to Shahan's. "Yes. The young lady I care for." Facing front again, he stuffed his frustration. "So ... why don't you tell me about this great grandmother and why I need to meet her. I've been in the Core for over two months and Becky and Michael ... well, it's not fair that they are trapped here. Will meeting her help me to help them?"

"Why did you come?"

Confusion warred with shock at the question and Lander growled. "What?"

"I heard Aurelius Hunt forced you, but that cannot be the only reason. With your gifts, you could have stopped him."

Lander gazed out to his right, back to where the Bec Timur disappeared in the darkness of the small tunnel from which it flowed. *Could I have stopped Hunt? Saved Becky and Michael before Michael was shot? Do I really care for Becky ... love her? If I did, wouldn't I have tried harder to see her?* He didn't have any answers, but Shahan's silence pressed against Lander's doubts.

"I don't know. Maybe I could have stopped Hunt. But ... I guess a part of me wanted to travel the Vortex, come through the Flux and see where my parents came from." He hesitated for a minute. "And there was the voice. I think it was my mom's but ... I don't know ... maybe it was all in my head." He chuckled at his use of words. "I..."

"But Cyanne is dead. How could you hear her?"

As the miles and hours passed, Lander confided in Shahan. The large Stone Sovereign listened with a patient understanding that calmed Lander's concerns and helped him release his doubts. In time, Lander broached the subject of the rebellion. "You're part of it, aren't you? That's why you told me about Navid and his family."

"Yes. I hoped you would understand. The chancellor and vice chancellor are not Core Dwellers. They belong on the Surface. We need to be as we were before they came. Then all had peace. All were ... equal."

"And my grandmother, is she involved? Is that why I need to meet her?"

"She prayed to Noah's God. You were called. You are the answer to her prayer."

The hissing of the boat slicing through the river and the light, steady slap and splash of the paddles masked the silence that descended on the two. Lander, lost in his thoughts, stared with unseeing eyes at the unchanging shoreline as he mechanically paddled.

An hour later, cliffs rose up on both sides of the river. The cavern closed in tight and the light coming through the Sentinel Band from the Flux weakened, illuminating the surroundings in muted shades of deepest maroon.

As the river tossed their boat and roared its protest at being channeled into the cramped tunnel, shock speared through Lander, seizing his lungs until they burned. He gulped in a shallow breath. Without warning, the narrow tunnel opened onto a high-roofed chamber, the river spilling out with force. Though not as vast as the city caverns, the sweeping expanse offered a bright and open vista. In the far distance mist shrouded a vertical, vine-laced wall.

Here, vegetation flourished in shades ranging through all the colors of the Core. Small trees bearing fruit lined the river on both sides. The air that had been heavy and hard to breathe now felt as light as that of the El'Ruhan Cavern.

"Quick now, Sovereign Lander. We must get to shore."

The small boat shivered as Shahan turned it to edge toward a small landing. Again, Shahan called for Lander's help. "The water heads to the great falls. We must leave it here."

The roar had grown so slowly, Lander didn't realize what he was hearing until Shahan's words pierced his mind. *Mist? From the falls! Whoa!* He dug his paddle in with effort and soon he and Shahan ran the stone craft up onto the landing.

CHAPTER 22

Shahan and Lander jumped from the boat, pulling it farther onto the shore. Lander wiped his hands on his trousers then looked up, his breath catching in his throat. Before him stood a line of more than two dozen Core Dwellers dressed in camouflage, armed with spears and slings. *Threat!* Instincts took over. Lander set a barrier while pulling his father's Stones from their pouch and balancing both on one palm. A spark and the beginning of a fireball formed on his other palm, he was focused and increasing the size of the flames when Shahan's shout broke through, pulling his attention.

"Lander. Stop! These are friends." Shahan walked past Lander to face the others, while speaking a rapid stream of Corish. Lander caught a few words. "Stop, our side, welcome, and then the name *Zorah.*

Allowing the flames to dissipate, Lander moved next to Shahan. Though the armed strangers obviously guarding the landing still scowled at him, mistrust evident in their tense muscles and expressions, they lowered their weapons.

A broad-shouldered woman with gray streaked dark

brown hair stepped forward. "I sorry, Shahan. Did no see it you." She inclined her head to Shahan then flicked a glance at Lander. "Come. Zorah waiting."

The muscles between Lander's shoulder blades twitched as he and Shahan followed the woman and the rest of the group fell in behind. He stifled the urge to glance over his shoulder to see how many remained by the river and how many now breathed down his neck. He hoped Shahan knew what he was doing.

As they followed a path of worn stone, half hidden by the short trees, voices flitted through the thick air. The sound grew. A break in the trees ahead allowed him his first glimpse of a small village of round, gray, stone huts. People filled the area, and as the party emerged from the trees, gathered around them. Everyone spoke at once and the rush of Corish set Lander's head to throbbing. Soon they were leading a throng of Core Dwellers as if in a kind of procession and the sense of vulnerability he had experienced when he first woke a prisoner of Aurelius Hunt settled on Lander. He didn't question his ability to protect himself if necessary, but there were so many people, armed, unarmed, children. *There's gotta be more than two hundred.*

"What is this place?" he asked Shahan as they wormed their way past tiny houses on a path that seemed to have no destination.

"It is a place ... of ... for those who seek ... escape."

"You mean a place of refuge?"

"Yes. That is the word."

They stopped in front of a larger dome. Unlike the others, this one glowed with the cinnamon hue common in the Al'Wisan Cavern. The stone door swung open and a bent, old woman with wispy, white hair stood in the opening, her weight supported by a tall staff. Though, no taller than Lander's chest, her sharp pewter eyes snared Lander's, trapping his gaze in an unbreakable hold. His mouth dropped open as a sensation of ancient power swept over him.

The woman shifted her focus to Shahan and Lander drew in a breath. *What was ... that?*

Her gaze drifted back to Lander as she spoke with Shahan. After more words, Shahan turned to Lander. "This is Cyanne's grandmother, Zorah."

Lander inclined his head as Shahan had done. "I am pleased to meet you, Zorah."

Zorah's mouth flattened into a tight line, surrounded by radiating wrinkles. "I no do Surface speak." She huffed, her gnarled fingers twisting on the staff. "Shahan. You speak for him. Come."

Inside, the house was spotless with sparce furnishings. Familiar curved walls were covered with colorful tapestries, most depicting Stone Sovereigns with glowing red Stones of Power calling up a variety of gifts; some healing, some creating bubbles of protection, others lobbing fireballs or shafts of light.

"Sit." Zorah's deep, raspy voice brooked no disobedience. Lander looked to where Shahan lowered himself onto a sofa covered in pillows and a tapestry throw. Uncertain what else to do, he followed the man's lead as Zorah eased herself down onto a well-padded chair.

A boy who Lander guessed was a couple years younger than he placed a tray with mugs and a stone pot of *ah'sim* on a low table in front of Shahan and Lander, the spicy fragrance of the warm drink permeating the air. The youth left and returned a moment later with a platter of fruit, goat cheese, and small rounds of barley bread. He spoke a few words to Zorah. She shook her head. Bowing the boy backed out of the room.

Lander had taken his first sip of the *ah'sim* when Zorah set her focus on Shahan and spoke a few words in Corish. He nodded and turned to Lander. "Like many of our older people, Zorah has not accepted the rule to speak only English—Surface Speak. I will speak between you and Zorah. Is that acceptable, Sovereign Lander?"

Lander nodded. "Yes … yes, that is acceptable.

For the next two hours, Shahan translated. Lander lost himself in Zorah's memories as she brought to life the truth of what happened sixteen years ago after Hunt and the Core Dwellers left for the Surface.

"Though none of us knew at the time, Chancellor Morrison and Vice Chancellor Jenkins had been the cause of the disease that rode the air through all caverns. All Core Dwellers trembled in fear until the Surface Dwellers convinced many younger Stone Sovereigns to work with them. They organized healings. It worked. Though many died, the sickness was conquered. But by then, the young Sovereigns had come to lust after the authority and wealth they now alone possessed.

When the older Sovereigns and Gifted refused to accept the outsiders' rule, Morrison and Jenkins sent Stone Sovereigns to kill off Stone Sovereigns who disagreed."

"Stone Sovereign against Stone Sovereign. Gifted against Gifted. No care for Ungifted." Zorah's voice broke as she spoke the words in the hated language. "This. Should. Not. Be."

Tears dribbled down Zorah's lined cheeks. Her quiet pain filled the room. Shahan could not speak for several minutes and Lander struggled to swallow past the burning lump at the back of his throat.

Shahan continued interpreting as Zorah picked up the story again. Fury built in Lander as she spoke of the affliction of the Ungifted, reduced to nothing more than slaves. The amount of suffering Hunt and his people had caused—and were still causing—in the name of self, power, and wealth staggered Lander's imagination.

For the first time, Lander understood, this was the purpose for which he had been called. For the sake of his people, it was imperative that he help send Morrison, Jenkins, and Hunt back to the Surface. And, in keeping his promise to his mother, Lander would also keep his promise to Becky and Michael. They too belonged on the Surface.

Becky and Michael had been living with Ungifted, sharing their low status and difficulties for more than two months. Would they understand Lander's need to confront Morrison and Jenkins before keeping the promise he made to them? Knowing Becky's heart, he had no doubt she would accept his decision. Michael too.

Shahan continued. "By now, many Gifted and Ungifted have joined Zorah and the few remaining loyal Stone Sovereigns. Some, like Castor who now speaks to El'Ruhan, stay in their home caverns. Others come here. They hide and wait for time of rebellion."

Zorah reached out and placed her veined hand on Lander's knee. His attention swept down to the warm, worn fingers then up to meet her intense eyes. The hint of a smile crinkled the skin around them. "I ... see ... Cyanne ... you." Without taking her focus off Lander, she spoke to Shahan in Corish.

He translated. "Zorah asks for Cyanne's Stones of Power."

Discomfort tightened Lander's chest. Though Zorah was his mother's grandmother, the thought of handing his Stones to anyone incited a sudden flow of adrenaline. They were personal, linked to him. The bond had grown even stronger since coming to the Core. But as he stared into Zorah's eyes, he released his breath and his concern. Understanding spoke from the deep depths of those wise eyes.

Trust, Lander.

Eyes still locked with Zorah's, Lander reached into the pouch at his waist and pulled out all four Stones. Pulsing in shades of red and blue, they glowed, the light drawing Lander's attention. The accustomed weight familiar on his palms, he pulled peace from the connection.

"Gud. Gud." Zorah smiled. Nodding she held out her hands.

Taking care to not drop the weighty Stones, Lander placed the two red gems on the outstretched palms.

Zorah's eyes closed. Her breath slow and deep, she flexed her fingers. The Stones flared, their deep crimson light brighter and stronger than any Lander had been capable of producing. Though he had grown accustomed to being hailed as one of the strongest Stone Sovereigns, Lander was now forced to swallow back feelings of inadequacy. Whatever connection he thought he had with his mother's Stones, it paled in comparison with what he now witnessed.

Zorah blinked, then met Lander's gaze. She smiled and nodded, signaling him to reach out for the Stones as their illumination reduced to normal levels.

Lander slipped his father's Stones into the pouch. He stretched out a hand, but then pulled back. "I … can't." Swallowing back his disappointment, he said, "They belong with you."

Nostrils flaring, Zorah gave a quick shake of her head and again shook her hands. Lander leaned in to take one Stone, but Zorah grunted.

"Place your hands over the Stones. Do not take them." Shahan's words sunk in and Lander placed first one hand then the other over the bright gems.

Zorah grunted approval. She blinked her eyes several times until Lander got the message and closed his. Warmth spread from Lander's fingertips through his body to the tips of his toes and the top of his head. The temperature increased and Lander feared the heat would singe his fingers. Then Zorah pushed the Stones up into Lander's palms and release them. Gasping at the sudden shift, he clutched them so they wouldn't fall. His eyes popped open in time to see Zorah collapse against the back of her chair.

Dizziness swept over Lander. He shoved the now dark Stones into his pouch, then rose to check on Zorah, wobbling, uncertain his jellylike legs could hold him.

"*Shiviah-sor.*" Shahan jumped up and pushed Lander back onto the couch, then went to Zorah. "I will see to her. You must not rise."

"What just happened?" Lander asked. "What did she do?"

Slow, soft Corish issued from Zorah and her eyes blinked open. Shahan knelt next to her chair, nodding at her quiet words. A moment later, he sprang up and fetched her mug of *ah'sim*, holding it for her as she took a couple sips. She waved him away, and he set her mug on the low table before returning to his seat next to Lander.

Lander's vertigo fading, his need for answers pushed him to turn to Shahan. "Okay. Now tell me, what just happened."

The man's eyes flicked from Lander to Zorah whose lids drooped shut as she crossed her arms and nodded. "Zorah ... bless ... you. She prayed to Noah's God for his help for a long time. For our people. Now you are here. She bless ... blessed the bond. She has released the Stones full to you."

Pressure settled on Lander as the realization of what had just happened sunk in. "What next?"

One of Shahan's rare smiles lit his face. "We meet with Castor and the others and prepare to face Chancellor Morrison and Vice Chancellor Jenkins." The smile waivered. "We will face those Stone Sovereigns still loyal to them. It will be difficult."

"Well, Pop-pop Ian used to say nothing worthwhile comes for free."

Lander glanced over at Zorah snoring lightly on her chair, a look filled with peace melting years from her face.

"Ready to go now?" Shahan questioned Lander with his eyes.

"If you are."

Shahan's smile surfaced again. "Let us go."

Lander rose. His heart warmed as he looked at the lightly snoring woman—his great grandmother. He leaned down and placed a gentle kiss on her cheek. "I hope we get a chance to talk some more … Grandma."

CHAPTER 23

Becky skirted the village where the Stone Sovereigns gathered once the Ungifted were locked in for the night. Stories of attacks filtered through the work camp and she had seen first-hand the aftereffects of such abuse. She had no desire to provoke some testosterone-laden male into doing something stupid.

Rounding a stone outcropping she gasped as a shadowy figure tackled her from the side.

"Becks?"

Her breath hissed out in a stream of relief from between clenched teeth. "Michael. You scared me. Don't sneak around."

His silence sent a shaft of anxiety through her until he whispered, "look who's talking. Like we don't all sneak around after lights out these days."

"Have you heard anything, Michael? Is Shahan coming tonight to tell us what's happening in Shavah Al'Wisan?"

"Sorry about running into you, but I can't talk now Becks. Come on."

Michael took off at a rapid sprint. With her heart already pumping from the scare and Michael's manner, Becky followed. The two flew from shadow to shadow, making their way to the meeting cave. As they got closer, Becky's eyes snagged on numerous slower moving shadows. By the looks of things, this meeting would be the best attended so far.

Electing Castor as head of the United Core Dwellers had been a wise decision. A natural leader, he breathed new life into the UCD rebellion that sought to expel the Surface Dwellers and return the political structure of the Core to the way it was before Morrison and Jenkins had wrested control from the guilds and elders.

A strident voice echoed off the walls as Becky and Michael slipped up the short tunnel. "There is no choice. Stone Sovereigns must be summoned, Castor. Three dead. Three! We cannot handle the Jerr'as alone."

"Please, keep your voice down." Castor motioned in a calming gesture as Becky emerged from the tunnel into the tiny cavern. A wall of heat and the mixed odors of food and tightly packed bodies smacked her in the face. She blocked her nose with her hand and started breathing through her mouth.

The man continued in a softer voice. "The Sovereigns here are young and useless. We must contact Shavah Al'Wisan and ask for help."

Heads around the room nodded in agreement.

"I know the fear these Jerr'as attacks are causing." Castor scanned the crowd. "But if we take this step, we will need to stop United Core Dweller activities until the Sovereigns leave. The timing here will threaten the whole rebellion. We are so close to putting our plan into action."

"But what good is gaining our freedom if we die in Jerr'as attacks?" a large-boned woman standing beside a light stick asked from along the back wall.

Grumbles of agreement spread like wildfire through the people creating a loud buzz in the cave.

"*Shiviah-zor.*" Michael grabbed Becky's hand and pulled her with him as he shoved his way to the front of the crowd. "Castor. We need to talk. Now."

Castor's gaze shifted to Michael; he nodded, then spoke to the group again. "If you will be patient. Please, give me a minute."

Castor motioned for Michael and Becky to join him as he stepped into a small alcove where they could have some privacy. He turned to face them. "What's wrong, Michael?"

"Talon and the others … they're gone. Two teams of Stone Sovereigns—and I don't mean cadets—barged into our quarters and took them. It looked like they were heading toward the Al'Wisan Cavern by way of the Bec Timur tunnel."

Castor's jaw dropped. He snapped it shut and licked his lips. "*Shiviah-zor.*" Though barely whispered, the Corish curse word carried the weight of Castor's fear and frustration.

"What are we going to do now?" Michael punched the wall, then grimaced and cradled his right hand in his left.

Catching sight of his bloody knuckles in the flickering light Becky suppressed the urge to punch a wall and swear herself as a shudder raced up her spine.

A measure of hope dawned in Michael's eyes. "They didn't take the guns. And you still have the two we experimented with, don't you?"

Castor shook his head, his mouth drawn into a flat line. He ran curled fingers through his beard. "Yeah, I have them. And the ammunition I created from gems. But losing Talen and his experienced soldiers is a fatal blow to our plans. No one here has experience with firearms. And, as it is, we have too few Sovereigns willing to help us. Once they learn we no longer have the Surface Dweller soldiers' help we…" He pulled in a breath, his brow crinkling in thought. "Why would they take the soldiers now. We were so close."

Becky's mind raced. "Could they have a spy?"

Castor lipped his mustache. "That is a good question. I can't imagine anyone from here betraying us. I trust Shahan and he gave me his word every Stone Sovereign he enlisted is committed to returning the Core to self-rule. But anything is possible. It wouldn't be the first time a spy turned the outcome of a rebellion."

"Well, what do we do now?" Michael picked at the torn skin on his knuckles, his body bouncing with pent up energy. "I mean, can we use the guns and work with the Sovereigns who don't desert us?" His brows drew down. "That's assuming Talen doesn't … you know … rat us out."

"I need to think things through before we make any moves. Right now, I have to explain what has happened." He glanced over his shoulder then turned his attention back to Becky and Michael. "Were you two planning to stay for the Bible study?"

Both nodded.

"Good. I think we need to pray. So many Core Dwellers are embracing the truth of Noah's God—funny, I still think of him as Noah's God, not my own. This delay is going to be a stumbling block for some, I think. Your presence at the meeting will be a big help.

"Of course," Becky said. "I planned on attending anyway."

"Sure." Michael nodded. "Me too."

Michael bounced on his feet as they headed toward the sleeping quarters a couple hours later. Though the Bible study had gone well, with Castor teaching from the book of Colossians, as soon as they walked out of the tunnel, Michael's frustration found an outlet in unceasing movement.

Becky suppressed the urge to grab his arm and force him to stop. She shared his irritation. The UCD's plan to kidnap Morrison, Jenkins, and Hunt and transport all the Surface Dwellers through the Avortex hinged on the cooperation of Talen and his men as well as Shahan's Stone Sovereigns. With the soldiers taken, Michael's and her chance to get home just vanished like a morning fog in sunlight. *God. I miss morning fog. I miss sunrises and sunsets. I want to go home.*

Michael kicked at a loose stone and Becky gritted her teeth. "Stop it, Michael. Just stop. You aren't the only one this affects." She blinked back burning tears. "I've been counting on this working ever since Castor and Shahan came up with the idea."

A sob broke through her determination to be strong. Michael turned and wrapped his arms around Becky's shoulders. "Ah, Becks, I'm sorry. I know this is hard on you."

She swiped a sleeve under her nose and sniffed. "I'm sorry, too, Michael. If it wasn't for me, you wouldn't even be here." She pulled away from his friendly comfort, wrapped her own arms around her waist, and started forward again. "I'm scared, Michael. I haven't been this scared since we first came to the Core. Think about it. What if there is a spy in the UCD? What does that do to our chances to get home?"

Becky's eyes widened and she pulled in a gasp of air as three forms broke from behind the house they were passing. Two held glowing Stones of Power. Though she didn't recognize two of the approaching Sovereigns, the third sent a shiver skittering up her spine. Kaleb Deklakh.

"*Shiviah-zor.*" The curse hissed from between Michael's clenched teeth as he pushed Becky behind him. "What do you want, Kaleb?"

The three fanned out around Michael. Kaleb stopped a

couple feet in front of Michael. "Who told you to speak, Ungifted? You need to learn your place."

"She is different. Are these the ones you told me about?" The words drew Becky's attention to the Sovereign on her right. Bulkier than Kaleb, he wore a deep maroon uniform with a more ornate insignia on the collar of his cloak. He brandished Stones that reminded Becky of Lander's mother's stones, red and sparking flecks of fire.

"Yes. Darrius. They are Lander's Surface Dweller friends." Kaleb's eyes flicked from Michael to Becky. The raw hunger in them pulled fear into her throat and she reached out to wrap fingers around Michael's arm. His tense muscles felt like rock.

A muscle bunched in Michael's jaw. "You were part of the group who took Hunt's people a few hours ago. What are you doing back here now?"

Darrius laughed. "None of your business, Ungifted. But we would like to get better acquainted with your pretty little friend."

"Not happening." Michael's words came out in the form of a deep growl.

"Come on, Michael. Let's just keep going." Becky tugged on his immovable arm.

"Come on, Michael," Kaleb mocked in a high-pitched voice. "Listen to the girl and go on back to your quarters. We will make sure she gets back to hers soon enough."

Michael stepped back into Becky as the Sovereigns to either side moved in closer. With a swift shift in his weight, he shoved Becky away. "Go Becky. Run."

She blinked back her fear. Seeing the mix of determination and grief on his face, Becky turned from her friend and sprinted back toward the meeting cave, yelling, "Castor! Help! Somebody! Anybody! Help!"

A large group people who must have been on their way back to their sleeping quarters were already moving toward her when she heard Michael's scream. Her heart thudded as if to crush her lungs and she slid to a stop. *Oh God, no! Please no! Not Michael!*

She fisted her hands and forgot to breathe as she pivoted, her focus on the spot where three Stone Sovereigns stood, their attention now on the crowd of people approaching. Michael lay on the ground, still. Becky pulled in a gulp of air and swallowed past a boulder sized burning in her throat as Castor barreled past her. On numb feet, she made her way back to fall on her knees next to Michael.

At seeing a small circle of burned material and red flesh on Michael's chest, still smoking, a moan started, worked its way through her lips, then swelled into an anguished scream.

"What have you done?" Castor spit out the angry words as he slammed into Kaleb. "You idiot. Stupid, blind idiot." He smashed a heavy fist into the young Stone Sovereign's gut, sending him sprawling and his Stones flying.

As if coming out of shock, Darrius aimed his Stones at Castor. "Stop. Now."

Castor straightened up to his full height and shifted his stormy eyes to Darrius. "Or what? You'll kill me?" He waved his arms at the surrounding people. "Kill us all?" He shook his head. "You may be good, Sovereign, but you're not that good."

Angry murmuring filtered through the violence-laden air but despite the tense activity around her, Becky's only thoughts were for Michael. A moan escaped his lips as she lifted his head and slid beneath, lowering it to her lap. His eyes fluttered open. "Becks?"

"Yeah, Michael. It's me."

She grabbed his chilly hand and kissed it, then lifted her gaze to find the third Stone Sovereign standing over her, his jaw hanging open. "Please. You are a Stone Sovereign so I know you can help. Please help my friend."

The man shook his head. "We did not mean—"

"I don't care what you *meant* … I know what you *meant*, but now you need to act like a Stone Sovereign, like my friend Lander." Becky gritted out the words her muddled brain sent to her mouth as she battled an overwhelming need to scream. "Lander would be down here next to me doing his best to save his friend. Now, do it!"

He made to take a step toward Becky, but Darrius called out, "Varro. We leave must go. Leave him."

"No!" Becky screamed. "You cannot do this and run. Stay and heal him. If you do not, I will make certain everyone will know Stone Sovereigns are cowards and liars."

Darrius took two steps toward Becky, fury written on every line of his face. Before he could take another step, a crowd of Core Dwellers pushed between him and Becky.

He scanned them with a look of repugnance. "You will pay for this, Ungifted. The next time you call for help because Jerr'as are threatening, do not expect us to come." His gaze met Becky's briefly, then shifted onto Varro. "The Ungifted is beyond help. We must go."

"But." Unexpected softness filtered into Kaleb's voice. "He is not Ungifted. He is Surface Dweller."

Darrius sliced the air with his hand. "It does not matter. We are Stone Sovereigns. Who will question us?"

Varro looked down on Becky, sorrow written in his eyes. "I am sorry." With a final glance at Michael, he followed Darrius and Kaleb as they made their way back toward Shavah El'Ruhan.

Michael's breath coming in uneven gasps, Becky cradled his head and looked up at Castor. "What do we do now. You have to help him."

CHAPTER 24

Aurelius Hunt stretched his legs out and a relaxed sigh slipped through his lips. His trip to the Core certainly didn't work out as he had planned, and yet, perhaps the current circumstances might work even better. He pulled in a deep breath of moisture-laden Mist Rise air and scanned the orchard that covered the slope leading to the Bec Jekesh. Taking a sip of his now-cold *ah'sim* he wrinkled his nose at the thick sweetness of the tea-like brew.

He leaned toward the table to ring the bell that would call a servant when Ryan Jenkins stepped out onto the Overlook. "Enjoying yourself, Aurelius?"

Hunt snorted. "More so now than when I experienced your *hospitality.*"

"You're still not over that? It's been months. And I did apologize."

"I suppose you are right. It was a unique experience for me. Something I will never forget; even if I forgive you."

Morrison plopped into the chair opposite Hunt's. "You deserved it."

"I suppose so. I'm just gratified that we can set aside our misunderstanding and come to terms with how to handle Morrison."

"Yes. Ever since he started getting sick and the Sovereigns couldn't help him, he's changed. He's been talking about returning control to the elders and guilds for the last six months." Jenkins poured a mug of *ah'sim*, took a sip and grimaced. "This is awful."

He rang the tiny bell and a few seconds later, a young girl with her hair tied up in a ponytail, wearing the tan garb of an Ungifted, stepped into the doorway. "Yes, sir?"

"Take this away. It's cold. Bring us something stronger."

She inclined her head and with a quiet efficiency, gathered the mugs and pot onto a tray she had retrieved from on the wall near the table, and carried the offending *ah'sim* toward the doorway.

"And bring us some fruit as well."

The girl turned and inclined her head again. Jenkins sighed his frustration and waved her out. He strode to the half-wall at the far side of the Overlook and stood at what Hunt suspected was parade rest. The man had always been military in his bearing.

Hunt examined his fingernails. *Shivah-zor! I need a manicure. It'll be one of the first things I do when I get back to the Surface.*

Elam came in place of the girl a few minutes later with a new tray. Thin stone tumblers sat around a pitcher of fruit wine and a bowl of fresh fruit. He placed the tray on the table next to Hunt and bowed, meeting Hunt's gaze. Elam looked to Jenkins as if expecting more orders. When Jenkins ignored him, he lowered his gaze to the floor for a minute before turning and exiting the Overlook.

Hunt poured a drink and took a sip. "Ah. That's much better. Ryan, come, sit. We need to talk."

Jenkins returned to the table and again took his seat across from Hunt, pouring himself a tumbler of wine and filling a small plate with fruit.

Hunt cleared his throat and waited. When Jenkins looked up, Hunt said, "My men. Are they coming?"

Jenkins slipped a sliver of apricot into his mouth and chewed. "My Sovereigns left to pick them up two Mist Rises ago. They should be arriving next Mist Rise. Morrison is in no state to protest our actions at this point, and I have several Ungifted ready to transport him. It should go smoothly. In a handful of Mist Rises, we will be on our way to Shavah Deklakh. Soon after, you will return home and I will have complete control of the Core."

"And with Morrison gone and your control of amenable Stone Sovereigns intact, we will make use of the Vortex and Avortex on ... shall we say ... a monthly basis?"

"I should have done it years ago."

Aurelius's icy blue eyes zeroed in on Jenkins. "Yes. You laid all the blame on me, but nothing stopped you from returning to the surface."

Jenkins sighed and downed the wine in his tumbler before reaching for the carafe and refilling it. "True. But it took longer than we expected to gain the level of control Phil and I wanted. By that time, it just didn't seem worth it. Why would I want to return to a menial job on the Surface if I can be a king down here?"

Hunt nodded. "Yes. Why would you?"

Jenkins cast a narrow-eyed gaze at Hunt. "I need to ask you something that has bothered me for the last sixteen years. How did you come up with that virus? I didn't know you were experimenting with biological warfare weapons."

Hunt leaned back and allowed a sly grin to emerge. "Ah yes. The virus. I wondered when that would come up.

"That virus didn't start out as a virus. It was supposed to be an insecticide. A good one. But sunlight killed the pathogen. What good is an insecticide that doesn't work in sunlight?

"So, I decided to reformulate it and experiment with it on

those kinds of organisms that never see the light. The ones that grow deep in caves. Remember? When Sullivan came back carrying a large lump of pure gold and spouting off about cave writing? That's when I had you and Morrison put together the team. We spent two weeks exploring deeper into the cave system before anything happened.

"Imagine my surprise when we came face to face with Ian. Of course, his name wasn't Ian, remember? It was Abiasaphel'ian or some such nonsense. But I could never pronounce it so nicknamed him Ian and the name stuck."

Jenkins nodded. "Yeah. That's right. I remember. Then you left Phil and me here with instructions to try and take control." He smiled and raised his glass in a salute. "Here's to our new partnership."

The trip up the Bec Jekesh to Shavah Al'Wisan took three times longer than the trip down. Shahan kept the boat close to the shoreline where the current ran with less force. Lander thought they would have made better time if they got out and pulled the boat upstream. Shahan nixed that idea with warnings that Jerr'as liked to prowl the shores along that stretch looking for unwary travelers doing just that. Lander thought his arms would fall off as the necessity to paddle never eased. If they slowed their efforts, the flow pushed them back. Turning the boat to position the bow upstream again, Shahan and Lander paddled even harder to make up the lost distance.

The trickiest part was working their way past the point where the Bec Timur flowed into the Bec Jekesh. Despite the threat of Jerr'as, Shahan had pulled to shore and attached ropes to the bow and stern of the craft. The two walked along the uneven, rocky shoreline, pulling the small boat while scanning for Jerr'as. But Shahan knew what he was doing so even when things got a little scary, Lander trusted him. A short while later, they drew the craft in, untied the ropes, and hopping in, resumed paddling.

By the time they docked, Lander had decided he never wanted to see another paddle for as long as he lived. Shahan threw a rope to an Ungifted dockworker who tied the boat while Shahan and Lander jumped onto the dock. Leaving the river behind, they turned onto the main thoroughfare and headed toward Lander's new home. They were walking through the busiest part of the city when a young cadet huffed up to them. "I finally ... found ... you." She leaned over, rested her hands on her knees, and pulled in several gulps of air. "Chancellor Morrison is looking for you." Another deep breath and the young lady pulled herself upright. "He wants to see you. Both of you."

Shahan nodded. "We will freshen then go see him."

"No." The cadet's eyes went wide. "He said now."

"I will not meet until I have cleanup. You. You go tell Chancellor Morrison, Stone Sovereigns Lander and Shahan will join him soon."

Though Shahan spoke the words in a soft voice, their force was unmistakable. The young cadet's mouth hung open as she bobbed her head several times in quick succession. Snapping her mouth shut, the girl took off in the direction of Morrison's mansion.

"My home is far," Shahan said. "I will cleanup at your home."

"Sure ... um. It's just that ... I don't remember the way."

"This is fine, Lander. I will lead."

Nearly an hour later, they arrived at Lander's mansion. Navid greeted them at the door while Olive and Anah scrambled to get food on the table.

"Don't bother." Guilt seeped through Lander as the three

stared at him, frozen like statues in mid action, the aromas of spicy lamb stew and baked bread filtering from the kitchen.

"Have we disappointed you?" Navid asked, his hands folded at his chest. "What do you require?"

"No." Lander choked. "No. You have done nothing disappointing ... to disappoint me. It's just that Chancellor Morrison has summoned us, and we need to wash and change before going. So ... though it's great you got food ready ... and I appreciate it ... we don't have time to eat."

A thread of suspicion wormed through Lander when, though he was talking, Navid's eyes were locked on Shahan.

"It is well, Navid." The big Stone Sovereign's gaze met Lander's then flicked back to Navid. "He has met Zorah."

Navid's clasped hands tightened, his knuckles turning white. "And did he—"

"No." Shahan interrupted. "We have not yet. Coming upriver is ... distracting. Be at peace. I will speak with him soon. Now, please, help us to freshen."

Lander felt as if he was watching a play he didn't understand and irritation at being left out simmered in his stomach. Maybe now wasn't the time to confront Shahan, but Lander wouldn't let it go either. It hadn't taken him long to realize Shahan's agenda, but he was tired of being kept in the dark.

"Where's the bathtub?" Lander growled.

He suppressed the urge to scream when Navid just stared at him again.

"The bathing chamber." Shahan explained.

Understanding blossomed in Navid's eyes. "Oh. Yes, sir. The bathing chamber is this way."

Still coming to terms with the luxury this dwelling represented, Lander lowered his achy body into the hot-spring-fed pool that served as a bathtub. When Shahan slid in across from him, Lander allowed his swirling emotions to drive him and he remained silent. He washed in a burst of nervous energy.

Ignoring his protesting muscles, he climbed the four steps out of the water and snatched up one of the bulky, cream-colored towels to dry himself. Though his mind warned him he was being unreasonable, he allowed his self-righteous resentment full sway. It just felt right to cut himself a break and release some of what he had bottled inside for the last several weeks. If Shahan happened to get the brunt of his anger, so be it. The man had broad shoulders.

Lander found a clean uniform set out on one of the chairs. A tray of fresh fruit, a pot of *ah'sim*, and a maroon mug waited for him on the small round table against the wall. The shutters, closed partway, allowed a low level of light into the room. His eyes shifted upward to his bedroom and he released a groan. *O to sleep. Yeah. Right.*

Guilt sent tendrils of common sense through his swelling anger. Shahan didn't deserve Lander's antagonism. And yet, Lander experienced a peculiar pleasure in the situation. After pouring a mug of *ah'sim* he gulped down a mouthful, wrinkling his nose as he swallowed the thick sweetness. He popped a couple figs into his mouth, finished toweling dry, and donned the uniform. His fingers did the work of a comb, pulling knots out of his hair. Another quick gulp went down as well as several slices of apricot, then he walked out of the room. He sprinted down the stairs to find Shahan already dressed and waiting by the front door.

Ignoring Shahan, Lander yanked the door open and took to the path at a rapid pace. Shahan followed. Neither spoke. That was fine with Lander. He clung to his self-righteous anger like a security blanket, wrapping himself in the resentment surfacing from behind the wall he constructed back on Zephryn Island and had continued to fortify over the past eight weeks. Warm, comforting. Easier than accepting responsibility for Becky's and Michael's situation or keeping his promise to his mom; easier than admitting he enjoyed the admiration of his peers. Oh yes, it was much easier to feed the anger than allow the guilt to surface.

CHAPTER 25

Lander and Shahan were crossing the Bec Jekesh when Shahan brought up a subject Lander wished he could bury.

"Aurelius Hunt will be with Chancellor Morrison. You have a history."

Setting his mouth in a flat line, Lander marched forward. The weightless air stirred. *Misfadura,* the Core's equivalent of night, when the residual moisture still left from Mist Rise dissipated, was setting in. He pulled in a deep breath savoring the fragrance of fruit tree blossoms on the light breeze.

He sucked in a breath, his hands curving into fists, when Shahan grabbed his shoulder and spun him around. Shahan's expression matched Lander's. Anger. Lander took a step back. Shahan, the calm center in any situation, faced Lander with a storm brewing in his eyes.

"Your anger makes you weak. Aurelius Hunt and Vice Chancellor Jenkins will see it and use it to mani ... manip ... control you." Shahan's gaze pierced Lander. "You must release this ... anger."

"Is that what you and Zorah were talking about? All that Corish I couldn't understand?"

"Some. There is much you do not know. I fear your emotions will betray those you wish to help."

"So? What? Are you telling me I don't have the right to be angry?"

"No. I am telling you, do not let your anger out when meet now."

Shahan's words sunk in. He was right. Like surfacing from a stream of ice water, Lander emerged from the swirling depths where he'd allowed the fury to take him. A shiver ran through him. *Where had that come from? I'm angry. Yeah. Sure. But this is just … out of control.*

Lander.

Whoa no! I'm hearing voices again.

Lander. Please. I need you.

"No. No. No. This is not happening."

Concern lowered Shahan's brows. "Lander? What is wrong?"

"I think I'm going crazy. It's like I can hear Becky calling … in my head."

Shahan stared until Lander shook his head. "I'm fine."

The large Sovereign turned and took two steps from Lander. His tunic taut across the tension filled muscles of his back. "You must understand, Lander, I have kept … things … from you. But the time for secrets is past. After we meet with Vice Chancellor Jenkins, I must tell you more of what is happening."

Lander's jaw dropped. "Now? You drop this on me now? When we're about to meet with Jenkins and Hunt? And I'm hearing voices?" He threw his hands in the air. "Great timing."

"It is not great timing. It is bad."

"Yes, Shahan. That was tongue in cheek."

Lander nearly laughed at the confused expression on Sha-han's face. "Means, I meant the opposite of what the words said."

"Why?"

"Doesn't matter. Are you finally going to tell me your part of this rebellion to return rule to the elders and guilds and gain rights for the Ungifted?

Once again, Lander almost laughed at the look on Shahan's face. "I'm not stupid, you know. We can talk about this later at my place."

"Yes. That would be good."

Lander breathed a sigh of relief. The remainder of the walk passed without the earlier tension between him and Shahan. He respected the Sovereign and his abilities, especially when he learned Shahan was more than two hundred and fifty years old. Though not nearly as old as Zorah, Shahan possessed a wealth of knowledge. Disquiet at his earlier anger settled in Lander's gut.

Reaching Morrison's mansion, Lander strode up the stairs to the entry with Shahan behind. Two cadets stationed at the double doors opened both sides without saying a word. Lander and Shahan walked in, down the empty hallway, and up the stairs to the second floor and the Overlook. Shahan slipped ahead of Lander and Lander bumped into the big Sovereign when he pulled to an abrupt stop.

"*Shiviah-zor!*" Though nothing more than a released breath of a whisper, Lander caught Shahan's word and the shock in his voice.

Stepping to Shahan's side, Lander pulled in a breath. Jenkins and Hunt sat at the small table on the far side of the Overlook. Talen and the other guards were seated at a larger table beside the outside wall near the olive trees. Darrius, his team, Kaleb, and several other Sovereigns Lander didn't recognize stood along the inner wall; Stones of Power already in their hands glowed with soft light.

A hand pushed Lander from behind. Deolah. She and her team crowded in behind Lander and Shahan forcing the two deeper onto the Outlook.

Jenkins pushed up onto his feet, his focus locked on Shahan. "Sovereign Shahan. Please hand your Stones of Power over to Captain Darrius."

Friction sparked between Jenkins and Shahan like a thick rope, unraveling and stretched to the breaking point. Darrius stepped away from the wall, passed Lander, and took up a position facing Shahan. "We have been friends and teammates for a long time, Shahan. Do not make this more difficult."

Shahan's gaze moved from Jenkins to Darrius. He blinked, then nodded. With slow movements, he fetched his Stones from their pouch and handed them to his captain.

"Very good." Jenkins said.

Turning his attention back to Jenkins, Shahan asked, "where is Chancellor Morrison?"

Jenkins nodded. "Yes. You would ask about him." Jenkins turned and walked to the wall overlooking the orchard covered slope. He stood silent for a moment, pulling in several deep breaths before turning back. "Chancellor Morrison is ill. In fact, he is so ill, we have decided to return him to the Surface for medical help."

"We?" Shahan asked.

A mirthless smile tipped the corners of Jenkins's mouth though his eyes remained cold and serious. "Mr. Hunt and I have come to an … understanding. He, his men, and Darrius's team will return to the Surface with Chancellor … no, make that ex-chancellor Morrison—I believe that title is mine now. Of course, you will not be part of that team effort."

"No!" The word slipped from Lander without thought. But once it was out, he continued. "If they are going to the Surface, I want to go too. I need to take Becky and Michael back."

Jenkins didn't acknowledge Lander's outburst but continued to stare at Shahan. "Did you think I didn't know what you and Morrison were up to?" He moved closer to Shahan until they were almost nose to nose. "That you were conspiring with Morrison to send *me* back to the Surface? I know what you've been planning with that old witch woman at the end of the cavern and those so-called rebels.

"Unfortunately for you, you underestimated me, *Sovereign* Shahan. And now you will pay the price for your treacherous actions. Your Stones of Power belong to me. Your rank is stripped. And if you are remembered at all, it will be as one of the Ungifted. Those you called friends and teammates, the ones you have betrayed, have been given orders to take you to the dark tunnels beyond the Bec Jekesh where you will be left bound, unarmed, and alone. We will see how well you fare against Jerr'as under those circumstances, traitor."

The entire time Jenkins spoke, his voice never rose. Though he didn't shout, Lander shivered at the evil infecting his words.

Jenkins waved at Kaleb. "Take him away. Burn his uniform, dress him in Ungifted garb. Lock him in a cell in the Cadet Quarters until Darrius and his team return and my orders can be carried out … with malice."

"Wait," Lander took a step forward and reached to grab Jenkins's arm. Before he could touch Jenkins, however, hands seized him from both sides, pulling him back. Deolah shifted to his front and with quick actions, opened Lander's pouch and pulled out all four Stones. Lander struggled to break away but could only watch as Deolah handed his Stones of Power to Hunt.

Lander stopped struggling as a weight of despair lodged in his stomach. Darrius, Kaleb, and Deolah pushed Shahan toward the door, but he resisted long enough to speak to Lander. "Do not doubt the words Zorah spoke."

And then, Shahan was gone. Lander lifted his eyes to see Hunt staring at him with a curious expression. He wanted to plant his fist in the man's face; he would wait. The time would come when he could smash the hated countenance. When, he didn't know, but the time would come. That Lander promised himself.

Jenkins had taken his seat opposite Hunt again. He took a sip of whatever he was drinking, pulled in a satisfied breath, and released it through his nose before looking at the remaining Sovereigns. "You may leave us now."

Once he was released, Lander backed up to the inner wall as the others filed past him and exited the Overlook. The solid rocks grounded him, holding his rising panic at bay.

Hunt nodded to Talen. "You, too. Wait for me in the lower dining hall."

Lander pressed closer into the solid support at his back as Talen and his men walked out.

"Well, Lander, it seems we find ourselves once again in familiar circumstances." Hunt motioned for Lander to take a seat at the table.

Lander almost refused, but curiosity squelched the urge. He moved to the table and sat in one of the two empty chairs, his mind already spinning, churning out plans to rescue Shahan, escape to the El'Ruhan Cavern where he would collect Becky and Michael, and then … home. He didn't think past that, refused to consider how he might help his people. For now, all that mattered was saving Shahan and getting his friends to the Surface.

Playing Hunt's game, Lander sat quietly waiting for whatever Hunt and Jenkins might reveal.

Jenkins set his mug on the table with an audible clunk. "Lander. Let me be frank. The fact is, I have no one else with the abilities you possess. If you are willing to pledge your support of my Chancellorship, Aurelius and I have agreed you may retain your status as a Stone Sovereign and remain in the Core."

Jenkins held up his hand as if to stop Lander from speaking. "This is a one-time offer. And it lasts only until second Mist Rise when Aurelius leaves for the Surface, so think about it before you say anything."

Lander's gaze shifted to Hunt. The man's unfocused stare turned Lander's blood cold and he set his attention back on Jenkins, who was still making a play for Lander's support. "If you remain in the Core, you will be given authority over all the Company of Stone Sovereigns; you will out rank Kaleb and even Darrius. The house you now live in will be yours permanently. You can have your choice of Ungifted servants. Any young woman who meets your eye, whether she is Gifted or not, will be yours for the taking. And you will receive honor. Think about it boy, unlimited power and wealth. It is an excellent offer."

Jenkins turned to Hunt, his eyes seeking out the man's acknowledgment. Hunt nodded. "Yes. The offer is more than fair. If I were you, I would take it." He pursed his lips, scanned the orchard below. "However, I must admit I'd prefer it if you rejected Ryan's offer."

Jenkins laughed. "Of course you would. Because, you see, Lander. If you reject my offer, you will be allowed to return to the Surface along with Aurelius and his people ... as their prisoner."

Hunt spoke up. "As you can imagine, setting you free on the Surface where you can run to the authorities could create rather a difficult situation for me. So, these are your choices. Remain here and work with Mr. Jenkins to keep order in the Core and be a hero to your people; or, return to your cell on my island."

Lander snorted. "Yeah. Right." He lowered his gaze to his hands resting on the table, his fingers twining in and out. He glanced back up at Hunt. "What about my friends? What happens to them?"

"If you elect to remain in the Core, we will escort them back to Zephryn Island and arrange transportation for them to return home."

"Aren't you afraid they will go to the authorities?"

"I am confident, once they understand the need for silence in order to protect you and the Core, they will cooperate. This whole time, these messy last couple months will fade from memory and life will go on as before. I will even arrange for the two to be offered full scholarships at the university of their choosing."

"So, you see, Lander." Jenkins picked up the conversation. "Your decision will affect not only you, but your friends' future as well."

Lander licked his lips. "And Shahan. Can I help him?"

Hunt narrowed his eyes at Lander. "Turning into quite the negotiator, aren't you? Well, that would be up to Ryan. What do you think, Ryan?"

"The man is a traitor and deserves his sentence. But perhaps we could negotiate a less harsh punishment."

"You see, Lander, the decision that you make is very important."

Lander nodded; his brow furrowed in thought. "How do I know you will keep your word? I mean, after everything, how can I trust you two?"

Hunt tented his fingers and rested the two pointer fingers against his lips. Shifting his hands down to the table, he nodded. "I see your dilemma. I can give you nothing more than my word. But I give that freely."

"Well, what's your answer?" Jenkins pushed.

"I ... I'll need time to think ... and a suggestion. You want me to trust you. Okay, I'll go along with that if you do one thing for me."

"Yes?" Jenkins leaned forward.

"Show that you trust me. Return my Stones."

Hunt laughed outright. "Well played, Lander. Well played."

Lander struggled to not let his jaw drop open when Aurelius Hunt pulled all four Stones from the pocket into which he had deposited them. He placed them on the table in front of Lander. "They are yours."

CHAPTER 26

Fully expecting Hunt to have him seized and his Stones of Power taken, Lander worked to cap the compulsion to run from the Outlook, down the stairs, and shoot through the streets of Shavah El'Wisan and disappear. Instead, suspecting another Stone Sovereign trailed him, Lander took his time leaving the mansion, then meandered through the streets eventually landing at his home.

Navid greeted him at the door with an offer of food, but his swirling thoughts made no room for anything except the need to rescue Shahan, Becky, and Michael, and escape the Core.

"Is Sovereign Shahan not with you?" Navid asked as he leaned out the door and his eyes scanned the street behind Lander.

Lander's thoughts collided. "Wait." He yanked Navid in and turned the man to face him. "You're part of it ... with Shahan ... the rebellion." He didn't ask. He stated the fact that stared him in the face. "Yeah. You, Zorah ... Castor. Yeah. You're all involved."

Navid's gaze dropped to the stones at his feet. "Sir. I do not know what you are—"

"No." Lander ground his teeth. "Don't. I know you're involved, and I need your help. Shahan has been accused of treason and locked in the Cadet Quarters. Jenkins plans to kill him once Darrius and Kaleb return from taking Morrison to the Surface. We need to rescue Shahan and we don't have much time."

Navid's eyes grew large and he stood frozen for a moment. But then, blinking, he turned and loped into the kitchen shouting, "Olive! Anah! Quick. We need to contact Sovereign Rahni. Yes. Yes. And send a message to Zorah. And one to Castor. Hurry girls."

"Rahni's part of this too?" Lander asked.

"Yes. Yes." Navid's head bobbed.

Within minutes, Navid and Lander were alone in the house. Navid bustled about the kitchen seeming to have no purpose beyond wiping tables and muttering to himself.

"What are you doing?" Lander grabbed the man's shoulders and gave him a quick shake. "Shouldn't we be doing something … more important than … cleaning?"

Navid looked up at Lander as if coming out of a dream. "More important? Yes. Yes. Of course. There are many more important things. But until the girls return, we must wait."

"Wait? No. I'm not waiting. I have an idea." Lander started toward the stairs but stopped and turned back to Navid. "I need clothing. To blend in. Better make it Ungifted. Can you get me some? Now."

Navid thought for a moment then nodded. "Yes. My nephew is about your size. He serves at a house up the street."

"Great! Go."

Navid stood staring like a deer in headlights again.

"Now." Lander resisted the urge to yell, concerned that if he shouted, Navid would lose direction and start cleaning again.

"Now. Yes, sir. Going now."

As Navid scurried out the kitchen door, Lander sprinted up the stairs, taking them two at a time, a plan formulating in his mind. But the plan hinged on his being able to get away from the house without his tail realizing he had left.

A moment later, Lander found himself praying for Olive and Anah which lead to prayer for a whole bunch of people. If Jenkins and Hunt suspected Lander was involved in the rebellion, might people be following the girls? Would Olive and Anah lead the enemy to others? Put them at risk? Lander had no control over that, so he did what he could. Pray. Pressure to pray for Michael rose in him like a vise squeezing his chest. *This is you, Lord, isn't it? There's something wrong where Michael and Becky are. So ... okay ... I lift Michael to you. I can't be where he is now, but I know you are. Keep him; help him. And Becky. And Castor. Navid sent a message to him so he's a part of this rebellion. Watch over them all. And, please watch over me. Help me to help Shahan. Amen.*

While waiting for Navid and the girls to return, Lander took scissors to his hair, then a sharpened stone that doubled as a razor. By the time he was done, he looked bald and older. He grimaced at his reflection in a mirror stone and was wiping a hand over his stubbly head, when the kitchen door slammed. "Navid. I'm up here."

Navid took a step back when he saw Lander. "What have you done, sir?"

"No time to explain, Navid. Do you have ... of course you're carrying them." Lander grabbed the bundle from Navid, tossed it on the bed and proceeded to strip. In less than a minute, he asked, "Well, Navid. What do you think?"

"I would not recognize you if I had not seen you change. Oh, my. You look like one of us."

Lander growled. "Not one of you. Not one of them. Isn't this rebellion about destroying the divisions Jenkins and Morrison put in place? Returning the Core to what it was before those divisions caused strife and hatred? I am a Stone Sovereign. I *am* one of you. And we are all Core Dwellers."

Navid's eyes widened. "I see what you mean. Do you think it is possible?"

"If I didn't think it was possible, I would just cut my losses and make a run for the Avortex right now."

Seeing confusion spread across Navid's face, Lander sighed. "I did it again. Okay. Cut my losses means I'd give up … stop trying.

"Now, how can I hide my Stones in this outfit?"

By the time the two stumbled down the stairs, Lander had an extra strip of cloth wrapped around one arm like a sling. Since injuries were common among the Ungifted, Lander hoped the additional material wouldn't raise suspicions. Hidden within the folds of the sling all four Stones rested, secure and readily accessible.

Lander pulled to a stop inside the kitchen door. A young Ungifted he didn't recognize sat at one of the worktables.

Navid slipped in front of Lander and raised his hands. "Please, sir, this is my nephew. If you want, he can dress in one of your uniforms and lead the one tracking you on a course away from here before you leave."

Lander stood for a moment as Navid's words sunk in. "That's a great idea. Thank you, Navid. I hadn't thought of that. Yes, please. It would help a lot."

In short order, Navid had helped his nephew into a uniform. Lander watched with interest as the young man strolled out the front door and headed toward the closest bridge. It wasn't hard to notice the young lady dressed in Gifted clothing following not far behind.

"Okay. Now it's my turn." Lander scanned the area behind the kitchen before slipping out. Navid waved and closed the door behind him.

Sticking to the edges of lawns and following the line of

walls, Lander headed back up the hillside. He didn't follow the main road to the Cadets' Quarters, but meandered along, frequently scanning behind him to check if anyone followed. Once he determined no one trailed him, he sprinted through an alley and picked up the main road, crossed one of the many bridges and headed to the quarters.

He pulled in several heavy breaths and waited for his heartrate to slow. He leaned against the side of another official building, using the shadows for cover, and kept watch for more than an hour. *Misfadura* was still a few hours off and there was little movement at the residence. Most cadets were probably at practice or serving in some capacity at this hour.

Though the activity level seemed normal, the two Stone Sovereigns stationed at the main doors were not. Lander stepped away from the wall. Shaking out his hands and rolling his shoulders, he slipped back along the side of the building, sprinted across the rear, and worked his way through a couple courtyards to a position where he could see a boarded up cellar entrance to the quarters. Nestled at the back corner where the trash was burned, the old entryway had been closed for years and forgotten by all but the cadets who snuck in past the fake barricade after curfew.

Lander raised his eyes to the ceiling, somewhere in the hazy distance above, and wished for blue sky and sunshine. He missed the Surface, the wind in the trees, the woods, and storms. He had always loved storms. Here the days melded one into another. Sporadic soft breezes filtered through the caverns but nothing stronger. He shifted his gaze back to the door. *It's time.*

Lander focused and went invisible. He gasped and went visible. Focusing again, he pulled in a deep breath and examined his body. Lander had always believed when he sought to disappear that was what happened. But after spending the last months building barrier after barrier he finally understood. He didn't disappear; instead, he created a snug, mini forcefield around himself that acted like smart camouflage. *Cool! I never knew...* He smiled. *I wonder? Could I cover Shahan too ... make him invisible? I guess I'll find out.*

He sprinted across to the side of the Cadet Quarters, scanned, then approached the blocked doorway. The rank odors of ripe trash assailed his nose. A moment later, he located the hidden handle. Reaching out with his unbandaged arm, he gave it a sharp pull. Though the stone slats looked like separate pieces, they opened together as a unit, just like a normal door. One last glance behind him, and Lander descended into the cellar. Sublevels were rare in the Core and this building was one of the few to possess one.

Allowing the door to close behind him, Lander turned and flicked fire on his palm, illuminating the dark room. He released his shield and became visible. Pulling his arm out of the sling, he retrieved his father's Stones from within its folds. Grateful that his curiosity had prompted him to explore all levels of the quarters while living there, he crossed the room and climbed a set of uneven stairs.

He had no doubt of his goal. The only place prisoners were kept here was in the tower, a soaring rock formation that abutted the main building, with only one way in and out. Lander concentrated and disappeared, chuckling at the effect. Keeping to the wall, he padded down the main hallway toward the senior cadets' rooms. Beyond them he came to a stop at the first obstacle, two more Stone Sovereign guards. He didn't recognize the two, but they wore the cobalt uniforms of Deklakh and he figured they were loyal to Jenkins.

Lander allowed himself to become visible, slipped his arm back into the sling, cradling his stones on his palm, then approached the guards, limping and mumbling to himself. Just as he hoped, the two reacted as if he was an Ungifted who had wandered into the restricted area.

"You! Ungifted. You do not belong here." Lander stifled the grin that threatened as the man dropped his Stones into their pouch. Lander stumbled forward. Reaching out, he clutched onto the man's uniform as if to break his fall.

"Hey! What—" the guard began, but then crumpled from the short, controlled beam of light Lander sent through his chest. Experience had taught Lander the man would be out cold for about two hours. He lowered the unconscious form to the floor as the other guard approached, her Stones glowing.

"What have you done to him?" Her eyes sparked with animosity.

"Um … nothing, good Sovereign. I do not know." He shrugged. "Your friend reached out to help me then … well, you see." Lander took a step closer to the Sovereign.

"Don't. Get back." Suspicion drawing her brows together, she motioned for Lander to back up. He raised his good arm as if in surrender. Still clutching her Stones, she knelt next to her partner and began examining him. From within the cast, Lander shot a beam into her, dropping her onto the other guard.

He dragged both bodies over, propped them against the wall, and prayed no one would find them until after he and Shahan were long gone.

Moving through the doorway the two had been guarding, he swallowed hard and prepared himself. The next, and most worrisome, obstacle awaited him. The massive entryway into the Tower.

CHAPTER 27

Scanning the dark hallway, Lander approached the fifteen-foot high door to the Tower. He had been here only once before when a senior cadet gave him a tour of the quarters. A sigh escaped as he offered a silent prayer of thanks that the corridor remained unoccupied.

It didn't take long to discover a controlled burst of fire wasn't enough to break the lock. Grinding his teeth, Lander fetched his mother's Stones from the cast and focused to bring all four Stones of Power into play. Hoping the sound wouldn't carry, he directed a blast of energy at the bolt. It hissed for a few seconds, then burst asunder with a loud crack that ran the length of the door from top to bottom. After replacing his mother's Stones in the sling, he shoved both sides of the break. With a grinding sound they parted, and Lander pushed through into another short hallway that led to a set of uneven steps.

He took the stairs at a quick jog, stopping at each floor to check the cells. Fortunately, there were only three rooms jutting from each landing. The first four stories proved empty. When he got to the fifth, and last, the cell to his left was locked. This time a swift, short burst of fire destroyed the lock.

Allowing his Stones to continue glowing, he raised one above his head to illuminate the small cell. A glittering eye reflected the light. Shahan's battered face caused Lander to grimace. One eye was swollen shut and blood dribbled from a slice across the other cheek.

Lander made quick work of the chains that held Shahan to the wall.

"You have come for me. Why?"

"No time to talk now. Just relax and let me heal." Once again Lander retrieved his mother's Stones and worked with both sets, focusing on healing a fracture in Shahan's right leg.

He cursed silently at the time needed to heal the leg before Shahan would be able to walk. Nearly fifteen minutes had passed by the time Lander helped a limping Shahan down the stairs. With shuffling steps, they slipped through the broken door, along the hallway, and through the other door to where Lander had left the unconscious guards. Seeing they still lay propped against the wall, unmoving, Lander released some of the tension clenching his muscles.

As they headed toward the entrance to the cellar, voices echoed through the hall. Lander pulled to a stop, Shahan leaning into him.

"Okay, Shahan. I need to try something. Hold onto me and, whatever happens, don't let go."

Shahan huffed, breathing heavily, and nodded. Sweat plastered his brow.

"You okay?" Lander studied the Sovereign's pain-filled eyes.

"Yes."

"Good." Once again, grasping his mother's Stones, he balanced all four in his palms and focused. The camouflage bubble covered Lander. He concentrated, directing the thing to grow. A crooked smile worked its way out when the shield expanded to include Shahan and then closed in tight like a second skin over both of them.

"Now. We've gone invisible together so stick with me. We are going down into the cellar and out through a hidden entrance. From there we will cut across the courtyards to the right and come up behind the administration building. Are you ready?"

Shahan nodded and Lander started them forward.

A group of four cadets stood in front of the cellar entrance and Lander breathed a sigh of relief to see the door already open. But as the two maneuvered around the conversing cadets, Shahan slipped, and a groan leaked past his lips. Laughter erupted and Lander kept Shahan moving as he prayed the noise would cover their movements.

Leaving the Cadet Quarters behind, fear of a misstep churned like sour milk in Lander's stomach as the two walked with hesitant steps across the alley, through the yards, and slipped in behind the opposite building.

They stopped for a bit so Shahan could catch his breath and rest his leg. After peeking around the corner, Lander pulled Shahan's arm over his shoulders and moved out.

By the time they got back to his house, the drain of sustaining the camouflage shield around Shahan and himself left Lander huffing for air. This bubble, though smaller and held for a much shorter time, consumed a lot of energy when he increased it to cover another person. He would have to think about that as his plans for the future began to take shape.

His head swiveling, Lander helped Shahan into the door Navid held open. Tension bled from Lander as he collapsed on a kitchen chair next to Shahan. Navid brought Lander and Shahan mugs of water.

Lander downed his water in one long swig, some of the

liquid dribbling down. He swiped a hand across his chin. "We can't stay here. They will be looking for us. Did you hear from Sovereign Rahni?"

Voices drifted from the other room and Lander held his hand out, stopping Navid from responding. "Who?"

Navid's mouth turned up at the corners. "It is Sovereign Rahni and another Sovereign who supports our goals."

Shahan's eyes narrowed. "Who?"

"Me." Siprian stepped into the kitchen.

Shahan sprang up then grabbed the table for support, his eyes narrowed with suspicion. "You did not want to hear the Ungifted truth. We cannot trust you."

Lander moved between the two. He nodded to Shahan and turned to face Siprian. "If Shahan doesn't trust you, neither do I." Lander paused, his gaze flicked to Rahni who stood in the doorway then back to Siprian. He capped the rising anxiety Siprian's presence had stirred. "Unless … unless you can convince us you are on the level."

Siprian's look of confusion clamped Lander's mouth shut. He blew out a breath. "Yeah, right. *On the level* means you are being honest with us."

His confusion melting, Siprian nodded. "May I?" He waved toward another chair.

"Okay." Lander hoped he wasn't making a big mistake. It seemed as though every decision he'd made in the last few months ended in disaster.

Siprian lowered onto the chair, his attention focused on Shahan. "You are right. I did not want to hear. Did not want to lose my … authority … prestige." He shifted his gaze to Lander. "That is the right word, Sovereign Lander, is it not?"

"Like respect, right?"

"Yes. I did like when others bowed to me. But not no more."

"What changed?"

"Navid knows. Rahni knows"

"They may know, but I want you to explain."

Siprian's eyes sought the window overlooking the small back porch as he pulled in a deep breath and worked his fingers in and out of each other. "Navid had another child. A son. Bast. Though he was Ungifted, Bast and I grew up together. He was my friend." He turned to face Shahan again. "When you spoke with me, I did not want change. After that, Bast did not follow an order quick enough and Kaleb killed him, my friend. Now I see you were right to be concerned, Shahan. I want to do what you and Rahni are doing. I want the Core to be safe for all again."

While Siprian was speaking, Lander watched Navid. Tears came into the old man's eyes and he grabbed the side of the table as if for emotional support. Siprian was telling the truth. Lander shifted his attention to Shahan. He had learned to trust the Sovereign and hoped he would see the truth in Siprian's words.

"As I know you, Sovereign Siprian, I know you speak the truth." Shahan's words calmed Lander's concerns. He knew he could trust Shahan with his life and now he could extend the same level of trust to Rahni, whom he had always liked, and Siprian.

Rahni slipped past Lander to stand at Siprian's side. Placing a hand on his shoulder, she turned to Shahan. "I speak for Siprian. Thank you for accept he tell the truth.

"But now, I think it is not safe here. Others will be look for Shahan."

"I know a place. It is not far," Navid said.

"Will it be safe?" Lander glanced out the window wondering how long they would have before Shahan's rescue was discovered.

"It is safe. Olive and Anha are there now. Come. I will show you."

With every step he took, Lander expected the shout that would bring a team of Stone Sovereigns down on them. Rescuing Shahan had been a no-brainer. But confronting and possibly killing other Stone Sovereigns rubbed against Lander's code of honor. They were colleagues, not enemies.

He stopped walking as the others continued, and stood frozen in thought. *That's not right. I can't call them all friends … not if I am a part of what Shahan and the others are doing. But can I kill another Stone Sovereign?* His thoughts triggered the memory of Hunt's guard he had killed back on the Surface. That dredged up Hunt's proposition. *"As you can imagine, setting you free on the Surface where you can run to the authorities could create rather a difficult situation for me. So, these are your choices. Remain here and work with Mr. Jenkins to keep order in the Core; or, return to your cell on my island."*

He even promised to get Becky and Michael scholarships. Lander shook his head as if to dislodge the unwelcome thoughts. *No. If I don't help the Ungifted and join Jenkins, I'll be trapped.*

"Lander," Rahni called, her voice a harsh, loud whisper. "Keep up."

Siprian dropped behind Lander, scanning for enemies and after several more turns and a short walk along a swampy path, they arrived at a modest home. Round and a worn, pale pink, it sat amongst other rundown dwellings.

Navid knocked softly and a moment later, Anah opened the door a crack. Her eyes rounded. Pulling the stone slab open all the way, she beckoned everyone in.

"We did not know if you would come," Anah said, hugging her father. "Torem and his family have left for Shavah El'Ruhan. We are alone here."

Lander's gaze roamed the small room and everyone standing, cramped together. How could they hold a meeting like this, he wondered? But just then, Olive stepped through what Lander had thought was a wall hanging.

"Come." She held the cloth back and motioned for the group to enter.

Lander slipped under the cloth. A small entryway to his left, lit by a bright light stick, led to a stairwell. He plunged down the stairs and at the bottom pulled in a gasp. Beneath the house was a large room. Several chairs and a couch—all with soft-looking padding—and a heavy table surrounded by carved stone chairs filled the area. The glow of a dozen light sticks bathed the area with warmth and comfort, illuminating two area rugs made of the long-fibered mosses common in the Bec Jekesh Cavern.

"This is the great room," Olive said. "We often meet here. You should be comfortable. Anah and I will prepare some food and drinks. We will be right back." Both girls disappeared up the stairs.

Moving into the unexpected great room, Lander helped Navid and Siprian push the chairs into a semi-circle in front of the couch. When they finished, Shahan took a seat on the couch and Rahni knelt in front of him to continue healing.

Lander, Siprian, and Navid sat in chairs and began juggling ideas for a plan to get all the Surface Dwellers back to the Surface. A short while later, Olive and Anah brought in trays of fresh fruit and *ah'sim,* the aroma of the sweet tea-like drink suffusing the air and setting Lander's mouth to water.

After depositing the trays on the table, Anah sat on the arm of her father's chair and Olive plopped down on the couch next to Shahan.

Lander suspected it was late when the group finalized their plans, perhaps even heading toward Mist Rise.

"We have made good plans," Siprian said. "Rahni and I

will leave word we are going to the Bec Jekesh Cavern to hunt Jerr'as. Then we travel to Shavah El'Ruhan where we will stay hidden and wait for you to bring Chancellor Jenkins. If you do not arrive by eight Mist Rises, we will know something went wrong and we will return here."

Lander nodded. "That's right. Next Mist Rise, Darrius and the others will leave to return Hunt, Morrison, and Hunt's people to the Surface, so Jenkins will be short on Stone Sovereigns. Shahan and I will make our move the Mist Rise after, kidnap Jenkins and head to the El'Ruhan Cavern. If all goes well, we should meet you two days—*Mist Rises*—later."

Shahan rose, his eyes meeting every other conspirator's. "This is good. Now we pray to Noah's God."

"Just God," Lander said, also pushing up onto his feet. "Not Noah's God. He is not just Noah's God; he is God of all."

Shahan's expression clouded. "That is what Castor says." He cleared his throat and closed his eyes. "God. The God who had power to flood the world. You warned Noah and he listened. You kept your promise to bring the waters. You are more powerful than Chancellor Jenkins. You are more powerful than any Stone Sovereign. We trust you." He paused then raised his hands. "Thank you."

Lander smiled at Shahan's simple prayer. Simple. Like believing. Simple. But so hard. That kind of faith and trust. And yet his parents believed.

There's no greater love than to lay down your life for a friend. The words circled in Lander's mind. He was beginning to understand why his parents had given their lives to save others. Perhaps in the next few days, he would follow in their footsteps. To save Becky, Michael, his people. To lay down his life for others. He shook his head, dispelling the image of his death.

Then Rahni reached out to him, and clasping her hands behind his neck, pulled his head down and planted a soft kiss on his right cheek. "Siprian and I will go now. We will meet you in time and finish this."

Lander nodded. "Yes, ma'am." She patted his cheek and stepped back. Siprian approached and gave him the Core arm clasp. They turned and headed back up to ground level. Lander lifted a silent prayer to keep them safe. His thoughts turned to Becky and he prayed for Becky, Michael, Castor, and Desma as well. As he was praying, a disturbance arose in his spirit. He didn't know what it meant, but whatever it was, it wasn't good.

By the time he turned back, Shahan lay sound asleep on the couch, his soft snores ruffling the covers at his chin.

CHAPTER 28

Lander peered around the side of the mansion below Jenkins's. As expected, two guards flanked the doors. And they weren't cadets. The new chancellor preferred to have full-fledged, experienced Stone Sovereigns guard him. Lander also suspected there was a team inside as well.

He glanced over to where Shahan and Zorah hid, still processing the fact that this nine-hundred-year-old woman had come to help. When she arrived last *Misfadura*, they had talked for over an hour with Shahan once again translating. Before going to sleep, Lander had given her his mother's Stones. Her response, spoken in English warmed him. "You are family. To you will go Stones of Power when … this … thing … is done." She had risen and reaching out, pulled Lander to his feet, and wrapped him in a surprisingly strong hug.

Shahan signaled to proceed, pulling Lander from his thoughts. Lander focused. Going invisible, he sprinted from his hiding place, banked left onto the road, and raced up the hill. He didn't slow as he took the steps two at a time up onto the porch, using his momentum to smash bodily into the first of the two guards. The Sovereign whoofed out a breath and fell onto his back. Without waiting to see if he got up, Lander plowed into the second guard, a heavy-set, older woman, while releasing his hold on invisibility. By that time, Shahan stood over the first man, his hands fisted, shaking his head in warning. Though the Sovereign glowered at Shahan, he remained on the ground.

Lander's gaze flicked back to the second Sovereign. She held out her hands in surrender. "You are Sovereign Lander? The one who came from the Surface?"

Lander nodded as Zorah hobbled up to the landing and moved to stand next to him, leaning heavily on a stout staff. She spoke a few words in Corish and the female guard nodded. To Lander's surprise, she handed her Stones of Power to Zorah who passed them to Shahan.

"What just happened?" Lander looked from Zorah to Shahan as the female guard pushed upright.

"She is with us." Shahan said. "But this other," he waved at the sullen man on the ground, "he is not."

Zorah pushed Lander and pointed toward the guard, a flood of Corish pouring from her.

"What?" Lander wished she would speak more English. He knew she could if she wanted. *Stubborn old lady.*

"There is no need, Zorah," the female guard said. "I will take care of him."

Zorah released a sound that reminded Lander of a growl. She grabbed the Stones of Power from Shahan and handed them back to the woman, who fixed her attention on her partner and spoke in a stern voice. "You need to hand your Stones to Shahan and follow me."

Lander felt the power in her words and relief flooded through him when the man obeyed.

Zorah, Shahan, and the woman exchanged another quick

dialogue in Corish then the man and woman headed down the stairs.

"Are you sure they aren't going to betray us?" Lander watched the two as they moved off at a quick trot downhill, toward the river.

"Marrias will not betray Zorah," Shahan said. Lander's gaze shifted to Shahan as the large Sovereign continued. "There is little time. We must proceed."

Shahan pulled the door open, then he and Lander slipped inside while Zorah headed back to the place where she had hidden. There, she would watch and wait in case they needed help escaping the mansion with Jenkins.

Shahan moved in next to Lander and Lander reset his concealment shield, this time including Shahan within the bubble. The entryway was empty. They moved together up the stairs to the Overlook, hoping Jenkins would follow his normal routine and be out there enjoying his Mist Rise mug of *ah'sim*.

Lander ground his teeth. None of the doors to the Outlook were open. That meant Jenkins wasn't there yet. Voices from the foyer pulled his attention. Jenkins and several others. Shahan waved Lander farther down the hallway. Creeping past the four doors to the Outlook, he breathed out a huff of relief when he saw the hallway didn't end but bent to the left ahead. The two just made it past the turn when Jenkins halted half-way up the stairs.

"You four remain here. See that I am not disturbed." He thumped up two more steps before stopping again. "Elam. Make certain my *ah'sim* is hot today, the muffins sufficiently warm, and the fruit cold. Last Mist Rise, the *ah'sim* was tepid. Do not make that mistake again. Morrison might have overlooked such incompetence in his Ungifted; I do not."

"Yes, sir."

One door banged open as Jenkins walked out onto the Overlook, and Lander dropped his shield. Quiet, steady movements defined Elam as he opened the other doors before heading up the hall where Lander and Shahan hid. The man pulled in a gasp and his jaw dropped open when he saw them. His shock lasted only a second, then a soft smile filtered onto his face. "Sovereign Lander. Is there something I can help you with?"

Lander grinned back. "In fact, Elam, there is something you can do for Sovereign Shahan and me." Lander pulled the small packet of sedative powder Zorah had mixed before heading to Jenkins's from his pouch. "Chancellor Jenkins sounds out of sorts this Mist Rise. I think he needs more sleep. This should help."

"Ah, just the thing sir. I am certain he will appreciate the addition to his *ah'sim*." Elam held out his hand and Lander dropped the tiny package on his palm. "If the young sir is interested, I am alone in the kitchen at this hour." He paused and dipped his head. "There is *ah'sim* and fresh muffins … if you are interested. I must go there now to prepare the chancellor's Mist Rise meal."

Lander looked to Shahan. Shahan shrugged but the hint of a smile crooked the side of his mouth. Stepping out of the shadows, the two dogged Elam's steps through several twisting turns and down a narrow set of stairs into a large kitchen. Several light sticks sat in urns stationed around the room. Two heavy worktables took up most of the area with curved cupboards scattered along the umber walls.

"Please, sit." Elam scurried around the room, getting together Jenkins's meal. He lifted a kettle off the small stove and poured hot water into an *ah'sim* pot to steep. The sweet and spicy fragrance arose on a cloud of steam. The warm aroma of baking blended with that of the *ah'sim* as Elam pulled a tray of fresh-baked muffins from a stove powered by heavy-duty light sticks that threw off controlled amounts of heat. After setting a half-dozen muffins on a platter, he drew out a pail of milk from a hole cut in the wall and lined with water to keep things cool. He also retrieved a crock of white, goat-milk butter and another of apricot preserves from the cavity.

With great care, he pulled the strainer of steeped *ah'sim* leaves from the pot then emptied the contents of the packet Lander had given him into the hot liquid. Placing everything on a tray, Elam turned to Lander and Shahan. "Please help yourselves to what is here. I will return shortly."

Shahan shook his head. "No. Do not return until Chancellor Jenkins sleeps. We will know what to do then."

"As you wish, Sovereign."

"Do you think it will work?" Lander asked Shahan after Elam left. "I mean, it's just some ground up plant."

"It will work."

"But you were going to use something else."

Shahan's eyes met Lander's. "Yes. But Zorah knows more. This is better."

Lander's knee bounced and he drummed his fingers on the table. Surging up, he roamed the room, checked out the stove, then made his way back to the table where he grabbed a muffin and took a generous bite. "Ummm. These are good. Elam knows what he's doing."

"Yes. That is why Jenkins keeps him."

Lander picked up another muffin and tossed it to Shahan. "We might be here a while. Eat."

They were each finishing their second muffin when Elam returned. "It seems you were correct, Sovereigns. Chancellor Jenkins must be very tired. He has fallen asleep. I have told his guards he is resting and will not need them for the rest of the morning."

"Elam, you are a genius." Lander grabbed the man's hand and pumped it. Elam's eyes rounded and his jaw dropped.

A few minutes later, Shahan had the unconscious Jenkins slung over one broad shoulder as he followed Lander back to the kitchen. Elam held the outside door open. "May Noah's God be with you."

Threading through the olive trees on the far side of the house away from the main road, Lander and Shahan picked their way back to where Zorah waited. She flung a ragged cloak over Jenkins, then Lander and Shahan each took an arm, pulled it over their shoulders, and proceeded down the main road staggering a bit as if drunk. Though it was early, the sight of drunk Sovereigns was not unusual regardless of the time.

The trip back to their hideout took longer as they meandered their way past several taverns and wove back and forth on the stone roadway. Lander feared Jenkins would wake before they made it to their destination, but whatever was in Zorah's little packet proved effective. After maneuvering Jenkins down the steps, they dropped him, still slumbering, onto the couch.

By that time, sweat dribbled from Lander's shaved head into his eyes and soaked the back of his shirt. A tired, but grateful smile emerged when Olive handed him a large mug of water. She gave mugs to Shahan and Zorah as well before skipping back to the main level.

Zorah spoke to Shahan in hushed Corish then Shahan turned to Lander. "He sleeps for long time. We will eat now."

Though Elam's muffins had been tasty, Lander was ready for some real food. Something hearty. So, when the spicy aroma of Core lamb preceded Navid down the stairs, Lander's mouth began to water. He licked his lips as Navid placed a plate of lamb chops on the table. Anah followed with a bowl of greens, and Olive with a tray of biscuits in one hand and a container of thick, beige gravy in the other. The three made the trek back up and down one more time bringing plates, eating utensils, and pitchers of water and fruit wine.

After Shahan lifted another hesitant and simple prayer, they plowed into the feast and no one spoke for a while. When Lander had eaten his fill, he looked around the table to see the others had also finished eating. "Well. So far, so good. Now we move on to part two of the *grand plan*, getting Jenkins to El'Ruhan and picking up Becky and Michael … and Castor and Desma if they still want to return to the Surface."

"I go with." Zorah locked her gaze on Lander.

Lander's immediate reaction was to say no; she was old and slow and couldn't walk without her staff. But as he gazed into his great grandmother's eyes, her determination induced him to say nothing, just nod.

Her stern expression morphed into a confident smile, as if she had read his mind. He just hoped she wouldn't slow him and Shahan down. He had no doubts about her abilities to wield Stones of Power; he had witnessed their reaction to her back at her home. And she still held onto his mother's Stones. Her physical endurance, however, was another story.

"It is good to have you with us," Shahan said to Zorah. "We rest now. We leave at Mist Rise."

Navid, Anah, and Olive stood and began clearing the table. "We will clean up here then return to Sovereign Lander's mansion. If anyone comes looking for him, we will say he has gone with Sovereigns Siprian and Rahni to hunt Jerr'as."

Zorah checked on Jenkins. Stirring a bit of her powder into some water, she motioned for Shahan to hold his head and dribbled a few drops into his mouth. Jenkins swallowed automatically and though his eyes shifted in their sockets, they never opened.

Lander, Shahan, and Zorah climbed to the upper level to wash up. Soon after he returned to the cellar, Zorah and Shahan joined him. Jenkins was sleeping on the couch, so the three pulled cushions from chairs and spread them out on the floor. With his nerves still zinging, Lander expected to take a long time to fall asleep, but within minutes of his head hitting a pillow, he plunged into a dream world where he chased after Becky, but she kept disappearing.

He woke long before Mist Rise, a feeling of apprehension choking him. *This has been way too easy. Something doesn't add up. Hunt's up to something.*

CHAPTER 29

Soon after Lander woke, the soft sounds of movement alerted him to the fact that Zorah and Shahan were also awake. Zorah moved to the couch and checked Jenkins.

"Are you awake, Lander?" Shahan asked.

"Yeah."

"We must go."

"Yeah."

They gathered supplies and carried them out to the small donkey cart Zorah had procured. The Ungifted handler stood near the head of a small brown donkey with large ears. The animal flicked its tail and watched with wide curious eyes as Lander and Shahan loaded the bed of the cart. Several blankets were spread for Jenkins to sleep on.

Zorah leaned on her staff and waited with the handler while Lander and Shahan trudged back down to collect Jenkins. Getting him up the narrow stairwell proved to be as difficult as getting him down had been, but with some juggling and effort, the two made it through the door and carried him to the cart.

Shahan propped Jenkins upright; the man hung like a puppet with cut strings. Lander jumped into the wagon and, grabbing Jenkins's shoulders, levered him over the side while Shahan lifted his legs. Once they had Jenkins flat on the bed, Lander covered the man with a blanket and jumped out.

Shahan and Lander walked to where Zorah and the handler stood, talking. "Shahan. Lander. Dis is Dov. A friend." Though Zorah's English was rougher than even Shahan's, Lander appreciated her using it for his sake.

Dov bobbed his head a few times. "Good to meet you." He rubbed his hand on the side of the donkey's face. "This is Sheba. She is a good girl. We are happy to help our friend Zorah."

"Thank you." Lander reached out and they clasped arms in Core fashion. Dov's grasp was, like the man, strong. Lander's mind pulled up the image of a grizzly bear. His gray-streaked hair and beard enhanced Dov's bear-like appearance.

When Lander moved back and Shahan stepped in to grasp arms, Lander studied Sheba. He had seen few donkeys in the Core; they were rare and prized for their ability to carry loads or pull carts. Dov's willingness to use his donkey and cart to help them spoke volumes about his relationship with Zorah.

"Wait," Olive called. She, Navid, and Anah came running, each holding a wrapped package.

"Here. Take these. They are food and wine for you." Navid's eyes lit up as his face broke into a broad smile. "You did not think we would send you off without food, did you?"

Lander and Shahan took the bundles and added them to the back. Navid and his daughters waved from the small front yard of the rundown dwelling as Zorah and Dov led the way with Shahan and Lander following.

Dressed as Ungifted and with hoods pulled low over their faces, Shahan, Zorah, and Lander blended in. As they made their way through the streets of Shavah Al'Wisan, Dov's popularity shone through. Many Gifted and Ungifted waved or stopped to speak a few words with the handler. At one such stop, Lander stormed ahead, muttering to himself. "We don't have time for this … *chatting.*"

Shahan caught up to him. "You must be patient. Dov speaks to many. It is his duty to the UCD." He nodded, his eyes asking Lander to understand. "He is a messenger."

Lander swallowed the protest forming on his tongue.

"You must not talk of what you see." Shahan's serious demeanor broke through Lander's frustration. Lander turned and continued walking, but this time with an increased pace. The others must have sensed his need to be alone with his thoughts because, though they could have caught up to him at any time, they kept their distance.

Lander's mind sifted through the events of the last few months. His relationship with Becky, his fear when he was Hunt's prisoner, the awful trip through the Vortex when he thought Michael might die impacted Lander in ways he was still struggling to understand. The significance of the words his mother had spoken to him from beyond the grave beat against his common sense like never before, tearing apart the last shreds of unbelief. The realization that he was just a small part of something bigger shattered his pride, leaving it in tatters, and landed squarely on his heart.

He had grappled with this before. But now, seeing the number of people who spoke with Dov as they walked the streets of Shavah Al'Wisan, put faces on the faceless crowd of nameless people who had populated his thoughts. Before, the words his mother had spoken to him almost three months ago had seemed abstract; now those words were clothed in humanity.

For the first time, Lander considered returning to the Core after he got Becky and Michael back to the Surface. What would it mean to stay with his people? To be part of rebuilding the trust between Stone Sovereigns, Gifted, and Ungifted? To help people like Zorah and Shahan re-establish the elders and the guilds? Until now he'd thought about the privilege and admiration being a Stone Sovereign brought. Or he dwelt on his feelings for Becky; even though his feelings were strong, he still placed his wants over her needs. The words circled in his mind. *Greater love has no man. Greater love … love. Have I ever loved anyone but myself?*

He struggled with the pain that question churned within him and almost missed the way the cavern ceiling lowered. By the time he noticed his surroundings, walls of deepest maroon were closing in and he pulled to a halt, staring into a dark, narrow tunnel. *When did that happen?*

"Do not stop, Lander." Shahan's direction started Lander moving again as they blended in with the large crowd flowing into the narrow opening.

They had left the city behind and were now passing through the tunnel which connected the Al'Wisan Cavern and the El'Ruhan Cavern. The shortest of the connecting tunnels, he had not traveled this way before, and the shadow-drenched passage sent pangs of claustrophobia zinging through him. But it wasn't long before soft, golden light shown at the end of the stuffy tunnel. Stifling the desire to run into the brightness beyond, Lander fell back to walk alongside Dov and Sheba.

Not long after, leaving the tight space behind, Lander pulled in a deep breath of fresh, light El'Ruhan air as he filtered out with the crowd pouring onto the wide roadway. The sound of gushing and churning to his left issued from the Bec Timur as it flowed into the adjacent channel, its waters eddying and swirling as it resisted the tapering passage.

Lander moved to the side of the road and took in the shimmering vista before him. Shahan and Zorah stopped next to him while Dov and Sheba wandered off the beaten path for Sheba to nibble at some fresh meadow plants.

Like every other time Lander had traveled into the golden cavern, he drank in the magnificent landscape. It reminded him of the Surface; the only things missing were clouds and sun … well, maybe more … like storms and rainbows.

Two more Mist Rises until he saw Becky again. He wondered for what seemed like the millionth time if she thought of him, what she thought of him. Had she given up hoping for him to return. *Soon. We'll be there soon. Then I'll keep my promise.*

Beads of moisture decorated Sheba's blanket, glistening like myriad jewels in the golden light of the Flux. Mist danced in the familiar patterns of Mist Rise, soaring and falling, spiraling in shades of gold and green. Lander ran a hand over the hood of his cloak and droplets skittered down his face.

He stood with Shahan on a shallow knoll alongside the highway, overlooking a vast expanse of sparkling turquoise water in the distance to their left. The Jekesh Bec'Stor. A cluster of small, rundown dwellings and one larger building occupied the area at the base of the rise, comprising the work camp where Becky, Michael, Castor, and Desma had been assigned.

The sounds of shuffling feet and multiple conversations filled the air as the crowd of people passed behind them, continuing on the main road toward Shavah El'Ruhan.

Before reaching the city, the Bec Jekesh split into dozens of smaller streams which flowed down into the Jekesh Bec'Stor, the largest lake in the Core. Sitting along the closest of those streams, the work camp looked deserted.

Shahan shook his head, his eyes narrow and searching. "Some … thing is not right. It is too quiet."

Lander scanned the camp. Though he saw no one, it was early. "Mist Rise is not far along. Maybe they are eating?"

Shahan's mouth flattened. "No. Ungifted here start work before Mist Rise."

Zorah walked over from where she had been talking to Dov. "Dov say tings bad."

"Well, what do you want to do?" Lander slipped his hand under the hood of his cloak and scratched the back of his neck where the hair seemed intent on standing at attention. He felt it too. Tension filled the air. Like they had reached the pinnacle of a roller coaster and everyone was holding their breath in anticipation of the drop.

Shahan's silence spoke volumes.

Lander shifted his feet and blew out a puff of air, then pulled in a deep breath. The faint aroma of baking drifted on the slight breeze that shifted the mist. "Smells like someone's making bread. Maybe things just seem quiet."

Still focused on the camp below, Shahan shook his head again. "We will stay on main road. Follow crowd and go direct to Shavah El'Ruhan."

A weight dropped into Lander's stomach. Despite his anxiety, his desire to see Becky pushed against the need for caution. "No. Becky's down there. We need to check it out."

Without waiting to see if the others followed, Lander left the main road to plunge down a beaten path to the empty work-camp. He slowed as he got closer and looked over his shoulder. A sigh of relief filtered through his lips when he saw Shahan helping Zorah down the shallow slope as Dov followed, leading Sheba.

The relief was short-lived. As he turned back, several people stepped out from behind one of the small buildings. His eyes snagged on Hunt. The man moved to the forefront, leading Talon and his men as well as Darrius and Kaleb and their teams. A boulder the size of the El'Ruhan Cavern dropped into Lander's stomach. Siprian and Rahni approached with the rest. And they all balanced glowing Stones of Power on their palms.

"This was too easy." Hunt chuckled as he pulled a wide-brimmed hat from his head. "Did you really think I would just return those Stones to you and let you go without protest?" His gaze drifted over to the cart. "I suppose you have Mr. Jenkins stuffed in there?" He nodded. "Not a bad plan. It's just a shame you expected me to be a man of my word."

His attention shifted to Shahan and Zorah. "Nice of you to return to me, Sovereign Shahan. And I would wager a guess that the unassuming woman with you is the elusive Zorah, ex-Stone Sovereign and ex-elder of the Core." His gaze shifted back to Lander. "Thank you for delivering one of the prime leaders of Morrison's quaint revolution to me."

He signaled those behind him forward. "Mr. Talon. Sovereign Darrius. Take those rebels into custody."

Lander froze. The realization that his reckless action now divided him from Shahan and Zorah battered his ego. If he had just been patient, he could have constructed a camouflage bubble that encompassed all of them.

Darrius stepped forward a few steps, Kaleb at his side. Kaleb's anger seared Lander as his captain stared daggers at him. In a moment, Kaleb's Stones crackled and grew brighter. Lander dove to the side and rolled. Pulling his father's Stones, he focused and went invisible, then sprinted back toward Shahan and Zorah. He expected to hear gunshots or the whoosh of fiery Stone whips from behind, but the only sounds were huffing breath and pounding feet—his own.

CHAPTER 30

ov and Sheba remained behind on the slope as Shahan and Zorah approached. A dense shield shimmered in front of them, reminding Lander of the air above hot pavement after a quick shower. Shards of color sparked off its curved face. The two came to a halt near where the path levelled out, Shahan supporting Zorah on one side, her staff thumping to rest on the other. Lander skidded to a stop a few feet in front of them.

He wrestled with what to do; his thoughts bogged down as if trapped in quicksand. He loathed the thought of injuring, maybe even killing, his fellow teammates, but if they left him no choice, he'd need to deal with it. Whatever happened next, he'd chosen his side and he wouldn't back down now.

Still holding onto invisibility, Lander turned to study the situation. Darrius's and Kaleb's Stones continued to flare though both captains stood as he left them. A flutter of wings tickled his stomach when he realized that after those first few steps, no one had moved. Hunt, his men, the Sovereigns, all stood frozen, as if waiting. *Waiting for what?*

Avoiding the edge of their shield, Lander swung into a position alongside Shahan. "I'm here." Shahan's eyes flashed in his direction. "No! Don't look at me. Until we find out what's going on, I don't want them to know where I am. I don't see Morrison, do you?"

Shahan's head shifted slightly as he scanned from side to side. "No."

They moved forward again until they were about twenty yards from where Hunt and the others stood, blocking the road. Lander could sense Zorah's and Shahan's rising concern at their enemies' lack of action. He shared it. *What are they doing?*

"Lander, I know you are there," Kaleb shouted. "Show yourself."

Yeah, right! Like I'm going to give up my only advantage. He whispered to Shahan, "Keep them talking. I'm going to try and slip behind."

Shahan nodded. "Darrius, I have been your friend since you were … birthed, stood with your family at your Kinship ceremonies. Why, now, do you challenge me?" Shahan's words filtered through the misty air, halting, but clear.

"Why do you force me to challenge you, Shahan? If you truly were my friend, you would not have put me in this position. You are a traitor and because of you I have a black mark on my record."

"What record?" The normally stoic Shahan raised his voice. He snorted through clenched teeth. "The record these Surface Dwellers have kept on us? It means nothing. Where is the pride in your heritage? You have become their *khzir.*

"*Shiviah-zor.*" Darrius's mouth flattened into a flat line at the slur. His Stones of Power flared.

"No." Hunt stepped forward to stand between Kaleb and Darrius. "He's trying to provoke you, to distract you from discovering what Lander's up to." Hunt circled a hand over his head. "Find him. Now. Before he … just find him."

His attention slid back to Shahan and Zorah. "And break through that shield. I want those two taken alive."

Lander had slipped past the line of enemies and around one of the stone outcroppings to come up next to the only large dome in the camp. He reached out to pull open the stone slab that served as a door, but it wouldn't budge. A quick glance over his shoulder told him a few things; Darrius was pounding Shahan and Zorah's shield with heavy blasts while the other Sovereigns had spread out searching for him. Talon and his men, however, remained in place, a quiet presence behind Hunt. *Weird! No time to wonder.*

Palming his Stones, Lander sent a quick burst into the locking mechanism of the door. Unlike his attempt to shatter the lock in Hunt's office, this time his precision resulted in a light click and the slab shifting open a quarter of an inch. He stuck his fingers into the opening to pull, but something slammed into him from behind, knocking him to the ground. He lost focus as his Stones skittered away on the rocky path. Scrambling onto his feet, he faced off against Kaleb.

"Looks like you lost something, Surface scum." Kaleb's Stones sparked as he slipped past Lander and scooped up his now dark Stones. Turning back, he motioned for Lander to move to where Hunt and the others waited. "Move."

Gritting his teeth, Lander sought his focus again.

"Oh no you don't." Kaleb's words were punctuated by a spear of flame.

Fire shot through Lander's left leg, buckling it and sending him to his knees.

"Try that again," Kaleb sneered, "and I'll take out the other leg. Now, get up and move."

Pushing up, Lander hobbled forward one step. He looked over to where Shahan and Zorah were still holding strong against Darrius and his team. He grinned. "Looks like your friends are having a hard time."

Kaleb shoved Lander. "I said, move."

Lander wasn't ready to give up yet. If he could just distract Kaleb. *Just need a diversion.* As if in answer to his prayer, the door he had unlocked burst open, the stone slab banging into the side of the building with a loud crack, drawing Kaleb's attention for a few seconds, just long enough for Lander to disappear.

"*Shiviah-zor.*" Kaleb's outburst echoed off the side of the building. Lander followed the curve of the wall and started to hobble away when the realization of who led the dozens of people pouring through the door he had unlocked struck him like a bolt of lightning.

Castor, waving one of Talon's guns, was shouting commands. Next to him stood Desma. The slight person beside her drew Lander like lodestone to a magnet, Becky. She too sported a weapon … and it looked as if she knew what she was doing.

Lander dropped his invisible shield again and called, "Becky." But she was already moving away with Castor and Desma while dozens more people poured out of the doorway, shoving and yelling, brandishing make-shift weapons, and blocking Lander's view.

A heavy hand dropped onto his shoulder and spun him around. Once again, Lander found himself face to face with Kaleb. Behind him guns spoke; and screams of pain began to punctuate the rising tumult. Energy sizzled. Becky was somewhere out in that chaos and Lander ground his teeth, his heart pounding to break out of his chest at the thought. He'd need to deal with Kaleb before he could find Becky. Staring into his captain's spite-filled eyes, Lander's mind scrambled. Injured and with Kaleb now palming Lander's own Stones, things looked hopeless.

Words, unspoken yet undeniable and clear, imprinted Lander's mind. ***Go to Hunt. Change hovers.*** The truth sunk deep into Lander's thoughts. The only way to stop the insanity was to get to Hunt. He didn't know what he would do once he got close to the man but allowing Kaleb to capture him—*no problem; he already has*—was his best option.

Yet again, Lander struggled with the fact that the only way to help Becky was to let her go. Sweat beaded his forehead and he forced himself to cap the urge to lift his head and scream out his frustration into the mist-laden air. Instead, he curled his fingers into tight fists, his fingernails cutting into the skin of his palms, and limped in the direction Kaleb had waved. Right toward where Hunt stood toe to toe with Talon arguing, while the other guards faced outward around them, alert ... guarding ... observing the skirmishes now raging throughout the area.

Unrelenting in his attacks, Darrius continued to keep Shahan and Zorah trapped within their own shield while blocking incoming fireballs from Siprian. *If Siprian is keeping his word, Rahni must be as well.*

He scanned the field searching, and the surge of hope he felt died an untimely death. The Ungifted fought with an intensity born of anger, but they were no match for trained Stone Sovereigns. Though they attacked the Sovereigns with guns, farming implements, and even rocks and bare hands, many of the Sovereigns had bonded together in tight-knit units and formed shields like Lander had practiced, raising and lowering them to combine attack with defense. Bodies littered the ground around each group. Only other Stone Sovereigns could break through those defenses.

Lander's jaw dropped and a tendril of hope ignited in his heart as a large group of Core Dwellers appeared on the road, pouring over the crest of the hill. He recognized several from Zorah's community. Though, like their fellow Ungifted, most brandished farm tools, several carried crafted weapons, including staves, and swords, and even a couple pikes. Battle cries sounded as those in the lead charged down the hill and plowed into the battle. Sheer numbers drove the Sovereigns back.

Kaleb shoved Lander past Hunt's guards to a position near where the billionaire argued with his head of security.

"… guard you, get you home, but we will not fight these people for you." Talon's voice was a sharp hiss. Lander couldn't miss the meaning behind his words.

Hunt's reply was soft and carried a dangerous edge. "This is not over." He shifted and turned toward Kaleb, holding out his hand. "Well done, Sovereign. Now, give me those and go help your fellow Sovereigns before they are overrun."

Kaleb hesitated, clutching Lander's father's Stones to his chest, but Hunt's expression darkened, and the captain handed them over with a growl of disapproval. With a final glare aimed at Lander, Kaleb sprinted toward where Darrius fought.

Becky blinked when the sharp sound of the door unlocking pierced the gloom. A thin line of muted light shown through where the door shifted ajar.

Hunt and several teams of Stone Sovereigns had locked everyone in the dining hall sometime before full *Misfadura*. Throughout the ensuing, dark hours, Castor kept the nervous Ungifted calm. Using the remains of a broken light stick, he read from his Bible and spoke courage and peace into the tense situation. Becky could only guess at the time now as muffled voices filtered in through the doorway.

"This is it," Castor whispered. "Like we planned, everyone who has a Surface weapon, stay close to me; we will lead. The rest will follow. We must move quickly before they realize we are free. Now. Go!"

Still refusing to accept Michael was gone, Becky recognized she was in denial. She'd studied the stages of grief in school. Understanding didn't make dealing with the pain any easier. But as she clutched one of the rifles Castor had reworked to use his stone bullets, the first inklings of anger wormed their way through her, and she set her teeth.

Initially, Castor had refused to give her a gun, thinking she was in no shape to take part in what was coming. But once she demonstrated her proficiency, he relented. She thanked the Lord her father had insisted she learn to shoot, and her range instructor for allowing her to practice with his Mossberg. Pushing up onto her feet, she moved into position behind Castor and Desma. Keeping pace with them, she exited the dining hall and broke into a sprint as they raced toward a group of Stone Sovereigns she didn't recognize.

Pandemonium reigned as Ungifted fought Stone Sovereigns in a one-sided battle. But it was their hopelessness that drove them. Within minutes, several Ungifted lay on the ground, wisps of smoke rising from their bodies, reminding her of the way Michael died. Her anger spiked a notch. She searched out the Stone Sovereigns who had been there that night. In all the insanity of noise and the swirling lights of high Mist Rise, disorientation set in as she tried turning a full three-sixty. A scream sought release as a woman she had served with in the kitchen stumbled and fell at her feet, her chest smoking.

She lifted her eyes. Anguish blended with her seething anger and set her heartbeat to pounding in her ears as tears streaked down her cheeks. Not twenty yards away Kaleb stood speaking with Aurelius Hunt. And Lander was with them. She lifted the gun, but indecision muddled her thinking and then Kaleb sprinted away. Part of her wanted to follow the Sovereign, kill him slowly, one bullet at a time, but seeing Lander with Hunt sent a tremor of emotion through her.

Becky didn't know what to feel. Lander had betrayed her and gotten Michael killed. Now he stood with Hunt. *With Hunt! He's with Hunt. Everything is his fault!* The strength of love she felt for Lander birthed a nascent hatred fueled by fury. It roiled in her stomach like bad sushi. And she welcomed it like a controlled grief that pulled her attention from a harsher, deeper pain.

Her gaze sought out Kaleb. He now stood next to the man most responsible for Michael's death, Darrius. The two were intent on working to destroy a translucent barrier held in place by Shahan and an old woman Becky didn't recognize. Though three other Stone Sovereigns protected Darrius's and Kaleb's backs, no one looked in her direction.

Becky raised her rifle, took careful aim, and shot. She thought seeing Darrius crumble would give her satisfaction—ease her pain—but it didn't. The hole of grief within her spirit still felt hollow. Anguish at taking a life threatened her sanity. ***Not now, Becks. Don't think about it now. Just keep moving.*** "Michael?" She shook her head and pulled in a deep breath, then another. Her shot had drawn Kaleb's attention. She watched as if seeing a movie unfold as he leveled his Stones in her direction.

With Darrius down, however, Shahan and the woman dissolved their shield. Shahan sprang forward, wielding Stones of Power. Forcing Kaleb back. The young captain twisted away from a lance of fire directed at him, then slipped behind a knot of Ungifted and vanished.

Shahan strode to Becky. "I thank you, Lander's friend. It is good to be free to fight. Where is Castor?"

She shook her head, then shrugged. "Somewhere."

Shahan's attention riveted on Lander. "I must go help Lander."

"Why? Looks to me like he's made a new friend. He and Hunt should get along just fine."

Confusion crinkled Shahan's brow. "He is not with Hunt. He came with us. Kaleb injured and took Stones."

For a second Becky pushed Shahan's words away, needing to hold onto her new-found hatred. But what Shahan was saying filtered past her guard and looking over, her eyes met Lander's. The cold vise in her heart melted a fragment and she released a sob.

CHAPTER 31

With Mist Rise coming to an end, a faint breeze kicked up and the air began to clear. Chaos marked by the odor of burning flesh and punctuated by screams swirled around Lander as his head swiveled and his eyes burned at the carnage before him. His breath caught but then whooshed through his teeth when Darrius went down, allowing Shahan and Zorah to drop their shield and come to the aid of the struggling Ungifted. Bile climbed Lander's throat as Stone Sovereigns he had accepted as friends were, one by one, overrun by the sheer numbers of Ungifted. His promise to his mother had landed him in the middle of a war he couldn't stop. *How am I supposed to help?*

Hunt's powerful presence at his side held Lander in place. And any attempted escape while unable to walk was plain stupid. He'd be more of a liability to Shahan and Zorah—to the Ungifted rebels—than a help. He needed to recover; then, he needed to reclaim his Stones of Power. Keeping his hands low, he worked healing into the injured limb.

Standing helpless and watching without taking action as

people were falling—injured or dying—around him, sickened Lander's spirit, but with Hunt holding his Stones and Talon hovering directly behind them, Lander continued to heal and prayed for a chance to act.

Hunt's shout next to his ear broke Lander's concentration. At first, he thought the man was yelling at him but then realized Hunt had turned and was now glaring at Talon. "Why aren't you out there? I gave you a direct order. Now get out there and aid the Sovereigns who are working for us. If we can't stop these fools, we'll lose all control here. We must keep the power in Jenkins's hands."

Talon's response rumbled deep and low as he took a step forward and stood toe to toe with Hunt. Lander fought to keep his jaw from dropping as Talon's words confirmed Lander's suspicions.

"No. I am sorry Mr. Hunt, but I told you already. We will not fight these good people. They were kind to us, accepted us when they should have hated us. Castor has become a friend. I will not do them harm. We are warriors, not assassins. It's time we went home."

"You can't do this, Mr. Talon, remember who signs your paychecks. I can make it so you'll never find work again. Now, do what you were hired to do and obey my orders. Earn your pay."

"You do what you have to, and we'll do the same."

Lander turned in time to see sparks flying from Hunt's eyes as mottled red warmth crept into the man's face. "You will regret this." Hunt waved his arms to encompass all the guards. "I'll pay you double what I'm paying ... triple." He growled when not one of the men responded. "You will regret this. You're all fired! Every one of you."

"Whatever." Talon said as he stepped in and scooped Lander's Stones from Hunt's hands. "For now, I'm going to take these, then I'm going to see if Castor needs any help."

His gaze shifted to Glen, the wiry man who had helped Michael. "Keep Mr. Hunt out of trouble ... and safe."

Glen nodded. Talon faced Lander. "I still don't like you. Don't trust you. But ... these are yours, not Hunt's." He juggled Lander's Stones. "Tell me, kid, if I give these to you, what are you going to do with them? I know you're part of Kaleb's team, a Stone Sovereign like them; are you fighting with them or against them?"

Looking Talon in the eye Lander waved behind him. "Becky's out there somewhere fighting with the Ungifted. Michael too. So are my friend Shahan and my great grandmother. I don't want to fight, but if I have to, I'll be fighting with them. Did you mean what you said about getting Hunt home?"

Talon's eyes narrowed and he nodded.

"Then I want to help you. The Core needs to be rid of all Surface Dwellers."

"Including you?"

Lander blinked. "We don't have time for that now. Are you giving me my Stones or not?"

The hint of a smile crinkled the skin around Talon's eyes as he dropped the Stones of Power onto Lander's outstretched palm. "Okay, kid. Maybe you're not all bad. Let's put an end to this." Talon waved his men forward and jogged into the swirling bands of combatants.

Lighting up his Stones, Lander sent a final burst of healing into his leg. Behind him, Hunt stayed silent, his brow crinkled in thought, while Glen stood at his side. Ready for action, Lander, pocketed his Stones then scanned the shifting mob for Becky. Their eyes met and he froze.

She held a rifle and stared. A moment later, she marched toward him, slipping past knots of struggling Core Dwellers. Lander stepped forward when she got close, a crooked smile worming out onto his face. She marched right to him, her face set in a scowl, and slammed the stock of her rifle into his stomach. He stumbled back. "Becky ... what—"

She hit him again. "I hate you." Slam with the butt again. "I hate you."

He grabbed the gun and twisted it from her grasp. "Becky. What's ... Why..."

"Michael's dead. Michael's dead and it's all your fault."

A sick feeling flooded through Lander and he froze, numb, confused. He wanted to wrap his arms around Becky and tell her everything was going to be all right, but he couldn't. He couldn't process her words and he stood gaping at her anger, a chasm ripping open in his own heart. *Michael? No ... can't be. No. I'm going to save him ... keep promise ... get him...*

Tears flooded Lander's eyes then overflowed onto his cheeks. He reached out to Becky, but she batted his arm away, her own tears dribbling off her chin unnoticed. She looked so lost and frightened, Lander reached for her again and this time, though she struggled against him, he pulled her into his embrace and held her tight. She went stiff then crumbled into his chest, crying out in loud, racking sobs, wetting Lander's tunic.

He would have held her like that forever, wishing he could carry the pain for her rather than just share it. But as he looked out over her head, Darrius, breathing threats and murder stumbled toward them. Blood dribbled from a wound on the side of his head. Flames from his Stones of Power reflected off his eyes, turning them red and reminding Lander of pictures he'd seen of demons.

Releasing Becky, Lander grabbed her arms and set her aside. Dropping the rifle, he snared his father's Stones from his pocket and paced toward Darrius.

Darrius pulled to a stop, rubbing at the blood oozing down the side of his face. It caked the ends of his hair over his temple and smeared as he wiped.

"You killed Michael! Murderer!"

Becky's shout sent a wave of heat through Lander. "You? You killed my friend?"

Darrius curled his lip. "You mean the Ungifted upstart? Your *friend*? No true Stone Sovereign would lower himself to be friends with an Ungifted. And a Surface Dweller at that. But, then again, since you were raised on the Surface, you are not any better. Give it up. You will never be a proper Core Dweller, just a joke. Save yourself some pain and hand over those Stones before you get hurt."

Lander shook his head as he stuffed down his fury; for now, he would hold it at bay. He needed to keep his cool if he was going to fight Darrius. He'd seen the Sovereign in action. He was tricky and brutal. Though his words were meant to cut and unbalance him, Lander allowed them to slide past like Mist Rise moisture on a slick rock. He wished he could brush off the pain of Michael's death as easily. He locked memories of his big friend behind a sealed door. He'd come back for them later, when he had time to grieve.

Becky slipped in front of Lander. "Michael was more a man than you will ever be you self-satisfied, piece of garbage."

Concerned for Becky's safety, Lander pulled her back and shifted to block her from Darrius's gaze.

But Darrius ignored Becky, his ire fully fixed on Lander. "We accepted you despite your inadequate upbringing. Welcomed you. Gave you full Stone Sovereign status. You could have had anything you wanted, power, wealth, luxury, taken anyone you desired. But no. You chose to side with these vermin who cannot even protect themselves from Jerr'as without our help."

"Enough." Lander bounced his Stones on his palms. "You want to talk or fight?"

"No." Shahan dropped a large hand on Darrius's shoulder, causing the Sovereign to flinch then glare up at his old friend.

Shahan shook his head. "It is over. You will not do this. The battle is over. Now is time to begin helping wounded. Darrius, I have respect for you, but you will give me your Stones of Power. Now."

While Shahan was speaking, Zorah hobbled up behind him, leaning heavily on her staff. Her eyes narrowed and she spoke a few lines of Corish to Darrius. His mouth opened as if he would protest, but after another, single, emphatic word from Zorah as she thumped her staff on the ground, he snapped it shut.

"This is not over." Grunting, Darrius slammed his Stones onto Shahan's outstretched palm. He flicked his gaze over those around him, then whirled and headed toward the main road.

"Wait." Becky moved from behind Lander and took several steps after Darrius before turning back to the others. "He needs to pay for his crimes! He killed Michael ... and he's ... hurt a lot of people here. He tried to hurt me. He needs to be punished."

Zorah stepped up to Becky and took her hand. "Be peace. He will ... punish. We will punish." She tilted her head. "You be peace."

Becky's shoulders slumped and she nodded. Lander draped an arm across her back, grateful she understood Zorah's strange way of speaking. Becky was right, Darrius needed to be brought to justice along with those who joined him in committing crimes against other Core Dwellers. But, scanning the area, Lander knew Shahan was right too. Injured Ungifted and Stone Sovereigns moaned; bodies of the dead and dying needed to be gathered.

Rahni, Siprian, and several Sovereigns Lander recognized from Deolah's team were moving about, checking the injured, giving orders to Ungifted who helped move those with more serious wounds into the dining hall. *When did Deolah's team get here?*

His focus lifted. In the near distance, Castor and Desma talked with Talon. There was no mistaking the fury etched in the lines of Hunt's face, but Desma's look of satisfaction completed the story.

"Becky, why don't you go over to Castor and Desma?" Lander swallowed the lump stinging at the back of his throat when she turned cold eyes on him. "I know … I know … you blame me for Michael. We need to talk. But right now, I need to help. Can we talk later?"

Some of the ice melted from her gaze and a sliver of hope settled in Lander's heart. "Sure."

He watched her walk away, admiring her strength, then joined Shahan and Zorah as they moved to where Rahni sat next to an injured Ungifted, her Stones pulsing with power.

"How can we help?" Lander hunkered down next to the older Stone Sovereign.

A tired, grateful smile lit her face. "Thank you." She glanced up at the threesome. "Zorah. I am gladdened to see you. The more injured are in the dining hall. Your experience will do well there."

Zorah nodded. "I go."

"Shahan, please take over here. He has burns on his side." Rahni pointed out where the man's shirt had been blackened by fire. "Lander. Come with me. We will move to check the new wounded Castor's people are bringing here."

After stopping to assess the first couple victims, Lander left Rahni behind and moved forward on his own. He had a knack for judging the severity of injuries and started directing who went where: the worst went to the dining hall, lesser to Shahan, and those with mid-level wounds to Rahni. As he became more aware of the half-dozen other Sovereigns' abilities, he directed the injured to them accordingly.

Things slowed and Shahan had come over to take a break with Lander when several Ungifted raced up to where

Castor stood with Hunt and Talon, panting and waving their arms.

"That does not look good." Shahan twisted as he watched Castor's reaction. "Come Lander. Dov is with them. We must hear what they tell."

CHAPTER 32

Lander skidded to a stop behind Shahan, his gaze landing on
Becky. She stood next to Castor and Desma and after a
quick glance in his direction, looked away.

"They took my Sheba. Took my Sheba." Blood oozed from
a cut on Dov's temple and the man kept hopping from leg to
leg. "You have to go after her ... save her. My Sheba..."

Shahan rounded on the man, grabbing his arms and putting
a stop to his antics. "Jenkins? Did they take Chancellor Jenkins?"

Dov, a wild look in his eyes, shook his head and moaned.
"My Sheba."

Lander had never seen Shahan so upset. He shook Dov,
rattling the man's teeth. "Did they take the cart? Jenkins?"

A level of control came over Dov. "Yes. Two Sovereigns.
I recognized the one, Darrius. The other I did not know. They
found Chancellor Jenkins. I tried to stop them but..." he ran
his fingers over the bloody cut on his head, "they took ... took
the cart, Jenkins ... and they took my Sheba." His eyes sought
out Shahan's "Please, sir, please save Sheba. She is all my family.
All I have..."

Siprian and Zorah had come over while they were talking. Siprian wrapped an arm around Dov's shoulders and guided the man toward the dining hall. "I will care for him."

"Wait," Shahan shouted. "Dov, which way did they go?"

"Upriver. Up toward the Bec Jekesh Cavern."

Her face a stern mask, Zorah hobbled up to Lander. "Here … you … take."

Lander's breath caught when she held out his mother's Stones of Power. "Are you sure?"

Zorah huffed and shook her head. "You take."

Siprian began walking again and after dumping the Stones in Lander's hands, Zorah followed, her staff thumping on the path.

"Thank you, Siprian," Castor said. After a moment, he pivoted to face Shahan. "Shahan, you want to tell me what that was all about?"

Lander spoke up. "Jenkins was in the cart. Zorah drugged him. We were taking him to the Avortex. Planned to stop here and pick up Becky and … Michael." Lander's voice cracked. "Now Darrius has him. Everything's falling apart." Lander ran his hand over the back of his neck, the fingers coming away sticky with sweat.

"Lander. Come. We will catch them up." Shahan's words took a moment to sink in before Lander looked up with an ember of hope burning in his chest.

"Take help with you." Castor waved a group of Ungifted holding rifles over. "Hovan, you and Alef go with Shahan and Lander. They are going after Sovereigns, so be prepared." Turning back to Shahan, he continued. "Hovan and Alef are best with the guns. Hovan's son was killed by Darrius so he will do what needs to be done."

"I will go too." Talon's voice rose behind Lander, causing him to flinch.

"No," Castor said. "You need to keep Hunt in line."

270

"My people can do that without me. Just give me one of those Mossberg's you reworked."

Shahan's brow crinkled. "We will take Hovan and Talon. No one else. Come. We must hurry."

Becky approached as Alef handed his weapon to Talon. From the look on her face, she was about to demand she accompany them. Lander held up a hand and shook his head. "No, Becky." He cringed at the look she gave him but plowed forward. "Castor, do you still want to return to the Surface?"

Castor released a growl, his focus on the distant town. "No. I can't leave now. Perhaps ... Desma.

"No." Desma's response carried the weight of determination. "I will stay with you. You're right Castor. There's too much at stake, we can't leave now."

Lander huffed out a breath and grabbed hold of his confidence. "Okay. This is how it's going to work. While Shahan and I track down Jenkins, Castor, you get Becky, Morrison, Hunt, and the others to the Bec Jekesh Cavern. We'll meet you on this side of the cavern. Make sure they are ready to travel when we get there with Jenkins because we're going right to the Avortex and I'm taking everyone up before anything else goes wrong."

Castor's mouth drifted open, but he snapped it shut. "Yes, Sovereign Lander. It will be done. And if you get there before we do, will you wait?"

Lander gave a stiff nod to Castor and Desma before setting his focus on Talon. "If you are joining us, you need to know, Shahan is in command. Not you."

A look of reluctant admiration slipped across Talon's face before his features returned to their normal closed expression. "I understand."

Their need to move pressed on Lander but he took up a position in front of Becky. "I don't even know what to say. I understand your anger. But I also need to see you safe. Please go with Castor."

She refused to meet his eyes. Tears flowed again. "I will."

It was all she said before walking away, but the soft, husky tone of her voice held the promise of forgiveness out to Lander.

Lander, Shahan, Talon, and Hovan sprinted up to the road and continued at a rapid pace through Shavah El'Ruhan.

"Are you certain they didn't find a place to hide in town?"

Talon's question sent a quiver of doubt through Lander, but Shahan's answer helped set his nerves at ease. "No, they will try to get to Shavah Al'Wisan. Jenkins has ... support ... there."

For the next few hours, they continued to jog stopping only briefly to drink. Shahan bent over the path often, but shook his head when Talon asked if he found any indication Darrius and the others had been there.

"Darrius knows. Staying on the path means leaving no trace of their passing." Shahan's gaze snagged on a patch of green to his right and he stopped to check it out. "No trace except a donkey's. See. Here."

Lander walked over and looking at the vegetation, smiled. Sheba had been there not long ago—and left a deposit to signal her passing.

"But if they head back to Shavah Al'Wisan by boat, we'll never catch them." Lander surveyed the road before them. "They have too much of a head start."

"This is true, Sovereign Lander," Shahan said, moving forward at a trot. "But if they decided to head toward Shavah Deklakh instead, we will catch them in the Bec Jekesh Cavern. Either way we must try."

"But you said they would head for Al'Wisan."

"That would be their best. But we must not discard another choice. They are not far now. We will know when we reach Dock Town. If they could not get boat, we may catch them there."

With renewed hope they could catch their quarry, the four pushed into a run as *Misfadura* set in. Sweat trickled down Lander's back and he wished for a cool breeze. Not much chance at this time. Except for Mist Rise, breezes were rare and usually confined to narrower spaces like the Bec Jekesh Cavern. He sucked his tongue to generate more moisture in his mouth, but with a chance they might catch Jenkins and Darrius if they didn't stop, he kept running.

Not long after, they jogged past the pasture where Lander had first demonstrated his abilities for Jenkins, disturbing a flock of sheep that ran across to the far side of the field, bleating their protest. Coming around the bend, Dock Town lay spread out before them. Light glittered off the surface of the river while the damsel fly like insects flitted about above the churning current.

The sound of braying came from near the docks. Sheba. Lander's pulse raced and he pulled to a stop. "Shahan. How do you want to handle this?"

Shahan's brow crinkled as he scanned the town, his eyes narrowed. He scrubbed a hand over his chin. A minute passed and Lander squelched his rising anxiety.

"Hovan. Do they know you?"

His face set like iron, Hovan shook his head. "I know them. They do not give attention to Ungifted."

"Go down but keep near huts. Look like you belong. Hide your weapon." Shahan's gaze shifted to Talon. "They know you. You sneak behind huts. Join Hovan there." Shahan pointed out a spot between two rows of huts across from the docks. "You shoot with that?" He indicated Castor's reworked rifle.

"If Castor hasn't messed it up too much, yeah, I can shoot."

"Good. Lander and I will approach in the open with our Stones. Darrius and Kaleb will respond to threat. We distract;

you get Chancellor Jenkins. But if you cannot. Do not let him escape."

Talon swiped at a trickle of sweat dribbling down his brow with the back of his hand as he studied the river. His mouth a tight line, he nodded once. "That'll work."

"Try to capture not kill. But we will do what we must to stop." Shahan's eyes flicked to Lander. "You understand?"

"Yes."

"You can do this?"

"Yes."

"Good. Hovan. Talon. Go. We will start after you."

Lander shook out his hands as he juggled from foot to foot attempting to control the level of adrenaline coursing through him as he waited with Shahan. He lifted a quick prayer when Shahan said, "Now."

Following Shahan into Dock Town, Lander pulled his four Stones, balancing two on each hand. As if they sensed his tension, all flared. Fire flickered from his mother's two. He locked away his fear and steeled himself to face what would come.

The connection between Lander and his Stones strengthened. Doubts faded. This moment in time, whatever happened next, was part of what his mother had called him for. He couldn't fail. He owed it to his people. And he owed it to Michael. The memory of Michael when he fought with the lightsaber back at Crossways Mission filled Lander's mind. *I will not fail.*

Walking into town down the main path, Lander moved into position at Shahan's right side. Ahead, Darrius and Kaleb were helping a wobbly Jenkins into one of the small stone crafts.

Dena stood guard on the dock. Her eyes widened when Lander and Shahan came into view. "Darrius. They are here. I cannot face them lonely."

Lander's heart thumped so hard the rushing blood echoed

in his ears. He had hardened himself to face Darrius and Kaleb, but Dena had always been kind to him, and her presence here threatened to undo him.

Shahan must have sensed Lander slowing and understood the cause. "Dena made her choice. Do not lose nerve. Remember. We lose, and all who died at camp died for nothing."

"I know. I know. But why Dena. I thought she'd…"

"She has chosen. So have you."

Lander pulled in a breath and released it with a harsh sound through his clenched teeth. "Yes. I made a promise." Under his breath, he added, "and I've messed up on too many promises already."

Leaving Jenkins in the boat, Darrius and Kaleb hopped onto the dock and flanked Dena. Darrius walked out, two glowing Stones in hand. Lander shoved his confusion about whose Stones Darrius now carried to the back of his mind as the Sovereign spoke. "What are you doing, Shahan? We have a good thing going and you are ruining it over some stinking Ungifted. Think. You used to enjoy our games too. Remember. You are the one who discovered Ungifted make great lures for hunting Jerr'as.

"We have power, prestige. We can take anything we want … *anyone* we want … with Jenkins in charge. Morrison was going to ruin that but Jenkins … he's on our side."

"You know he is right Sha." Dena stepped up to Darrius's right. "Give up this silly notion about Ungifted being equal. You know they are not." A seductive smile curled her full lips and softened her face. Her tongue peeked out. "Come on. Join us. We will forgive your little blunder. Go back to the way things were."

Lander focused on Kaleb as the captain shifted away from Darrius and Dena. Skitters traced up Lander's spine, igniting a new wave of adrenaline. Kaleb shuffled again; his gaze locked on Lander as he moved alongside one of the small, round huts.

Kaleb inched closer while Dena and Darrius had stopped moving.

No problem. I'm onto you, Kaleb. With one side now protected by the dwelling, Kaleb continued to approach Lander and Shahan, his advance controlled. Lander caught the flicker in Kaleb's eyes as the captain's Stones flared to life. At the same instant Darrius and Dena attacked Shahan, spears of light igniting the air between. A second later, Kaleb's shield hovered in front of Darrius and Dena.

Lander ignored the impulse to set a shield. Their only chance of winning lay in attack, not defense. Engage the other Sovereigns. Give Talon and Hovan a chance to grab Jenkins. Lander's Stones vibrated with restrained power. Releasing his hold, he unleashed a barrage of fireballs at Kaleb.

Anguished screams echoed off the stone house where Kaleb had stood as Lander rounded on Darrius and Dena. He didn't want to think of the carnage his attack might have caused a man he had called friend, but he prayed it would incapacitate Kaleb without killing him.

The shield protecting Darrius and Dena faltered, then collapsed. A quick glance to his left, revealed Shahan on the ground. He prayed the big Sovereign was alive as he turned his full attention on Darrius and Dena. Already the two had split up, moving in opposite directions, seeking shelter behind the closest huts.

He considered going invisible, but that would defeat the purpose. *Keep them focused on me. Shahan can't help. I need to ... do ... alone.*

"Hey, Darrius, you made Shahan an offer, what about me?"

CHAPTER 33

Stillness hung heavy in the air, the only sounds the white noise of the churning river and the whirring of insect wings, as Lander waited for Darrius's response. Fear the Stone Sovereign leader wouldn't take his question seriously battered at Lander's confidence. *Come on. Come on. Think.*

His Stones hot on his palms, Lander waited. Limping and bruised, a seething Kaleb shuffled out onto the road and took a stand next to Darrius.

Casting another quick glance to his left, Lander released a pent-up breath when Shahan groaned and stirred. Shifting his weight from leg to leg, Lander fought the urge to push Darrius. *Give him time. Let him think.*

Seconds dragged by like eternities.

"You would join us?" Not Darrius's, but Dena's voice rose.

Okay, Lander. Play the game. He juggled his Stones and stepped out to the middle of the road, praying Darrius and Dena didn't attack. He flicked his eyes to the dock. He needed to know; had he given Talon and Hovan enough time. Motion in the boat. It pushed away from the dock. Tension drained. Paddles dipped and rose. Talon and Hovan. They had Jenkins. *Time to end this.*

Lander concentrated and set a bubble of protection around Shahan. He didn't know if he could create two separate shields at the same time, but grunting with the effort, he established a second, thin barrier in front of himself. *Light, but it'll do.*

Lander pulled in a deep breath, released it, and began walking forward.

"Hey, Dena. Thanks for asking. But ... no. You see, I was taught that all people are created equal. Yeah, *created.* Not *evolved.* Jenkins led you to believe Stone Sovereigns are higher creatures, more *evolved.* He fed you a lie. So, I'll take my chances protecting fellow humans, even if they are weaker than I am."

Ignoring Shahan who struggled into a sitting position within Lander's bubble, Darrius, Kaleb, and Dena shifted into a line on the road opposite Lander. He had the impression of being in an old western gun fight and stifled the urge to holster his Stones like six shooters.

"Spoken like a true idiot, Lander." Kaleb waved his hand over his head in a circle. "Look around you. Without us, the Ungifted and lesser Gifted would all have been killed off by Jerr'as long ago. It's survival of the fittest. We keep them alive; they serve us."

Sorrow for his fellow Sovereigns settled in Lander's heart. He wanted to reach out to them, but they were past listening. They understood one thing: power. So he would show them power.

"Last chance, Kaleb. Surrender now. If this becomes a fight, you will lose."

The three laughed. "You are the one who will lose," Darrius's words sliced through the town.

"Then let's do this and see who is standing at the end."

Spikes of fire launched from Darrius and Kaleb as Dena threw a whip of corded fire toward Lander's neck.

His instincts screamed turn away, but if he did the slight protection his shield offered would twist with him, exposing his back. Instead, adrenaline spiking, he threw all he had into a wall of fire to brace the flimsy shield. If it slowed the attacks aimed at him, they would lose power. He might be injured, but not seriously.

The result of his release flooded the entire street with a billowing wave of liquid fire. *Didn't know I could do that...*

Darrius's scream of fury rose over the roaring of the flames. He had reacted, encasing his companions and himself in his own protective shielding as the fire surged past them.

"I'm going to kill you," Darrius shouted as he dropped his protection and raced at Lander, his own Stones flickering with suppressed power. Behind him. Dena dropped to her knees; a smoldering arm held to her chest. Kaleb stood, stunned for a second, then joined Darrius.

Lander skipped back a few steps then turned and raced to the closest house. Skidding past the rounded wall, he pulled up and went invisible. Talon and Hovan were safe on the river with Jenkins. But Shahan was still exposed and vulnerable. Lander needed to reclaim the power he was diverting to Shahan's shield to challenge Darrius and Kaleb, but he refused to leave his friend defenseless. Together, the two captains posed a major threat. He had hoped his fire would take one of them out, but, instead, Dena had been incapacitated, not one of the two, stronger Sovereigns.

Footsteps thudded behind him.

"*Shivah'zor.*" Darrius's breath came in heavy gasps. "He is invisible."

Kaleb grabbed Darrius's arm. "Idiot. He will go back to Shahan. Hurry."

Lander released his own curse. He pivoted. He'd never

reach Shahan before them. Coming back around the house, he came to a stop and focused one, thin, tight beam like the one he'd used to break the lock on Shahan's cell. Like the stone around him, he stilled and concentrated, his teeth clenched in a snarl. *Must be perfect.* He released the tiny spike.

Darrius's back arched, his mouth flung open and a high-pitched scream rushed out, then he smashed to the ground squirming as his hands clawed at the back of his neck. A moment later, he went still.

Lander swallowed back the bile climbing his throat. Kaleb had stopped when Darrius screamed. Now, he stood over his fallen leader, disbelief distorting his features. His gaze rose to meet Lander's. "You … traitor. I will kill you myself."

"Kaleb stop! Just stop! You don't have to do this. Darrius isn't dead. I just … put him to sleep for a bit. But he will have to pay for his crimes. Please. I don't want to hurt you."

Something bit into Lander's waist. Pricking like a million hornet stings. Hot. Burning. Encircling. He looked down. A whip of sizzling flame. Holding the end, Dena stood glaring. Her uniform singed, and torn, and her eyes burning with the light of hatred. She huffed and yanked the whip, dragging Lander toward her.

He bit his tongue to keep from crying out as the narrow cord burned through his tunic and singed his skin.

"You forgot about me, Lander. So focused on Darrius and Kaleb. You didn't think I could pose a threat. Well, super special Surface Dweller, guess who gets the final laugh." Gone was the sweet persona, the slender imp Lander had hoped to know better.

"Surprised you, did I not? Do you know how many times Kaleb got the credit for things I had done? In a sense I am a bit like an Ungifted. I go unnoticed." She laughed; the soft tinkling sound Lander had enjoyed in the past filtered through the air. "I have you now, truly and complete."

As she spoke, Dena pulled Lander closer. He allowed his

Stones to go quiet. If he tried to use them now, the power in the cord touching his body would be amplified by their proximity. It was a mistake he had made once before in a training exercise. Then it had meant just a nasty burn; now, it could mean death.

When he was twenty feet from Dena, Kaleb walked over. "You idiot." He shook his head. "You could have had it all but instead you chose to be a hero. You and Shahan. You are going to pay for this. When we get Chancellor Jenkins back to Shavah Al'Wisan, he will sentence you both to death by Jerr'as. You will suffer."

"I do not think so." Shahan levelled his Stones at Dena. Lander's bubble still rested where Shahan had fallen, shimmering and intact, but somehow Shahan had managed to walk out, leaving it behind, then approached without notice. "Release your hold, Dena. Now."

She hesitated, her eyes flicking from Lander to Shahan. "Dena. When have I ever made a threat I did not keep?"

The cord of fire fragmented, and Dena took a step back. "I will not challenge you, Shahan."

Still keeping his focus on Dena, Shahan spoke. "Lander, do Kaleb like you did Darrius. Make him sleep."

Lander shook his head. "Can't. Unless he turns around."

Shahan grunted. "Kaleb. It is over. Give Lander your Stones … unless you wish me to kill Dena and you."

Kaleb chewed the inside of his mouth and huffed through several breaths before he extinguished the glow in his Stones and handed them to Lander. "You win. For now."

Lander slipped his Stones of Power into a pocket and took Kaleb's, then limped to Dena and took hers. After depositing Kaleb's and Dena's Stones into his pouch, he pulled his father's back out and walked over to Shahan.

"You can release my protection," Shahan said. "We need to bind them."

"How did you get out?" Lander stared at Shahan. "You

were injured and immobile, then you were outside my bubble and walking. How?"

A half-smile crimped one side of Shahan's lips. "I tell you someday when you are older."

Lander opened his mouth to protest but then closed it. A chuckle escaped as tension and adrenaline bled from him. "I will hold you to that."

A rare laugh slipped through Shahan's lips as Talen and Hovan approached, a bound and gagged Jenkins in tow.

Hovan picked up his pace and lifted a length of rope. "I will see to these." He stumbled to a stop when Darrius groaned. "He is not dead?"

"No. He will be judged. Tie him as well." The tone in Shahan's voice left no doubt he expected Hovan to cooperate.

"He killed my son."

"I know." Shahan said. "He will pay for his crimes. The Elders will form again and judge. This is how it must be if we want order."

Hovan grunted but obeyed. By this time, villagers began leaving their huts and gathering around. Shahan called one over. "Telia. You are Dock Master today, yes?"

Lander recognized the woman. She had helped Kaleb and the team a couple times in the past.

"Yes, Stone Sovereign. I am today."

"We must go. You will keep these prisoners until we return. Do not untie. Do not leave alone. They are dangerous."

The woman, a Gifted by her clothing, pressed her lips together in a tight line. "They have enemies here. Hurt many. And they strong. We will do best we can."

Shahan nodded. "As you can. Keep them in separate huts. Feed them. Watch them. We will come or send others to take them to Shavah Al'Wisan. They will face justice."

"It is good. We will watch."

"Thank you. We must go, but can you share food first."

"And a place to sleep for a bit," Lander added as he stepped up to Shahan. "I don't know about you but expending that kind of energy and being on the go for so long, I'm spent. Plus, I need to heal again." He touched the sticky wound encircling his waist with trembling fingers.

"Mist Rise not long off." Shahan studied the river for a moment. "We will move faster after resting. We will leave at Mist Rise."

"I will not go with you," Hovan said. "I will stay. Will watch prisoners."

Lander thought Shahan was going to object when he didn't respond at first, but after a moment's consideration he huffed. "You may stay. But do not harm Darrius."

"It is well," Telia said. "Hovan is cousin. He will behave."

While Hovan walked off with Telia, the prisoners, and a half-dozen men and women armed with spears, the remaining villagers conducted the three travelers to one of the largest dwellings, a green boulder with a second-floor balcony set on pilings and overlooking the Bec Jekesh. The hint of a breeze coming off the water enticed Shahan, Lander and Talon to bed down on the balcony.

Lander's thoughts were filled with Becky as he lay on a padded mat watching the water slip by. The loss of Michael weighed heavy on him. Michael and Becky were best friends and Lander couldn't fault her for blaming him for Michael's death. Seeing her again stirred his longings. He wanted to be with her. *Hey God! Why? Why can't things be … not so complicated?*

The river continued to chuckle below as if laughing at Lander's question. He pulled in a deep breath and released it as he turned onto his back and cradled his head on clasped fingers. The last thing he remembered before drifting off was the memory of his mother's voice. **You are destined. You must return to the Core and save our people.**

CHAPTER 34

Lander yawned, then stuffed a tiny barley round into his mouth, chewing without thinking. He blinked scratchy eyes, fighting the bleary sight brought on by too much energy expended and too little sleep. Mist Rise was a faint promise over the Bec Jekesh. Shahan had woken Lander and Talon, saying he wanted to get an early start. Yawning again, Lander pushed up onto his feet. Shahan and Talon had already left the house and he could hear them talking below, the aroma of their *ah'sim* floating up to the balcony.

He gathered his Stones, placing them in the larger pouch one of the locals had given him, then rubbed a finger over his teeth, then ran his hands through his greasy hair. He climbed down the ladder-like stairs. The need for warm *ah'sim* lured him into the small kitchen to grab a mug before heading out to where Shahan and Talon stood, watching the river.

No one spoke, they stood in silence. With no pressure to perform or excuse or talk, Lander relaxed into the moment. It wouldn't last. Soon the mist would dance, and he'd be on his way to the Bec Jekesh Cavern.

He'd see Becky. Would she talk to him? Forgive him? Could he have done anything different? Stopped Darrius? He wished he could take away her pain but knew he couldn't. He groaned. Until he saw Becky and talked to her, he'd have to live with unanswered questions. Lander wanted to see Becky. His heart hurt with the ongoing separation. And yet, he feared seeing her. He wanted to hide from her anger ... her hatred. He hated himself. And he hated his default setting of running from things. He refused to do it again. If he'd just faced Becky's need months ago, she and Michael would be safe at home, living their lives.

"Lander. Finish your *ah'sim*. We must go."

Lander gave Shahan a sideways look. The questions still hovering in his mind like insects over the Bec Jekesh, he dumped the rest of his now-cold *ah'sim* on a fern and walked back into the kitchen. Ducking his head, he thanked the Ungifted woman for her kindness. She blushed and said something in Corish. Lander thought for a minute, translating in his mind, then said, "you are welcome. Your *ah'sim* was delicious. So was the bread. Thank you." Her blush deepened into scarlet. Lander smiled then passed Shahan and Talon going in to return their mugs as he walked back out.

Misty tendrils trailed from the unseen ceiling above, meeting and swirling with the fog rising from the river. Mist Rise had begun. Lander pulled in a deep breath of the moisture laden air and coughed then yawned wide as his lungs cried out for more oxygen. He'd never get used to the heavy air of the Core.

Shahan and Talon exited the dwelling, both bearing packs on their backs. Shahan tossed one to Lander. Catching it, Lander slipped the straps over his shoulders and followed the two as they walked to another house where they collected Chancellor Jenkins. Though red in the face and huffing his fury, the man said nothing as his bindings were checked and he was forced to march in front of the others as they headed down the path paralleling the river.

Two hours later, the roar of the water rushing beneath the stone bridge that crossed the Bec Jekesh as it flowed out of the Bec Jekesh Cavern drowned out all other sounds.

"If Castor has come, he will be in the main cavern. We will not break until we arrive there," Shahan shouted in Lander's ear. "Be alert for Jerr'as."

As Lander walked across the narrow strip, he looked down into the swirling chaos rushing beneath. He caught his breath and his balance. Though he'd made this trip several times in the past few months, he still hadn't learned to not look down. Jenkins, Shahan, and Talon headed into the tunnel without waiting and Lander hurried to catch up.

Lander's eyes adjusted as he left the brighter golden light behind and moved into the dimmer green-hued light of the narrow tunnel. Shahan continued pressing for speed and Lander wondered why since they would end up waiting for Castor and the others anyway.

They had left the linking tunnel behind and were walking toward a small, secluded hollow off the path, next to the river, when Jenkins stopped, turned, and faced Shahan. "You still have a chance to make this right, Shahan. Help me stop this uprising. I'll forgive your past indiscretions and give you the Vice Chancellorship. You'll have even more power than before. What do you gain helping the Ungifted? Think. The Core needs me to keep order. Let Lander and Talon meet Castor and take Morrison up to the Surface. Return with me to Shavah Al'Wisan and together we'll rule."

Lander stumbled back a step when Talon growled a curse and grabbed the front of Jenkins's tunic before pushing the man down onto a patch of lichen. "Don't! Don't even try. I'm taking you home. I'm just sorry you can't be convicted for your crimes without revealing the truth of the Core. Keep your trap shut, or I'll gag you. Got it?"

It was the most Lander had heard Talon say at one time

and contradicted Lander's opinion of the man. *Castor must have really gotten to the guy.*

Shahan stepped up to Talon. "Thank you. I would not do … as … he…"

"I know. But his drivel turned my stomach. I've had my fill of idiots like him and Hunt."

Shahan leaned down and helped Jenkins to his feet. He led the way to the edge of the river where they all sat. Lander passed out slivers of dried meat and travel rounds of bread while everyone drank from water jugs, Shahan sharing with Jenkins. They were packing back up when the murmur of voices echoed through the cavern, increasing as a band of travelers approached.

"Wait here." Shahan motioned for Talon and Jenkins to remain sitting then waved Lander forward as he moved toward the main path.

A couple minutes later, Castor and Rahni, leading a large group, entered the main cavern. Behind Castor, Becky walked with Desma, followed by Hunt and his people. As Shahan stepped onto the path, Castor startled but then greeted the large Stone Sovereign. "Greetings and well met, Sovereign Shahan." The two grasped arms in Core fashion.

Lander couldn't keep his eyes off Becky as she and Desma stopped. When her gaze landed on him, he offered a crooked smile. She flattened her mouth and looked to the other side of the cavern. Lander's shoulders drooped. Determined to not cause her any more pain than he already had, he shuffled back to where Talon waited. "Come on. It's Castor."

Talon grabbed Jenkins's arm and pulled the man erect.

"I'm getting up you moron," Jenkins said as he struggled to find his balance. Talon pushed the man forward. Lander let the two pass, then followed them to the road.

"Are you needing to break?" Shahan asked as Talon and Jenkins joined the group. Lander made his way to the back where he stood kicking tiny pebbles off the path.

"We stopped before leaving the El'Ruhan Cavern so we should be fine walking for a while longer." Castor wiped the back of his neck and released a soft chuckle. "I forgot how humid this cavern remains."

Shahan, Rahni, and Castor started off, continuing to talk quietly among themselves; Desma and Becky, once again, trailed. Talon pushed Jenkins to a spot next to Hunt and joined his men guarding the two. Behind them a group of Ungifted took turns pulling a cart carrying Morrison. Huddled beneath a blanket, the man looked even sicker than the last time Lander had seen him, and Lander wondered if traveling the Avortex might kill him.

Lander positioned himself so he could watch Becky from a distance. He huffed and wiped away a tear that leaked from his right eye, walling off his sorrow at her rejection. He wanted to make her forgive him, but he couldn't force her, so he trudged along, watching, his senses alert for threats.

His dream of Becky pursued by Jerr'as arose as a vision in his mind, sending adrenaline spiking through him. Hours slipped by without incident as they continued to make good time through the cavern, the Bec Jekesh rushing and growling to their right. The sense that danger dogged their heels prompted Lander to slow, drifting farther back from the large group. He reasoned with himself that Jerr'as would never attack so many people, especially since there were Stone Sovereigns present. But the feeling persisted, like an itch he couldn't scratch.

They stopped for a long break near where Lander had last drilled the shield exercise with his team. Another thing he had lost. There was no team anymore. Surrounded by people, Lander struggled against his old habit of separating himself from others and hiding behind a shield of loneliness.

As the party started moving again, Lander, again, paced himself to keep his distance. He fought the urge to run up to Becky, grab her hand, and beg for forgiveness. Like sparring partners, the desire to reconnect with Becky fought the older habit of closing in and keeping to himself.

He'd begun to discount his earlier anxiety, chocking it up to his own internal battle when the hair on the back of his neck rose and the hint of a familiar stench drifted by. Instinct kicking in, Lander grabbed his four Stones and sprinted off the path to climb a rock outcropping that gave him a good view of the cavern before and behind.

If he doubted himself, Shahan's and Rahni's reactions affirmed his intuition. Both had their Stones of Power out and glowing. They separated to positions on opposite sides of the path and scanned the area as Castor pulled everyone else into a tight group. Talon's experience was evident as he directed his men to grab their firearms and form a cordon around the others. "Get ready. Eyes out."

"Lander," Shahan shouted. "What do you see?"

"Nothing … yet." His gaze shifted as he studied the surrounding vegetation. "But…"

"Yes," Rahni said. "We feel it too. And smell it. Jerr'as."

Lander's Stones of Power sparked as if sensing his fear. Not for himself, but for Becky. His eyes were drawn to where she stood like some kind of wild west woman, rifle in hand, ready.

Jerr'as howls erupted from the area they had passed through. An instant later, Lander, Shahan, and Rahni sprinted back down the path. They hadn't gone far when screams broke out behind them. Lander's heart leaped into his throat. There must be two groups of Jerr'as. Once the band behind had drawn off him and the other Sovereigns, those before attacked. Shots echoed off the cavern walls.

"Go, Lander. Rahni and I will continue." Lander heard Shahan's shout from over his shoulder as he turned and ran back. Chaos greeted him. Talon faced a Jerr'as as it circled the soldier. A second later, the floor seemed to quake when he fired.

The stone bullet flew into the Jerr'as's gaping jaw and exited the back of its head, collapsing the animal.

A quick inspection revealed the guns had turned the tide and, though a couple people writhed on the ground with injuries, the Jerr'as were retreating. Lander scanned for Becky. Skitters of fear traced up his spine. He couldn't find her. A scream from farther up the cavern drew his attention. Becky stood alone swinging her gun like a club.

Lander was already moving when the Jerr'as knocked the gun from Becky's grasp. Shades of the night he had saved her back at the mission hovered as Lander, for the second time in his life, moved outside the constraints of time. He ran up the side of a boulder. Springing through the air, he set his shield. Momentum from his flight propelled him forward as he touched ground, sprinting. He slid between Becky and the Jerr'as as time resumed and the impact from massive claws bowed his shield. His eyes widened as the claws came within inches of his face before they bounced back.

The Jerr'as howled its frustration and clawed at the jelly-like shield. Lander expanded the shield to create a full bubble around Becky and himself.

"You okay?"

"Yeah. I'm okay."

"It didn't bite or scratch you, did it?"

"I don't think so. I ... ran out of ammo."

"Becky. I can't kill it through the shield. I'm going to have to drop the protection."

"I understand," she said as the creature slammed into the barrier, scratching and biting.

"Get ready. When I say go, run."

"Leave you?"

Lander ground his teeth. "Yes. Ready?"

Warmth spread through him from the spot when her fingers touch the small of his back. "Ready."

"Go!"

His Stones flaring, Lander disbursed the bubble. The Jerr'as attacked. Teeth bared. Claws out, the creature slammed into Lander. The force drove him back. Staggering, he fell onto his tailbone. Burning pain shot up his back and down his arm. Blocking the pain, he focused. A spear of intense blue shot into the crazed Jerr'as. It dropped. Charred and smoking.

Sucking in large doses of air, Lander looked over his shoulder. "Becky?"

"I'm here." She knelt next to him. "Lander? You're bleeding. Did it bite you?"

Lander's eyelids drooped. A chuckle escaped. He tilted his head back and pulled in another deep breath before releasing it in a huff. "It's just a scratch."

"Are you sure?"

He nodded. "I'm sure. Just give me a minute to catch my breath."

She pushed up onto her feet. Her mouth firm, she met his gaze. "I … don't even know how to feel. Part of me still loves you, but a big part of me needs to hate you right now."

Before Lander could respond, they were surrounded by concerned friends. Rahni knelt where Becky had been and examined Lander's hand. The pain had traveled up his arm from where the Jerr'as had taken a chunk out of the back of Lander's hand.

Rahni shook her head. "Nasty. Full of pain. But not serious. You are lucky."

"Not lucky," Becky said. "Blessed." She met his eyes, then turned and walked away.

CHAPTER 35

Rahni insisted Lander remain sitting while she cupped his hand in both of hers, her Stones glowing and warming him, and focused healing into his hand. Lander bit down on his lower lip, almost drawing blood. Becky walking away had left a gaping hole in his heart.

He was running out of time. If he couldn't get her to talk before they reached the Avortex, would he lose her completely? The thought of talking about their relationship while surrounded by people like Hunt and Jenkins festered in his mind. They would be trapped together in his small bubble of protection for hours. *No. I have to get her to talk before we get there.*

Once Rahni proclaimed Lander fit enough to complete his healing by himself, Castor helped him onto his feet and the two followed Rahni to where Shahan worked to heal others who had been injured in the Jerr'as attack. Nearly two hours after the attack, Shahan, Rahni, and Lander finished healing all those they could help. Exhaustion plaguing everyone, Shahan decided they would camp there through *Misfadura* and resume the journey at Mist Rise.

They had lost two Ungifted and Glen, the security guard

who helped Michael when he was shot. Morrison's health had given out and he also died during the attack. As the customs of the Core dictated, they burned the bodies. They also burned the dozen Jerr'as bodies left behind.

Saddened by the losses and uncomfortable approaching Becky as she talked with Desma, Lander volunteered to take first watch and wandered across the path to sit alone on a rocky ledge that gave him a good view of the area.

Time slipped by and Lander must have dozed off because he startled awake. Senses on alert, he sat without moving, allowing the quiet sounds of the cavern to float over him, listening for anything out of place while he searched the area for signs of Jerr'as. Pulling in deep breaths as his eyes roamed, he sought any trace of the Jerr'as's peculiar odor. Nothing. Except for the white noise of the rushing river, all was quiet. Though surprised no one had come to relieve him, he decided to let it slide. At this point, it didn't matter anyway.

He rose to his feet, groaning at the stiffness in his hand and neck as he worked his fingers and bent his head from side to side, kneading the muscles. He stretched and yawned, then hopped down from his perch. Shahan and the security guards were already awake and moving about.

Crossing the path, Lander walked to where Shahan, Talon, Castor, and, surprisingly, Hunt were talking. Lander had noticed a difference in the billionaire after one of the Ungifted died when he flung himself between a Jerr'as and Hunt, taking a nasty bite in the process. It seemed as if the reality of Hunt's mortality had sunk in and stomped on his notions of self grandeur. That, or the fact he had to admit Core Dwellers weren't any less human than Surface Dwellers.

"...should reach the Avortex by next Mist Rise if we leave now," Castor said as Lander approached.

"Unless we run in with more Jerr'as," Shahan said. He turned to Lander. "Anything?"

"No."

"Then let us eat and go."

Lander smiled at Shahan's unique brand of English as he followed the man to where Rahni had a small fire going. The aroma of fresh brewing *ah'sim* floated by as the gentle movement of air signaled early Mist Rise. Soon everyone was enjoying chunks of cheese and dried fruit and washing all down with the warm, sweet drink

By the time they returned to the road, beads of heavy mist covered everything, glistening in the golden light, and turning the rocky surface of the path slick like a thin layer of black ice.

Becky walked with bent head, her hood sparkling with tiny droplets. Lander watched as he followed, unable to keep his eyes from wandering back to her irresistible presence every time he looked away or scanned for danger. He had decided to make his move when Hunt's voice claimed his attention.

"Lander. Can we talk?"

In truth, the last thing Lander wanted to do was talk to the man who had held him prisoner and oversaw his torture. But noting the humble expression on Hunt's face, he said, "Sure."

They walked for a few minutes without speaking before Hunt cleared his throat. "I need to say I am sorry." He coughed. "If there is one thing I've learned on this trip, it's that Core Dwellers may have different DNA but they are as human as Surface Dwellers."

Lander gave him a sideways look. "For real? Or is this just because Jenkins won't be here to send up any more *test subjects*?" Lander's mouth twisted on the last words.

"Touché. Well played, Lander. No. I'm giving up on that research. I have many other projects to advance. Longevity and military use of Stone Sovereign abilities were top priorities for me but no more." Hunt paused, his eyes flicking away to the far side of the cavern before returning to Lander. "And ... Castor makes strong arguments for the existence ... allowing the existence of the Core to remain confidential.

"And now, if you'll excuse me..."

Hunt slowed, waiting for Talon to catch up. Lander glanced back and wondered if Hunt was going to apologize to his head of security too. Whether it was a ruse or the truth, Lander breathed a bit easier at Hunt's words. The fear that Hunt might take him prisoner again after their trip through the Avortex had weighed on Lander. It was one of the reasons he'd asked Shahan to accompany him on the trip. Two determined Stone Sovereigns would be more difficult to stop than one.

A thought occurred to Lander, if Hunt was on the level, Lander would be able to visit the Surface ... see Becky ... without fear. The realization sunk in that he'd made his decision. Up to now, he'd bounced between staying on the Surface or returning to the Core. Though he felt he'd kept the promise to his mother, and had no further obligations, Lander wanted to return to the Core. Stay there for a time, see if he needed to do more. But the idea of visiting the Surface grew in him. He lifted his gaze to Becky again. As if she sensed him, she glanced back.

A slight smile played on her lips and Lander took it as a sign. He broke into a trot, slowing when he came alongside Becky. He didn't press for conversation, simply enjoyed her presence next to him.

The rest of the trip through the Bec Jekesh Cavern went by without incident. They passed two smaller groups heading toward the El'Ruhan Cavern and warned them about Jerr'as ahead, but since each was accompanied by a pair of Stone Sovereigns, they decided to proceed.

Lander trailed Shahan and Rahni as they took the other Sovereigns aside and explained what had transpired over the past few Mist Rises. They also shared that they were now returning the Surface Dwellers to the Surface.

"Aren't you afraid they will turn around, sneak up on us, and try to rescue Chancellor Jenkins?" Lander asked as he watched the second party disappear in the distance.

"No." Rahni said. "Most Sovereigns do not ... app ... approve what was done."

Shahan picked up the thread. "We work now to return rule to elders and guilds. It is what most want."

As the group started forward again, Lander took up his place next to Becky. This time, though she still didn't look at him or speak, she wrapped fingers around his hand, sending his feelings into a tailspin. He clung to the hope of her forgiveness.

They reached the large, open level overlooking Shavah Deklakh in time to witness the mesmerizing display of a final Mist Rise before returning to the Surface. Becky breathed in the familiar scent of moisture hitting warm rock as she gazed out over the blue city. *Will I ever get the chance to see another?* She watched with intensity, savoring every moment of the sparkling, glorious dance, wishing Michael were with her to share it.

Glancing over at Lander, she released another layer of anger. Michael's death wasn't his fault. It would take time ... and distance for her to accept this and forgive him fully. But did she have time and distance? If she never saw him again after he returned to the Core, would she ever get the chance to tell him how she felt beneath the anger? Ready or not, she needed to set the hurt aside and talk to Lander. Before he walked out of her life forever.

Lander's hand in hers, she turned to him. "I am sorry. I know..."

He placed two fingers from his other hand over her lips. "Shhh. You don't need to say anything. I know you don't hate me even though you have every right to. I'm just sorry we didn't get a chance to talk before entering the Avortex."

She nodded. "And now we're out of time."

He pulled her to him and wrapped his arms around her waist. "We'll sit together while we're traveling up. It's not ideal with everyone so close together, but we can make it work."

Becky nodded then rested her head against Lander's chest, the thumps of his beating heart echoing through her.

"We need to move." Castor's voice broke through Becky's peace.

The Vortex sat on the other end of Shavah Deklakh but the Avortex was located on this side. Castor and Rahni led the way across the length of the level and into another small tunnel.

Even from a distance, bands of pink and blue light flashed on the walls and the echoing noise reminded Becky of a freight train. The tunnel opened into a round cavity. Looking up Becky caught her first sight of the Avortex. Litter swirled on the floor. When pieces skittered onto the flat stone beneath the spinning aperture, they were sucked up into the center of the swirling air as if pulled into a tornado.

Becky's heart pounded in her ears, mingling with the roar of the Avortex. *They say a tornado sounds like a freight train. I believe them.*

"Those who are not traveling the Avortex, assemble here." Castor took up a stand at a spot outside the pull of the Avortex. Once those remaining behind with Castor and Desma gathered around the couple, Shahan directed the rest into a tight group around Lander.

"Don't do this Shahan. You can reign with me. Remember the power you craved when I first arrived here." Jenkins, his eyes wild, tried one last time to reach Shahan as the Stone Sovereign physically pushed him next to Lander.

"Lander, set the shield." Shahan motioned for Lander to enclose the travelers.

Two Stones of Power balanced on each hand, Lander pulled up a billowing shield. Becky gasped as the roar vanished and her ears popped. Once Lander's bubble stabilized, he and Shahan walked it toward the Avortex. Everyone else kept still as the two worked to move it into position while struggling against the pull. The moment they landed beneath the center of the swirling mass the barrier lifted. The force of the movement threw all the occupants to the shimmering floor, except Shahan and Lander.

The air whooshed from Becky and she struggled to pull in another breath. Lander dropped to his knees next to her. "You alright?"

She considered his question. "Yes. I am. Are we climbing?"

He grinned. "Yeah. We're climbing really fast."

It didn't take long for the passengers to find places to sit on the floor. Becky stayed by Lander, standing with him as they watched the spirals zip by, his Stones lighting the interior of his bubble with a soft glow.

Hours had passed before Shahan approached. "I will take over for a time. You take a break."

"You sure you can handle this?" Lander's brows drew down over his eyes.

"I have done this before you were born."

As Shahan's Stones flamed, Lander allowed his to dim.

Becky placed gentle fingertips on his arm. "Can we talk now?"

"Sure."

The two moved as far from the others as they could and sat on the floor of the shield. Lander reached into an inner pocket and pulled out some pieces of dried fruit. "Hungry?"

Becky shook her head. It was silly of him to even ask now,

but she figured he was nervous and trying to postpone their conversation. She glanced up to find him gazing out beyond the wavering side of the bubble. "If you don't want to talk, we don't have to."

He startled. "No. I want to." He sighed. "Remember when we came down through the Vortex?"

"That seems so long ago now. So much has happened."

"I'm so sorry. I should have gotten you and Michael back sooner... Now ... well, things will never be the same between us."

"Lander, I still love you. But, like they say, love and hate are opposite sides of the same coin. They're both strong and one can lead to the other.

"I wanted to hate you when ... you know. But, somehow, I can't. And yet I feel like I need time and, you know, space to process things before I'd be ready to ... be ... with you ... again."

"I get that. And I think you're right. I'm willing to wait." He scrubbed his hands over his face and Becky noticed the tracings of a thin beard on his chin.

"Lander? Have you decided what you're going to do?" A shiver raced through her when he picked up her hand and began tracing her bones with a gentle touch of his finger. Warmth climbed up her arm and face.

He huffed, his attention once again flitting to the side. "I need to return to the Core. At least for now. And if I do, that will give you what you said you need ... time and space."

She chewed her bottom lip. "I don't know. I think that gives a whole new meaning to the term *long distance relationship*."

He chuckled.

"Does this mean we're over?" Becky asked, torn by the implications.

"No."

His firm 'no' sent another wave of warmth through her.

"I have a plan."

"Oh really? What kind of plan?"

"Exactly one year from today you and I will meet at the entrance to Hunt's cave system. If that's okay with you?"

"And then we can go from there?"

"Yeah. Would you consider visiting the Core again ... under better circumstances?"

"If you'll spend some time on the Surface."

"Deal."

Lander pulled Becky into his side and leaned into her, his lips descending. She met the kiss. Images of words implanted on her mind. *Go for it, Becks. You and Lander are made for each other.* She pulled back, her head swiveling.

"Something wrong?"

"No. No. Nothing's wrong." She smiled up at him. "Let's see, where did we leave off?"

CHAPTER 36

The barrier shuddered and slowed. Lander had taken control from Shahan a few hours ago while everyone else slept. The tremor woke Shahan and he stumbled across the wavering floor to Lander's side.

"Shahan, what's happening? I don't remember experiencing this in the Vortex."

"We approach the Surface. It is normal. It get rough before we..." Shahan's brow crinkled as he searched for an adequate description of their arrival. "Pop? Yes, pop."

Lander drew his lips into a flat line. Shahan's word choice concerned him. "What do you mean 'pop'? Like *explode?*"

"I do not think so." He began to illustrate his meaning with hand signs.

Great. We're about to explode and he wants to play charades. But then Lander caught on to Shahan's meaning. "Oh. You mean pop out of the Avortex. Like a cork."

Shahan's expression alerted Lander to the fact the Stone Sovereign questioned his description. He thought then pursed his lips and made like he was spitting out a watermelon seed.

Shahan almost smiled and nodded. "Yes. That will happen. I will help make shield stronger for … pop."

Time seemed to slow as forces played against the shield, buffeting it like wind billowing lacy curtains. Soon everyone was on their feet, eyes glued to the sides and top of the translucent orb and the spiraling lights beyond. Becky slipped under Lander's right arm as he continued to cradle his Stones. Her warm presence brought a sense of calm.

Shahan's Stones ignited deep red when he pulled them, adding their power to reinforce the protective bubble. A moment later, they began to rise again, this time at an accelerated speed, as if the time of slowing was a preparation for a final push.

Lander understood Shahan's choice of terms when, with a sound that resembled the loud popping of a gigantic cork, the bubble shot out of the top of the sparking Avortex. It hovered in the air a second before falling off to the side and landing with a soft thud.

Catching Shahan's gaze, Lander released his hold of the shield while Shahan did the same. He slipped his Stones of Power into their pouch, draped an arm around Becky's shoulders, and stepped away from the Avortex.

The cave housing the Avortex reminded Lander of the one where they had entered the Vortex almost three months ago. Musty, with dim, bare bulbs lighting the room from above, casting moving shadows as individuals began shifting about, stirring dust particles that floated like sparkles in a snow globe.

Talon took control. "This way." He led off, pushing Jenkins before him and with Hunt at his side.

Shahan, eyes widened as he studied the room. "This is not as it was when I came here before."

"It wouldn't be." Talon pulled to a stop, keeping Jenkins in check with a hand on his shoulder, and turned to Shahan. "Mr. Hunt had a massive amount of work done exposing the

Vortex and the Avortex to make them more accessible." He pivoted on his heel and pushed Jenkins toward the only doorway.

"Wait." Lander's loud cry echoed off dull gray rocks. "We need to be clear about what's happening. Shahan and I are going right to the Vortex, no detours. We're heading back to the Core. Now."

"Now?" Becky's question pierced Lander's thin armor of emotional protection.

He ground his teeth. "Yes. I will not take any chances. We're returning before anything else goes wrong. Hunt has Jenkins and can make certain that *no one* from the Surface descends to the Core again ... unless they get permission first. Which ... would be impossible."

"You do not trust me," Hunt said, stepping back into the room. "I wouldn't trust me either if I was in your shoes. But you must understand I meant it when I said I am not the man I was three months ago." He snorted. "I'm not even the man I was three days ago." He turned away and paced a moment before returning to face Lander. "What you don't know—and I need you to understand—is that for the last couple months, while I continued to support Jenkins's grab for power, I had been meeting daily with Elam. Remember him? Jenkins's Ungifted servant?"

Lander nodded, a vision of the slight older man rising in his memory.

Jenkins lunged for Hunt. "You son of a ... I knew that little weasel was up to something."

Talon grabbed Jenkins's shirt collar and pulled the man back.

Hunt's focus returned to Lander. "The things he said ... I'm still trying to understand. I admit, I am a work in process.

"You see, every few days messages came from Shavah El'Ruhan. Castor was teaching ... or perhaps you'd call it preaching from his Bible. His talks were copied and sent throughout the three caverns. Without Jenkins's knowledge, Elam and I shared time together. He translated the Corish into English for me and then we discussed what he had read. The more we talked, the more the words confused me. Like I was getting a glimpse of something still distant … but something I wanted. Then when that Ungifted—I don't even know his name—jumped between the Jerr'as and me … and died." He stopped, pulled in a deep breath, his misty eyes locked on Lander's. He released the breath through pursed lips. "Please trust me. I can't say I believe what Castor was saying, but I am changed. I promise, no harm will come to you and Shahan. And you can return to the Core whenever you wish."

Lander shook his head. Of all Hunt said, he zeroed in on one phrase. "Three days isn't very long. Not long enough to change old habits. I'm not—"

"Lander," Becky interrupted, shaking her head. "Shahan should at least have a chance to see the Surface. And we're all here as witnesses. I know Mr. Talon has changed. He spent too much time with Castor to not."

Lander huffed out a chuckle of disbelief.

"I trust him." Shahan stood his ground, calm, his hands relaxed at his sides.

His friend's words caught Lander by surprise. He stared at Shahan with his jaw hanging open. Protest sought release but he snapped his mouth shut. Was he right to deprive Shahan of what might be his only chance to experience the Surface? It had to be Shahan's decision. Lander would back him whatever he chose.

"What do you want to do, Shahan?"

Talon stepped up to the large Sovereign. "Before you decide, Shahan, you need to know. The trip from here to the Surface proper will take almost an hour."

Shahan nodded. "I see. Sovereign Lander and I should rest

before we enter the Vortex. It will be good to see something new."

Stifling his protest, Lander walked beside Becky as they followed the others through the long tunnel. It amazed him to see how dim the light was compared to the Core. They passed the room that housed the Vortex, it's distinctive light flickering on the walls as they walked by.

Shahan's reaction to his first elevator ride melted much of Lander's tension and by the time they arrived at the entrance gate, Lander gaped at the brightness ahead with trembling hands and an overwhelming desire to run into the light.

Becky's reaction mirrored Lander's. "Oh my! Sunlight! Look Lander, it's sunlight." Her breath came in quick gasps.

A uniformed man and woman stepped out from a tiny guard booth beyond the gate. Talon waved them over. They stared at the group as if looking at ghosts. Hunt tapped his toes and Talon said, "Well, we're not going to wait all day. Unlock the gate."

"Y-y-yes sir."

After the travelers walked out, the woman pulled the gate shut and began wrapping the chain back around the metal.

"Stop." Hunt waved her to a halt. "Leave it open. Two of our number will be returning in a bit. Oh, and please call down to the Mansion and arrange for transportation for..." He paused, counting heads. "Yes. Transportation for seventeen. We will wait out front."

"I'm not going." Lander let go of Becky's hand and took a step back toward the gate.

Hunt's brow puckered as he considered Lander's words. "Yes. I can see what you are thinking." He shifted his attention to the waiting guard. "Change in plans. Arrange for transportation for two." He pointed to Jenkins. "Accompany Mr. Jenkins down to the main complex. But be cautious. He is not to leave custody until he has been escorted off Zephryn Island."

Hunt faced Jenkins; his eyes narrowed. "Remember who supported your wife and family while you were gone. If you remain silent about the existence of the Core, I will continue to send monthly checks; if not, you are on your own."

Jenkins grumbled but got the message. "Yes … *sir.*"

Hunt's attention returned to the guard. "Mr. Jenkins needs to be delivered to the mainland in all haste. I do not want him here on the island longer than necessary." As the male guard secured Jenkins and propelled him to the shack, Hunt slapped his hands together. "Now. It is good to be home. And I am hungry. Call down to the Mansion and tell the staff I am back and desire all the fixings for a picnic lunch to be set up here in the high meadow." His eyes met Lander's. "Will that suit you?"

The unease Hunt's earlier orders had caused diminished and Lander nodded. "Yeah. But Shahan and I stay here. In the meadow. For a bit. Then we're going back."

"Of course. Guard. Tell them the lunch is to be served immediately." She looked from Hunt to Lander and back again. "Go. Now. Chop. Chop. We're hungry."

Lander let Becky run ahead and stayed by Shahan's side as they walked toward the brilliance of a sunny day on the tropical island. Covering his eyes, Shahan took a step back. "It is too bright."

His eyes watering, Lander nodded. "It is bright, but your eyes will adjust. Don't stop now we're almost outside. Come on."

Becky ran back and grabbed Lander's hand. "Hurry." Laughing, she tugged him through the vast opening then stopped. Her eyes widened then drifted shut, a tear leaked. "Michael should be here." She opened tear-laden eyes. "Oh, Lander. I feel like I'm betraying Michael by being so happy. How can I feel such joy when he's … he's…"

Lander pulled her into his chest and rubbed fisted hands

up and down her back until she quieted. "Becky. Michael wouldn't want you to stay sad. He'd want you to find joy in this, not guilt. You know that; don't you?"

She nodded then looked up. Lander wiped away her tears with his thumbs. "Remember Michael the way he was and live like he lived. That's the best way to honor his memory."

Becky nodded, then tilted her head to catch the sunlight on her face. Wanting to give Becky some space, Lander stepped away and scanned his surroundings.

Vibrant greens, reds, and yellows competed for his attention while boisterous, incessant bird song hammered his ears. He glanced back to Shahan who stood frozen with his tearing eyes squeezed almost shut and his jaw hanging loose.

A strong breeze slid through the upper meadow and Lander cherished the feel of unseen fingers lightly caressing his bare arms and face. From behind, Shahan let out an exclamation of delight. "The Surface is ... amazing."

Becky walked over and grabbed Lander's hand. They laughed. Loud and long. It was a release. A turning loose of all the sorrows and fears that had pressed down on them like a heavy blanket for the last three months.

Talon led the way to a secluded hollow overlooking the meadow and the mountains beyond. Shahan's head kept swiveling as he attempted to see everything at once. Like a small child experiencing a theme park for the first time. Lander understood; for Shahan it was all new.

While they waited for the food, Lander walked with Becky, Talon, and Shahan answering as many of Shahan's question as they could. In time, Talon took Shahan off leaving Becky and Lander alone.

"Are you still sure you want to return to the Core?" Becky stood with her back to Lander.

He stepped in and wrapped his arms around her. "I have to."

"But won't you miss the Surface, all this beauty? Miss me?"

He turned her and studied her features. He wanted to remember her as she was now. Strong and beautiful. Caring and kind. He swallowed back the burning at the back of his throat as the thought of leaving her seared his spirit. "Remember. We promised. One year from today. Don't forget."

"I won't. I'll be here." She pouted and he resisted the urge to kiss her.

"You won't forget me and marry some Core girl?"

Laughter burst from Lander. "Forget you? Never."

Becky and Lander had joined the group just before the feast arrived along with Hunt's daughter Livy and Parrish, Castor and Desma's son. They approached Hunt with caution but when he flung out his arms and welcomed Livy with a hug, she ran to him, tears streaming down her face. "Oh Daddy. I was so worried."

While Livy and her father reconnected, Parrish walked over to where Lander stood with Becky, his eyes scanning. "My mom and dad?"

"Decided to stay for a while. You father has become a leader and he and your mother felt they needed to finish things they started there."

Conversations filtered through the sun-drenched afternoon. When storm clouds began building over the mountains and thunder rumbled in the distance, Lander turned to Shahan. "A storm is coming. The others will want to get down to the complex before the rain starts and we need to leave, but you can't miss this. Let's say goodbye. We'll watch the storm from the cave entrance, then head back. Okay?"

Shahan's brows lowered. "Storm? Rain?"

Lander chuckled. "You'll see."

"I will do as you save Sovereign Lander."

Shahan and Lander helped load up a truck, two jeeps, and

the stretch limo that had brought the feast, servers, and Livy and Parrish to the high meadow. After they drove off, Lander led Shahan back to the cave entrance. By then, lightning flashed around them without ceasing and thunder echoed through Lander's chest.

They stood together watching until the last booms filtered through the mountains behind them and evening set in.

"It is time?" Shahan asked.

"Yeah. It's time. Hey, you want to come back up with me next year when I visit?"

"Will you stay longer?"

Lander nodded. "Yeah. I think I'll be ready to stay longer then."

"Good. I will stay longer with you."

The two turned their backs on the evening breeze and headed for the Vortex. Lander counted this as day one. Only 364 more days to go. But he would spend them well. Fulfill his promise to his mother and help bring peace to the Core. He'd work to bring honor back to Stone Sovereigns … maybe even learn Corish. He patted Shahan on the back and smiled. He planned to have a lot to share with Becky when he saw her again.

REVIEW?

Reviews help others make informed decisions about the
Books they choose to read.

If you enjoyed *Lander's Choice* please consider leaving a review
on Amazon, Goodreads, and/or any site of your choosing.

THANK YOU!

Other books by C. S. Wachter

THE SEVEN WORDS
The Sorcerer's Bane
The Light Arises
The Deceit of Darkness
The Light Unbound

Demon's Legacy: A Worlds of Ochen Short Story
A Weight of Reckoning – Sequel to The Seven Words

STONE SOVEREIGNS
Lander's Legacy

Facebook: https://www.facebook.com/cswachter/
Website: https://cswachter.com/
Goodreads:
https://www.goodreads.com/author/show/17719497.C_S_W
achter
Instagram: https://www.instagram.com/ch.ris8443
Twitter: https://twitter.com/CSWachter1
Amazon Author Page: https://www.amazon.com/C.-S.
Wachter/e/B079Y2R2PJ/